The Major's Wife

By Debra Gaskill

First published by Dog Ear Publishing
4010 W. 86th Street, Ste H
Indianapolis, IN 46268
www.dogearpublishing.net

dog ear
PUBLISHING

ISBN: 978-160844-694-0

This book is printed on acid-free paper.

Printed in the United States of America

To the Teacher and the Blacksmith,
Who gave me wings
And to the Colonel,
Who taught me to fly

ACKNOWLEDGEMENTS

There are many people who made this work possible.

First and foremost, I would like to thank my family – husband Greg, son Scott, and daughter Rebecca, who endured cold meals, late nights, and insufferable flights of fancy as this novel began to take shape in 1989 in a small concrete-block base house at Eglin Air Force Base, Florida.

Four years later, at Langley Air Force Base, Virginia, I presented this story to the members of the Williamsburg Writer's Block critique group, who gave measured and valuable criticism as the novel continued to develop and weren't afraid to tell me when I wrote crap; for that I am eternally grateful. Mary, Reba, Marlene, Carla, and Jane, you saw the early drafts of this work and inspired me to keep going when I thought I should give it all up and go to welding school.

Now, all these years later, my children are grown and artists in their own right, responsible for the cover art for my last book, Barn Burner and for this one as well. It's nice to keep it in the family.

To other family and friends, who were never sure about this very different road I traveled down, but who loved me nonetheless, thanks.

And finally—to Bob, the one who believed in me when everyone else said he was crazy.

CHAPTER ONE

Marcus

"How's that for a press kit?"

Editor Jess Hoffman slid the release and a color photo across my desk. If he recognized the face, it's doubtful he would have shoved the story my way.

"The literacy center has a new director. I want a feature by Friday. Hate to see all that red hair wasted on a black and white head shot on an inside page."

Dumbfounded by her face once more in front of me, I nodded. Jess turned to go as, surreptitiously, I traced the image of a few unruly, red strands across the shoulders of her corporate black suit.

It had been seven years since I saw her last, eight since she married the Air Force pilot who took her away from me.

I still kept up with her, though. Through friends and acquaintances, information unfailingly came to me as only a small town can, about the major's assignments to obscure and forgotten corners of the world, and the dates her two children were born. *"I heard Kay's in Korea now. Do you ever hear from her? Can I get you some more coffee?" "Did you see the announcement in the paper? Your dream angel and her fly-boy husband had another kid last month in Florida. What's that make, two?" "Look, Marcus, I got a Christmas card from Kay…another APO address. Boy, they sure don't stay in place for long, do they? Bet she's back overseas again."*

Now here she was, right before my eyes. I got through to her secretary and scheduled an interview for Thursday. Just as my workday was ending, the phone rang again.

"Mr. Henning, Mrs. Armstrong has had a sudden change in her schedule."

"Oh?" My heart sank.

"She'd still like to do the interview. Are you available this evening?"

"Sure." Trying to sound casual, I scratched her address into my notebook. It was deep in the heart of the yuppified, east-side historical district. "Tell her I'll see her then."

As dusk fell, I parked my car across the street from her house. I quietly watched Kay and her children as they played in the front yard. She seemed more polished, more poised and grown up. Still lithe and petite despite two pregnancies, she wore slim jeans that hugged her hips and legs. Her white blouse was tailored and buttoned up severely across full breasts, letting just the hollow of her neck show. Her red hair still cascaded down her back, but she clipped it back with a barrette, taming it, like she apparently tamed so many other aspects of her life.

Her big, blue eyes still dominated her face – I could see that from across the street. As she played with the children in the yard, her lips parted in an unaffected smile to show perfectly white teeth. Despite the fact that we both said goodbye to our twenties just a couple of years ago, I never have guessed she was anything more than five years out of college.

And the major was nowhere to be seen.

She glanced my direction, then did a double take, covering her mouth to hide her surprise.

"Hello!" she called out shakily.

I could only smile and wave. I turned to pick up my notebook from the seat beside me only to drop it onto the pavement as I stepped into the street.

"Can an old friend come without bearing gifts?" I asked.

"Marcus, of course you can!" She stepped to the wrought-iron gate and let me in. Beneath that poise, I sensed a new toughness; the wild, blue yonder I seen in her eyes before her marriage had become the cold, gray steel of the aircraft that dominated her family's life. I heard it said that it was better to be a pilot than a pilot's wife. Maybe that was true.

She always had a vivacity about her, a passion for causes and campaigns that led her down roads her social-climbing mother would rather she not travel. This evening, though, brittle edges showed around the corners of Kay's mouth.

Had the hellion I knew succumbed finally to adulthood?

"Come on up, and we'll do the interview on the porch. I'll get you something to drink."

She led me to the porch, then slipped inside the door, returning with two Cokes and an ice bucket on a tray. She developed manners, too. Hmm.

"I hope you don't mind coming to the house for the interview." Kay poured the colas into two crystal glasses, carefully selecting two ice cubes with silver tongs. "I was so surprised you called. I knew the center was sending out a release, of course, but didn't think Jess would assign you to do an entire story on me."

"I don't think he recognized your photo. You certainly look a lot different than you did eight years ago."

Kay shrugged. "Time passes. People change."

"Don't tell me you found religion. Or worse—you mean you've grown up?"

A devilish look shone in her eye, a glimmer of the old Kay. "I seem to remember making you see God on more than one occasion."

"Indeed, you did," I answered.

Kay laughed, but I could sense her pulling back. I pulled my notebook from inside my jacket.

"So tell me how you ended up back here in Jubilant Falls and how you landed such a plum position as a director?"

Before she could answer, there was a squeal from the yard as the two children rolled around on the grass.

The boy was the image of his father, from what I remembered of the major. The girl was a baby-doll version of the Kay I had known, wild and raucous and full of life, pounding her brother without mercy. Ah, genetics.

"Mom! Make her stop! *Make her stop!*"

"Excuse me." Kay flew down the steps and pulled the kids to their feet. "Both of you, into your rooms until I tell you you can come out."

The little girl scowled, and the older boy stuck out his tongue until the root showed, but both marched dutifully inside.

"I hear that Daddy didn't see her until she was almost three months old." Nervously, I lit my first cigarette of the day as Kay resumed her seat. She always had that effect on me.

"Where do you get your information? Don't answer...I know how this town talks. Yes, it's true. He was TDY."

"TDY?"

"I'm sorry—on temporary duty. After you've been in for a while, you start to talk in acronyms, and your civilian friends don't understand. He was based in Korea for a while and couldn't get back. Part of the package, I guess."

"Is the major gone, now?"

"Yes." Kay nodded shortly. "He's back in South Korea, at Osan Air Base for a year. They all have to do it, it seems. Even though the war ended in 1953, that was a cease-fire, not an armistice. So even though it's 1989, the war is technically still ongoing. When he returns, we'll pack up for Lakenheath in England for two years."

"Ah, the land of the Bard and the Beefeaters! What I wouldn't give for a few years there."

"I guess." Kay's eyes focused on the traffic in the street. Her knuckles whitened on the arm of the white wicker lawn chair.

"You're not excited about going?"

"I've just done it too many times, that's all. We tried to get assigned here at Symington next, but couldn't do it. I just hate to pull Andy out of another school system. Pack, unpack, a new home, a new town, a new squadron. That's my life." Kay smiled tightly.

Symington was the Air Force base in nearby Collitstown in Evener County. Many Jubilant Falls' residents made the half-hour drive to the base, to work at high-tech government jobs in research and weapons development. The base had a small test wing, where the major had been stationed long ago. The folks that worked at the base were different somehow, more in tune with what went on outside the confines of Plummer County and Jubilant Falls, less constrained by the county line and this limited little town.

"But a good one?" I was fishing now.

She turned her face away. "Yes. A good life."

I took a breath and threw my line into deep water. "I would have given you a good life, too, Kay, if you let me."

She stared stonily across the lawn. "He loves me and the children. What more could a woman want from life?"

There was more to this than changing school systems, more than should ever find its way into a personality profile.

I covered her hand with mine and squeezed. "I'll be here, if you ever need me. Old friend to old friend."

"Thank you. I'll remember that." She drained her glass and stood up. Taking both my hands, she pulled me to my feet. Her eyes brimmed with tears, and I could see the Kay I once knew struggle to come to the surface. I wanted to take her in my arms and kiss away the loneliness and forced desertion imposed by her husband's career.

"I think it's time I go."

"But what about the interview?"

"I know enough about you to put something together."

"Yes."

"I always loved you, Kay."

She blushed.

I kissed the palm of her hand and curled her fingers closed. "That's for the major's wife. I hope the major knows how lucky he is."

"So do I." Her voiced quaked, full of emotion.

I turned to go. She was still waving from the porch, as I pulled away.

* * *

That night, I sat in the newsroom replaying what happened on the porch, examining every gesture and every word. What happened to the Kay I had known, the woman who had been so feisty seven years ago?

She had been married before the major; we became lovers within a year of her divorce. On and off through the next three years, she had drifted back and forth to me, my hoydenish Scarlett at the barbecue.

I had been Kay's confidant as each new affair began, her shoulder when it had ended, and her lover again when I had succeeded in proving, for the moment at least, that I was the one who really loved her. I had loved her, even when she had said she wouldn't marry me.

"Oh, I couldn't live with anyone more sarcastic than I am," she had said.

Probably. It was best for both of us, I'm sure. But there had not been anyone else like her. No one had even come close.

She was beautiful the first time I ever saw her, dancing with a big ox of a man at a charity ball I had been assigned to cover. Her red hair had cascaded freely down the low-cut back of an emerald green cocktail gown, as she danced barefoot and on tiptoes, holding the straps of her silver shoes in her hands.

"Why barefoot?" When the music had stopped, I cornered her beside the hors d'oeuvres.

"Heels are simply another way for women to sacrifice their health on the altar of what men have told them is beautiful," she answered. "And I refuse to spend this entire evening in pain."

"Interesting." I reached out to shake her hand. "Hi. I'm Marcus Henning, *Jubilant Falls Journal-Gazette.*"

"I'm Kay Matthews. My mother is putting this whole charade on." She pointed toward a woman whom I recognized as Marion James, one of the town's half-lit luminaries who considered themselves *cognoscenti.*

"I see. And are you accompanying the man I saw you dancing with? I wouldn't want to ask you to dance if you were..."

She opened her mouth to say something then thought the better of it. "Yes—I am. Excuse me." She pushed past me toward her husband, who was standing across the room, his beefy arms folded and his fists clenched.

Two months later, I saw the same fiery hair in the checkout line at the grocery.

"Still dancing barefoot?" I touched her back, and she jumped like a cornered animal.

My stomach recoiled at what I saw. Large dark glasses hid her eyes, but they did not entirely cover the bruises skirting across her cheek. Despite the lenses, I could see that both eyes were black. There was a line of blue sutures across the left cheekbone, and the whites of both eyes were bloodied.

"Ohmigod...it's you." Kay pushed both her hands against her chest, as if to contain her fear. "Don't you people ever leave anybody alone?"

"What?"

"Please, whatever you do, don't take my picture!" Her groceries fell in the aisle, as she bolted for the door.

"Wait!"

I caught up with her in the parking lot. "What's wrong? What happened? Are you okay?" The next question was out, before I knew it. "Who hit you?"

"I shouldn't have gone out like this." Kay shielded her wounds with her hands. "I can't have my face all across the paper like this! Please leave me alone!"

"What are you talking about?"

"Mother said you reporters are vultures, every one of you, following people around, looking for any smut you can dig up. Can't you just leave me alone?" She jerked open her car door. I threw my weight against it and grabbed her wrists.

"I'm not here to do a story, and you're not so goddamn important that I had to follow you to the grocery. I was out of goddamn toothpaste, and I saw you in line, okay? What the hell happened to you?"

"I divorced the bastard. He got ninety days for his handiwork."

"So your husband did this?"

She sagged against the car door and nodded.

"Most women don't take such drastic steps the first time."

"Who said it was the first time? I just made sure it was the last."

I was silent.

"He's gone. I'll heal," she said.

"I like to buy you a drink sometime, maybe take you to dinner? You're still a beautiful woman, and I like to get to know you better."

"Really?"

"Really." Something made me draw her into my arms. "I could never hurt you."

She would become the love of my life, and then – before I knew it – I lost her.

That was seven years ago. Now Kay was home. Again.

* * *

Jess persuaded me to come to Jubilant Falls after I had bought too many beers in a Jefferson City, Missouri, hotel bar, trying to get a juror on a high-profile murder case to spill his guts. It wasn't much of an expenditure. Four two-dollar beers, and I figured I had a story. The case was thrown out of court; I was thrown off the paper. There's nothing more unemployable than a discredited journalist. Within the month, I left the state.

In college, Jess and I had promised that if one of us needed to pull himself up by the bootstraps, the other would at least help buy the boots. To that end, Jess hired me as the *Journal-Gazette's* lifestyle reporter.

Jubilant Falls sat on the banks of Shanahan's Creek, deep in the heart of the Ohio Rust Belt. What an ironic name! This town was anything but jubilant, and the only thing that was falling was the number of people with jobs. Life in this rural county ebbed and flowed with the financial tides of Traeburn Tractor. And, like most other manufacturers in the late 1980's, the tide was out more times than it was in. In Jubilant Falls, the trickle-down theory had indeed trickled out.

The drive into town from the two-lane state highway that ran north and south through Jubilant was deceptive. A former interurban line was now a well-groomed bike path that ran along the west side of the highway, as you entered Jubilant Falls. It was filled with families on Rollerblades, or groups of students from the local church college on bicycles. At the north edge of Jubilant, a renovated caboose sat on a siding where the owner rented skates and bicycles and sold ice cream.

From there, the two-lane highway turned into Detroit Street and curved past older well-kept, middle-class houses, former homes that had been converted into insurance agencies or dental offices and the occasional Victorian relic that lived on as a funeral home.

In the center of town, at the crossroads of Main and Detroit Streets, stood an enormous brown limestone courthouse, its clock tower chiming on the half-hour and counting out the hour like it was announcing the death of a monarch. City hall and county offices to the north and east flanked the courthouse. Small, greasy spoon restaurants and stores of various types, including a fading department store, followed each other like beggared children down West Main and South Detroit.

Heading south on Detroit, the houses and their residents got a little grubbier and a lot poorer. Jubilant Falls' Chamber of Commerce's image began to falter here; it was no accident the bike path didn't run through these neighborhoods on its way into the next county. It was from here that the Literacy Center drew its clients.

The *Journal-Gazette* was on South Detroit Street, in an old building that had once been a hotel in stagecoach days. The paper itself was a rarity, family-owned in the world of corporate journalism. We sometimes dodged stories for the sake of keeping an advertiser, but with Traeburn's slow death, there weren't many advertisers to piss off, and the staff – that is, everyone except me – was taking on more sacred cows and more big stories in an effort to show readers we were truly worth appearing on their evening doorstep.

I just covered the fluff, the goddamn, worthless fluff of debutante balls at the Jubilant Country Club. What were they so Jubilant about? That anyone whose skin happened to be a little darker could only hope to enter as a waitress or janitor or whose name ended in -*berg* or -*stein* could never hope to play golf, except as a guest? Not that there were any Jews in Jubilant; the population was overwhelmingly white here, although some of the larger farmers had begun transporting Mexican migrant workers from Texas for the planting and harvest seasons.

God, I hated this town. I hated every empty Traeburn smoke stack, every hungry face, every dirty child. If you weren't one of the Swedish or Scot or Irish immigrants who originally populated Plummer County, you came up from the poverty of Appalachia with the hopes that Traeburn would give you the false security of a job on the line. Then, division after division, Traeburn had cut production. The combine division went first, then the small lawn tractors, all of them slowly disappearing, until every convenience store clerk and janitor had a story to tell about how life was when they were making $20 an hour welding the rear transaxle on some agricultural behemoth. Jubilant Falls' unemployment doubled from the national average, and the county's infant mortality rate skyrocketed. Ironically, it seemed that only the farmers and the folks who worked at Symington had any economic security.

I thought of a woman who was widowed when McNair Machine Tool fired her husband three weeks before his retirement. She had come home to find him hanging in the garage. She settled out of court, according to police reporter John Porter who did the story, but scuttlebutt in the newsroom was that someone had gotten to her, pushing her to take a measly settlement.

I hated my beat most of all, only because it glorified the small island of wealthy families who controlled Jubilant Falls. Living on the north side of town in what Jess scornfully called McMansions, ensconced in their country-club dances and their flashy cars, they held poetry readings and debutante balls while hunger and unemployment ran rampant through the town.

Through an accident of birth, Kay was part of that.

She had tried to escape it, throwing herself into causes of one kind or another. Apartheid was big for a while; after her divorce, it was battered women, abortion rights, then protesting American intervention in South American banana republics. She never stuck with them long enough to see them through. She had her mother's money to fall back on, although the relationship between the two women was far from cordial.

Kay and I dated sporadically after she turned down my proposal. I knew she was stringing me along until someone better came along, but I couldn't let her go.

Then came the day when she waltzed, singing, into the newsroom, saying that she met a pilot with the call sign of Bear, stationed with the test wing at Symington.

"He's just such a big man, he says he can hardly fit into the cockpit, and that's why they call him that," she had gushed, the wild blue shining in her eyes.

"Huh?"

"Marcus, he's just so wonderful. A real hunk," she had babbled. "His name is Paul Armstrong."

"Sounds wonderful. Good-looking, courageous, tall... everything I'm not...and a hero to boot."

"Stop it."

Two weeks later, the phone rang. It was Kay.

"What are you doing Friday night?" she asked, trying to sound nonchalant. I could hear her fingers drumming on the kitchen counter in the background. Scarlett was never happy, unless she had a beau nearby.

"Anything you want, my dear."

"Dinner? Movie? What sounds good?" Her agitation increased.

"Either one—you can choose."

"Fine. You can pick me up at eight o'clock."

"So the pilot never called back, huh?"

She slammed the phone down, disconnecting us with a loud click. She was right; she couldn't live with anyone more sarcastic than she was.

She stayed all night. It was so good to hold her. I whispered, "I love you," into her red hair all night long. Kay held me tightly, but was silent.

In the morning, I woke before she did. I had converted the apartment's other bedroom to a study and bought myself an old Underwood typewriter. I still held grand delusions then, forcing myself to spit out three pages a day on a novel that would later go up in smoke one drunk and sodden night. Like everything else in my life, it, too, would fail. But I didn't know that at the time. Dreaming of greatness and Papa Hemingway, I persisted.

Before long, Kay entered, that morning's *Journal-Gazette* under her arm and a cup of coffee in her hands. I was too involved with my characters to do more than look up and smile. We sat silently, as the room filled with the typewriter's metallic clamor.

"Do you want some coffee?" she asked, after a while.

"Sure." Without looking up, I handed her my mug.

I don't know how long she was gone. My story had gotten away from me and a bad case of writer's euphoria was setting in, that wonderful high that must have prompted Thomas Wolfe to march down the street one evening, chanting *I wrote ten thousand words today, I wrote ten thousand words.* I remember hearing Kay swear as the coffee pot shattered into the sink. The back door slammed, and, before I could catch her, she was gone.

For two weeks, I tried to call, but she was too busy to talk at work, or her answering machine was always on at home. I knocked on the door, but she never answered. What the hell happened?

When I finally nailed her down at work, I could see the wild, blue yonder in her eyes. She had fallen in love. Every sentence was *Bear does this* and *Paul says that.*

I said something about hairy backs and palms.

She showed me to the door.

It was six months before I saw her again, accidentally meeting her on the street.

"So, how are you and the colonel doing?" I asked.

"He's not a colonel, he's a captain," she laughed, but there was an edge to her voice. I pushed a little harder.

"I'm sorry," I drawled sarcastically. "How are you and Steve Canyon getting on?"

"Stop it."

I changed the subject. A few sentences later, we said goodbye. I walked away feeling as though my intestines were falling out onto the sidewalk.

In another few months, I received an engraved wedding invitation. No personal note, no phone calls the night they set the date. I thought I meant more to her than that. I declined to attend, on the grounds that I refused to play the old boyfriend at weddings. I spent the afternoon of the ceremony with my head cradled in my arms atop the Underwood. I had really lost her.

Now, seven years later, she was back. I wouldn't lose her this time.

* * *

Jess ran the story on Monday. When Kay's secretary put me right through to her office, I knew she liked it.

"Marcus, I loved it! You haven't lost your touch."

"Thank you. How about lunch at the Colonial Café? We can celebrate my journalistic expertise and your new job." I bounced my pencil nervously against my blotter.

The Colonial was the basement restaurant in Jubilant Falls' only department store, Hawk's, on North Detroit Street. It was shadowy and overpriced, like most of the legal community who dined there daily, mainly because of its proximity to the courthouse across the street.

"Oh, today is pretty full, but I think tomorrow is open," Kay hesitated then rushed on. "Let me check my schedule and see. I'll have Barbara call you...."

"Don't do that. This is friendship, not business."

"You're right. Tomorrow, then?"

"Yes. See you then."

The following day was filled with rain, a hard, driving downpour that brought the hot July temperatures within tolerable limits. Kay was waiting behind the literacy center's heavy glass doors as I pulled up. I sheltered her with my umbrella, and – together – we ran for the car.

At the Colonial, we slipped into a discreet corner table. Kay surveyed the other diners from behind her menu.

"This town is too damn small," she whispered. "It figures that the first time I go out, I run into someone I rather not know."

"Who?"

"My mother's best friend, Lovey McNair. If we're lucky, she won't come over and ruin our lunch." Kay waved politely, a tense smile pasted on her face.

In the shadowy darkness, I could barely see the scar on her cheek. While time had given her the beginnings of crow's feet at the corners of her eyes, it had mercifully lightened that memento from her first marriage.

Kay searched absently through her purse. "One of these days, I'm going to have to clean this thing out."

"What's that?" I pointed to an airmail envelope sticking out of the corner.

"A letter from Paul that I got today."

"And you're not going to read it?"

"No."

"Why not?"

She gave me a look that told me I was prying.

"Okay."

Abruptly, she stuffed the letter deeper into her bag. "Look, here comes the waitress. What do you think you're going to order? Is the cream of broccoli soup as good as it used to be?"

"Are you okay? Is everything okay with the major?"

"He's fine. Tell the waitress what you want for lunch, and then you can tell me what you've been doing with yourself these last few years." Kay gave the menu a cursory glance and slapped it shut. "I'll have the cream of broccoli soup and a salad please, with iced tea." Her smile was forced.

"Chef salad and tea. Kay, what's going on?"

"You know, it feels so strange to be back here in my hometown again. It seems to change and not change. You know what I mean?" I let her steer me away from the letter into neutral territory. When our food came, the smile on her face became less strained, more genuine. The major, however, remained conspicuous, even in his absence.

"We'll have to do this again," Kay said. The waitress came to clear our plates, and we stood to leave. More at ease now, Kay slipped her arm through mine as we headed for the stairs.

"Yes, we will."

"Most everyone I grew up with doesn't live here anymore. They've all moved on to greener pastures. You're about the last person left that I know in town...besides Mother and her country club cronies." Kay made a face.

We reached the top of the stairs to the outside exit. I took her hands in mine and chastely kissed her cheek. "Then we'll have to get together even more frequently. You're still very special to me, Kay."

"Oh, Marcus."

There was a plodding of heavy feet on the stairs behind us. A woman cleared her throat.

"Kay Armstrong, however are you, my dear!" A heavy woman with fat feet spilling over the tops of her too-tight shoes lumbered to the top of the stairs. Her face was red from exertion. The deep blue, ostrich plume on her hat waved haphazardly in front of her, a wispy flag atop an overdressed and overweight battleship.

Kay jumped back a foot, scrambling for composure. "Lovey, so good to see you. I'd like you to meet my friend, Marcus Henning. Marcus, this is mother's friend, and my landlady, Lovey McNair. Mr. McNair owns McNair Machine Tool."

I remembered the widow's story, and acid curdled in my stomach.

The battleship sized me up, over her half-glasses. "Pleased to meet you, Mr. Henning. You write for the paper, don't you? We do so enjoy your little stories about our tête-à-têtes at the country club." Her voice was icy, with perfect pear-shaped tones, resonant with privilege and superiority.

"Why thank you," I said. "Is McNair Machine still in the business of fleecing widows, or have you moved on to orphans now?"

"Marcus!" Kay was aghast.

The battleship took the hit broadside, her heavily made-up eyes blinking in shock. "Mr. Henning, I'm sure I don't know what you mean."

"But Mrs. McNair, I'm sure you do."

"Mr. Henning, I assure you the accounts of that poor man's suicide were completely fabricated by your compatriots for the sole purpose of making my husband's firm look bad! She received a generous settlement, simply to quiet the whole thing down." She drew herself up to her full square height.

"Then all those shattered windows in that poor woman's house were from a Little League team run amok?"

"Lovey, I must apologize for all this," Kay broke in.

"No need, my dear. No need. I must say that I now understand why your dear mother was so relieved when you married Major Armstrong. It is so nice of you to remember your friends who have not been as fortunate as yourself in their climb up the ladder."

"You old bitch!" Kay snapped. Now it was Kay's turn to get angry. She opened her mouth to say more, but turned on her heel and ran out the door into the rain.

"Kay! Wait!" I ran after her, grabbing her elbow as I caught her at the corner.

"Take your hands off me! Don't you dare touch me!" She whirled around to slap my face. I deflected the blow with my arm. "I don't know what you're talking about, or what information you have, but you weren't on a story, Marcus. We were having lunch, plain and simple. Do you have to ruin everything?"

"Kay, I'm sorry, it's just that—" People on the street stopped to stare at us. I glared at them, until they averted their eyes and began walking again.

"Lovey's probably on the phone to my mother, right now." Kay ran her fingers through her red hair nervously. "By the time I get home tonight, Mother will have the whole story built up into some torrid affair! Do you realize what you've done?"

"I could live with an affair."

The force of her slap knocked me back a step. The rain on my face made it sting even more.

"Don't be so stupid, Marcus!"

"Jesus Christ, I was only kidding!"

"I wasn't! Get the hell away from me!" She turned sharply and began to run.

"Kay, please!"

Sensing I was close on her heels, she quickly hailed a taxi. "Wait!"

The cab slid into traffic even before she had the door closed, the driver glaring at me as if to say, *don't try anything buddy.*

Thunder rolled overhead, sending the rain down in sheets. I pulled the collar of my raincoat close around my neck and walked miserably back to my car.

* * *

That night, I knocked on her door. The rain was still pouring down. My head was drenched, and icy drops were running down my neck. I watched through the door as Kay tied a light seersucker robe around her waist as she came down the wide mahogany stairs. Her red hair was pulled back from her face with a brown plastic barrette. She recognized me in the cut glass of the heavy door and jerked the door open angrily.

"What do you want now, Marcus?"

"I wanted to apologize for the scene with Lovey McNair."

"You got me out of the tub." She ushered me in.. "You could have called."

"I had to apologize to you in person."

The shell of the perfect hostess enveloped her. "I'm sorry. I'm not being very polite. I was pretty horrible, too. Give me your coat." She pointed toward two French doors to the right of the stairway. "The living room is right through there. Go on in and sit down. I'll hang this up where it can dry and make up a couple of old fashioneds. That will warm you up."

"Sounds wonderful."

I made myself comfortable on the federal blue couch, flanked on each end by antique butler tables and matching brass lamps. Two leather, wingback chairs sat squarely facing the couch from each side of a pale blue rug. In front of me, a polished Queen Anne table held a model jet fighter and an oversized book on Air Force history. Overhead, a large, restored crystal chandelier illuminated a black marble fireplace ornate with scrolls and swans.

The walls above and beside the mantel were filled with the major's achievements. Military medals were interspersed with photographs of his glory days on the Air Force Academy football team. Apparently, all the major needed to do was flash his perfect teeth and boyish good looks, and somebody at the Pentagon rewarded him for it. There were plaques from former squadrons and a photo of him shaking hands with Ronald Reagan, one gunslinger to another.

It was perfect – all too perfect and as cold as the cover of a design magazine.

"My God," I said to myself.

"That's what Paul calls his 'I love me' wall. Impressive isn't it?" Kay padded across the living room and handed me my drink.

"I didn't come here to talk about Major Golden Boy."

"Paul. His name is Paul. He is not his rank." Kay curled into the opposite corner of the couch, playing with the maraschino cherry in her glass.

"Yes, well, I came to apologize for what I said to you about having an affair. If you want me to apologize to McNair, I'll do that too."

Kay sipped her drink silently, shifted herself more comfortably into the blue corner.

"Would you like to try it again sometime?" I continued, desperately. "We'll do it right…dinner, not lunch, someplace out of town if you like. I'll make sure McNair is nowhere near the place, before we even walk in."

Kay's blue eyes softened. "Thank you. I accept the apology and the dinner invitation. Paul's letter had me a bit off center. I apologize for my behavior, too."

"Apology accepted. So what did the letter say, anyway?"

"I'm not ready to talk about that just yet." Kay chased the cherry around the bottom of her drink, with her index finer. She

wiggled her shoulders further back into the blue cushions, exposing the top of her bare thigh, and sucked the alcohol from her finger. My heart caught in my throat.

"Are things not well between you and the major?"

Kay ignored my question. "How's Jess?"

Once again, I let her lead me. "He's fine. He was surprised,
when I told him that photo was you."

"I'm sure he was." Her voice low, Kay leaned forward and
gently brushed my cheek with her lips.

I drew her to me and returned the kiss, once, twice, three
times, savoring the taste of whiskey on her lips. When she didn't
push away from me, I unfastened her barrette and buried my face in
her hair, drinking in her sweet, clean perfume, exalted that she
would still want me.

"Hold me."

I couldn't believe it…here was the dream I had waited for so
long. I was holding my long-ago Kay James in my arms again. She
tightened her hold around my neck, bringing her body completely
against mine. We kissed once more.

"We shouldn't do this," she whispered into my ear.

"I know." I kissed her forehead, then her cheeks, her chin,
and the hollow of her neck. Gently, the seersucker fabric parted, and
my hand slipped tentatively over her warm breast. Beneath my fingers, I could feel her nipple harden as Kay inhaled in pleasure. Here
she was, in my arms, and she obviously wanted me.

A dam burst inside me, and guilt flooded in. Regretfully, I sat
up and sighed.

"Would a happily married woman be doing this?" I whispered.

Kay opened her eyes and brushed a few stray hairs from her
forehead. The lights from the chandelier shot sparkles from the dia-
monds in her wedding band. A wistful smile played across her lips.

"You're right. This is getting out of hand." Kay rose up on her
elbow. "Let me get your coat."

I sighed again and picked up a small photograph from the
end table beside me. It was the major, kneeling on the wing of his F-
15, his red helmet under his arm, giving the photographer a thumbs-
up.

What an all-American ego, I thought in disgust.

Kay returned with my coat. Without words, she pulled her
barrette out of the couch and pinned her flaming hair back in place.

"I suppose I owe you another apology for acting like an animal—again?"

"No, we're both responsible for what went on here." Kay laid her cool hands on my cheeks. "There's a lot of upheaval in my life right now. It was good to just have you hold me."

"You're very precious to me, Kay."

"Does that mean we're still on for dinner?"

I smiled. "Sure."

I slipped out the door and into the night. The rain had stopped, and the full moon glowed silver through swiftly moving clouds. As Kay shut the door behind me, I heard a small voice:

"Mommy, who was that?"

"Nobody, honey. Now go back to sleep."

* * *

The most lasting memory of my father will always be his hands – big, thick, workingman's hands that always had grease under the nails and in the lines of the knuckles. One thick hand would sometimes squeeze my face; often it was the only physical contact he made with me, throughout my life. Sometimes those fingers squeezed my face in affection, although it was in anger, more often than not.

There was the time I told him I wanted to be a writer when I grew up. His greasy hands squeezed my face so hard that I thought my pudgy boyhood cheeks would kiss each other across my nose.

"I'll have no pansy-assed fairy writers in this house. You understand that, boy?"

Boy. That's all he ever called me. I guess he assumed that any creative endeavor indicated some sort of deviant sexual behavior and that his son would not be the real man his father wanted him to be. Continued threats were not enough to make me quit. From then on, I wrote in secret and hid my manuscripts under my mattress.

When I finished college and his garage became more successful, my father became a grudging contributor to the arts in our little town. His contributions were made in the same spirit that someone would contribute to cancer research to keep the disease from crossing the threshold.

Both my parents were unschooled Kentuckians from the hills of Appalachia who moved up Route 23 North in search of work in southern Ohio. Neither of them graduated high school. Still, in spite of her abbreviated education, my mother loved Roman history. Its profound effect on her showed in her children's names: I was her only son, the philosopher-king, Marcus Aurelius Henning; my sister was Caesar's perfect wife, Calpurnia.

I was meant to be the family's success story. I wasn't – not in my father's eyes, anyway. I inherited my mother's love of reading, words, and the glory that shone in history's past. Poor math skills kept me out of the fields my father had chosen for me. I lasted one quarter as an accounting major and five weeks as an engineering major, before he gave up in disgust, and I changed to a double major in English literature and journalism, graduating with a *cum laude* diploma in my right hand and a job offer at a small upstate daily newspaper in my left.

"You'll never make any money," he spat out at graduation. "I got kids straight out of high school mechanics programs making more dough in a week than you'll ever see in a month."

His disgust was never so vocal as the time I left Missouri. I would always be his personal failure, and nothing I could do – not even the story of a lifetime – would fix that. Spending my days as I did writing up poetry readings and engagements, I never would gain that.

* * *

My father's assurance of my continuing failure still rang in my ears, as the next day's violent thunderstorms gave way to oppressive heat and outrageous humidity in Jubilant Falls. The editorial staff dragged through the day, with sweat running in rivulets down our faces and slowing the computer systems down to a crawl. Jess wiped the moisture from his forehead and leaned over my desk.

He had all those good looks that ensured success – tall with high cheekbones, dark hair, perfect teeth, and a John Kennedy, Jr., poise and assurance that came from knowing you were the best there was, at least in your family's eyes.

New female reporters and staff members often swooned over him – his crackling gray eyes never missed a new haircut or a nice dress. Not that these compliments were any kind of a come-on; he was married to his high school sweetheart, Carol. They had a daughter named Rebecca, and Jesse Foster Hoffman was as much a candidate for an interoffice romance as the Pope. Over lunch in the employee break room, I confided to him the details of my lunch with Kay, but not all of the details of my visit at her home. He didn't respond, sitting and silently shaking his head as he chewed on his ham sandwich.

"You're not planning to see Kay again, are you?" he asked.

"What is it to you, if I do?"

"She's married, and her frigging husband is in the trenches someplace! If I knew some guy was dancing around Carol while I was gone, I …."

"Shit, Jess, keep your altar-boy self-righteousness to yourself! Kay is a consenting adult. If she doesn't want to see me again, I'm sure she'll tell me."

"If Kay were my wife…."

"You still be paying alimony! You just don't like her, pure and simple. If she were the Virgin Mary, you wouldn't like her."

"That's not it." The phone rang at the desk next to mine. Automatically, Jess answered it. "Newsroom, Hoffman. Yeah…just a minute…he's right here." He covered the mouthpiece with his hand. "It's Kay. For you."

"Speak of the devil," I smirked.

Jess rolled his eyes and handed me the phone.

I had no idea how my life was about to change.

CHAPTER 2

Kay

"Marcus, I have a client here that you might be interested in talking to."

Tapping my red fingernails on my desk blotter, I smiled at the ragged scrap of humanity sitting on the other side of my desk. Tucking an uncontrolled auburn curl behind my ear, I leaned the receiver against my shoulder.

"Oh, yeah?" Marcus asked, at the other end of the line.

"Her name is Ludean Tate. She's been coming to the center for about six months now, and she's running into some trouble with her landlord that can't seem to get resolved."

"So? Tell her to get a lawyer."

"Legal Aid hasn't got the staff, and she hasn't got the money to pay for one."

"So, what's the problem?"

"She said she can't get repairs done, and she's concerned for her kids."

"This isn't my normal beat, Kay..."

"I don't have anyone else to call."

"Okay, I'll be right over." The phone went dead.

It had taken me too long to cultivate this thin veneer of serenity. I had a client who needed help from a system that couldn't or wouldn't give it to her, and Marcus was my last hope. I couldn't let all those turbulent feelings for him come bubbling out into the sunlight, even for the short time Paul was overseas. Exposure was too dangerous.

People die from exposure, too. I learned that later.

* * *

I introduced Marcus to Ludean, who only nodded in greeting. As he took her hand, Marcus blanched briefly at the diagonal scar running from her nostril to her upper lip. I was used to her strange appearance – her bony arms, the Goodwill store clothing, the stringy hair. But each time I saw other people's reaction to her, my heart broke all over again, and I knew I had to help her.

"Ludean has had a substandard repair of a congenital hare-lip and has had no speech therapy." It was hard for me to lay the facts of this poor woman's life out on the conference table as if she were a cadaver under examination. "Ludean, tell Marcus about the problem you're having at your apartment."

I heard her words as if for the first time, each honking sibilant making her words almost unintelligible. She couldn't make the system work for her; the system wouldn't take time to decipher her mangled language.

"I'm sorry. Can you repeat that?" Marcus asked.

I cringed. *Oh, God, Marcus, please. Don't.*

She slammed a bony hand down on the arm of the conference room chair. Once again, the words were honking and incomprehensible to him. I knew what she was saying: "Rats. I've got rats in my apartment."

She ran her fingers across the table.

"Rats?" he asked, taking over the interview.

She grinned toothlessly at his comprehension.

"Have you contacted your landlord?"

She nodded.

"How many times have you talked to him about the situation?"

She held up four fingers. It had often been this way. Once she figured out they couldn't understand her—and it didn't take long—she resorted to an odd sort of signing with her fingers, head movements and body language.

"And he has not taken any action? No traps? No exterminators?"

She shook her head.

"How do they get into your apartment?"

I cringed again as she spoke; Marcus still couldn't understand.

"You mean the window is…is broken? And the rats climb through the open window to get into your apartment?"

Ludean nodded, relief her crossing her bony face that someone had finally understood.

Marcus looked across the table at me. "Absentee slumlord?"
he asked.

"I'm not sure," I replied. "She's got more to tell you."

Ludean threw me a hurtful look.

Further conversation was slow difficult work. Ludean had to
repeat answers three or four times before Marcus could understand
what she was trying to tell him. I refrained from helping, just so he
could see how helpless she really was.

She managed to tell him the toilet didn't work, that she'd contacted her landlord on a multiple occasions, but had received no
response. Her status as a welfare mother of two children didn't
seem to carry much weight with getting things done.

As the strange, halting conversation ended, the sound of
Marcus's pencil scratching on his notebook echoed through the
room.

"You've got to help her." I said. "Nobody else will."

He sighed and nodded. "Let's go take a look at your place,
Ludean. I think we may have a story."

* * *

She lived on one of the dark, twisted, south side streets, in
an old clapboard house that had been divided up into four apartments. The sagging steps creaked painfully as Marcus, Ludean, and
I climbed to the porch. Boards were missing between the graying
slats. Like old soldiers who could no longer make formation, they fell
at an angle into the crawl space below.

Ludean opened the front door, and I gagged at the stench of
urine in the hallways. By the time we got to her second-floor apartment, the stench of human waste was even stronger, bringing water
to my eyes.

Marcus noted everything he saw, rapidly firing questions at my
client as we worked our way up the stairs. I had never seen him work,
except for the few times he covered one of Mother's society functions.
Now, an intimidating ferocity enveloped him. If he had any sympathy
for Ludean, it wasn't showing as he shot rapid-fire questions her way.

"Does everyone have problems with their plumbing? Does it
always smell this bad? How come you never spoke up before now?
What was the deciding factor in coming forward?"

Marcus seemed to understand her speech now.

"I got drunks hanging around — they pee on the porch at night. It always, always smells bad. Nobody here's got the nerve to go up against the landlord, we stay quiet and pays rent," she answered.

"What made you decide to come forward," he repeated.

"A rat walked across my baby's bed one night. I said I wasn't going to live like this any more."

Ludean unlocked the ragged door to her apartment, and two little faces appeared.

"This here's Aaron. This 'un's Priscilla."

The children were fairly clean, considering their abysmal surroundings. The boy looked like he was about eight, with dishwater blonde hair and hard, blue eyes. I knew from the orphans I had worked with when Paul and I were first in Korea that it would be a battle to keep Aaron from a life on the streets, if we didn't start now. Ludean depended on him too much, and it showed. It wouldn't be long before he found an easy way to bring money into the household through selling drugs or theft. He'd be in the justice system and his mother would see him only on prison visiting days, if we didn't do something before he reached adulthood.

Priscilla, with her curly, black hair and her honey-colored skin, was probably about kindergarten age. Neither child spoke, as we entered.

Their surroundings weren't fit for a dog.

Ludean had taped cardboard over two broken windows in the front room; the paint was peeling, but there were scratch marks where she had attempted to scrub them clean. In the hallway where Aaron slept on a folding cot, the bare brown wall was exposed, but again showed where Ludean had tried to clean it. The battered linoleum showed the same attention.

Priscilla had the luxury of the one bedroom, but the one broken window was taped over with cardboard. Rats had eaten through a corner.

Marcus roamed the apartment quickly.

"Is he from the welfare office?" Aaron asked, suspiciously.

Ludean shook her head. "Ssshhh."

"You say you have contacted your landlord repeatedly, and he has refused to make repairs?" Marcus asked sharply.

She nodded.

"Who owns this place? Where do you pay your rent?"

"I go to Detroit Street, the big brick building with all the windows...."

"You don't know the number?"

"I don't look for no numbers. It's next to Hawk's." Her chin lifted defensively. "Give my money to the man sitting behind the desk. Four doors from the elevator."

"Do you have a receipt from the last time you paid your rent, Ludean?" I asked. "Can I see it?"

She fished through a pocket and handed me a tattered receipt.

"Aurora Development Corporation is your landlord?" I asked. "That's one of the biggest businesses in town."

"It's right downtown." Marcus looked over my shoulder. "Close to the paper."

He took the receipt from me. I felt his hand brush mine, and I closed my eyes as his familiar scent encircled me.

"Can I keep this?" he asked Ludean.

She nodded.

"Thanks. Sit tight, and either Kay or I will get back in touch with you. I need to get a photographer. C'mon Kay."

I took my client's bony hands in mine. "He's going to help you, Ludean. Right, Marcus?"

"I've got to get back to the newsroom. Let's go."

* * *

"What do you think?" I asked, as we drove through the twisted South Side streets.

"Well, the only thing standing in my way is Jess. He could give the story away to the crime reporter, John Porter, or he can give it to the city government reporter, Addison McIntyre, although I don't think he will. Or he can say that the whole thing is not worth a story at all."

"He wouldn't!"

"He's the editor. He can do any damned thing he wants."

I looked over to see Marcus chewing the end of his pencil. "But I gave you the story and I want you to do it!"

"Who owns Aurora Development?"

"I don't know. I know they also developed all those god awful, garish homes on the north end of town. I didn't know they had any rentals, much less anything that run down."

"Another option is to sit on it for a day 'til we find out. It's close, a couple blocks down from the paper," he mused. "Basically, what happens with these things is that a judge establishes an escrow account, and the tenant pays the rent into the account until the repairs are made. I could walk down tomorrow and pay a visit. I could present the problem to the rental agent, and everything would be taken care of. A place that big doesn't want publicity like that."

"What if it doesn't work?"

"Then Jess can't turn down a front-page story, even if I've done all the leg work."

"What if Jess doesn't think it's a story? What happens then? She's absolutely helpless. She can't read anything above the most basic kids' books yet, and you saw she can barely talk. If the system won't help her, and the paper won't expose that, she's back to square one."

Mother's words echoed in my head: *"Kay, I don't understand why you waste your time with those kinds of people."*

"Because I'm here to make a difference," I'd replied. *"Because I have so much, and they have so little."*

"What are you doing tonight?" His question shook me from my thoughts.

"Why?"

"I can get a couple of bags of groceries together pretty easy…"

"I have some hand-me-downs from the kids…" I pulled Paul's Porsche behind Marcus's battered Ford that was parked at the curb in front of the literacy center.

"They'll say we're getting too involved," Marcus whispered, as he leaned across the seat, close enough that I could smell his mix of cologne and cigarettes.

"Who cares?" I smiled, feeling pulled into his orbit.

"See you tonight, then?"

"Wouldn't miss it."

"Great." He winked and jumped out of the car.

A match dropped into the dark night of my soul, and I knew why I loved him all those years ago…and why I shouldn't go with him tonight.

* * *

What was it about me that always made me choose the wrong man?

Later that afternoon, I lay across my bed, amid newly laundered stacks of Andrew and Lillian's outgrown clothes. The kids were playing in the yard; their laughter, along with the repetitive folding, made me pensive and thoughtful.

First, there was that disaster with Grant, followed in a couple of years by another disaster...Paul. Of course, no one except me thought he was a mistake. Especially Mother.

"If this marriage ends in divorce, too, you'll only have yourself to blame," she had whispered the day of my wedding, as she pretended to fuss with my veil. "I am aware that we all make mistakes," she continued, her whisper loud enough to carry all the way to the altar. "And I am willing to completely forget that little to-do with Grant Matthews. But *this*, Kay! You couldn't have done better, even if I had picked him for you myself! If you do anything to ruin this marriage, there is something seriously wrong with you."

Nothing like a mother's love.

She made it sound as if I just bought the prize pig at the Plummer County Fair. Thank God an usher stepped in to escort her to her seat. I wanted to run from the church in tears. Maybe I should have.

Paul and I had met on a blind date in the officer's club at Symington Air Force Base, which sat across the county line in Evener County. We had been set up through a mutual friend of mine, Kate Miner, who worked civil service there. He had seen a photo of Kate and me – we been roommates at college – but I never knew what he looked like.

"It makes for a little suspense," Kate had giggled. "Don't worry, this guy's an Adonis, a god. After all you've been through, I think you deserve one like this."

I slipped into a seat, at a table in the darkened corner of bar. In a few minutes, I saw blonde perfection in a flight suit break from the knot of uniformed men surrounding him at the bar and pull a photo from a pocket on the leg of his flight suit. Glancing at it, Michelob in hand he scanned the tables, and I waved. In two steps, he was beside me.

"Hello, I'm Paul Armstrong," he said, as he offered a strong hand. He had green eyes sharp as an eagle's and an air of untapped strength and danger that made me weak in the knees, even though I was sitting down. "You must be Kay James, Kate's friend."

I don't remember what blather had escaped from my mouth. Something, no doubt, that had made me seem like I never spoken in English before, or was really in need of a brain transplant.

He had slid, panther-like, into the chair beside me. My eyes took in his perfectly sculpted face, his broad shoulders that held embroidered silver captain's bars Velcroed on each shoulder, and broad chest with another patch with his name, Paul 'Bear' Armstrong.

I had pointed at the nametag. "Tell me Bear isn't really your middle name."

He looked down at the name patch. "Oh, that's my call sign. What they call me on the radio when I'm flying."

"Oh." God, where had my voice gone? Why couldn't I speak intelligently to this man? Maybe it was because I had been looking for a hero. I had caught myself rubbing the scar above my left eye and, embarrassed, locked my hands together in my lap.

He stood up. "Listen, I like to take you to dinner, if you're interested."

I nodded like a six-year-old.

"How does lobster upstairs in the club dining room sound?"

I nodded again. "Th-that would be gr-great."

"Club regs say I can't wear this flight suit in the dining room, so I'm going to duck into the men's room and change. Then we'll go up."

In two minutes, he was back wearing tailored khakis and a polo shirt. His bare arms were muscular and covered with blonde fuzz.

"Shall we?" He offered me his arm. I stood up and knew from that moment, I was falling for him...hard.

God, just don't let this one be a loser, I prayed, as we ascended the stairs. *Don't let him be like Grant Matthews.*

"I don't believe in luck," he told me over dinner. "You take life by the throat and make your own opportunities."

"Is that why you asked for the picture of me?"

He pointed his fork at me playfully. "Hey, I didn't ask for it. Kate gave it to me. Said you be the girl of my dreams."

"And what if I wasn't? If I had three eyes, or a zit the size of Texas in the middle of my forehead?"

"I thought you were gorgeous from the minute I saw your face."

Here was the man I thought I was waiting for.

I waited for over two weeks after that first date, cursing him and myself like any lovesick schoolgirl as I sat beside the phone. Finally I gave up and spent one last disastrous night with Marcus, wishing the whole night that he was my flight-suited hero.

Paul was waiting for me at home when I pulled up, choked with guilt over how I used Marcus. Paul had been TDY since our first date, he explained, and came right over to Jubilant Falls when he returned.

I never saw Marcus again.

Six months after our marriage, we were transferred to Eglin Air Force Base in the Florida panhandle where Paul was assigned to the 33rd Tactical Fighter Wing. I became everything Paul (and Mother) wanted me to be, volunteering with all the right organizations, attending all the right parties, smiling the right smile to the right general's wife, assuring that my husband moved up the career ladder.

I learned to speak in the language of this new world I married into. People didn't move to another base, they went PCS (permanent change of station). They didn't fly just fighters or bombers or cargo planes, it was F-15s, B-2s and C-130s. I watched Paul shine through UEIs (unit evaluation inspections) and ORIs (operational readiness inspections). It was a new life, completely separate from Jubilant Falls and my past, and I loved every minute.

Then something changed.

I got pregnant.

The first time I heard other wives whispers, we were at a cocktail party at the Eglin Officer's Beach Club. Paul and I walked to the bar, to get our drinks—I'd sworn of my usual glass of wine for diet soda. Paul ordered a beer. In the corner, I noticed a petite blonde lift her chin, thrust out her miniscule breasts, and smile in his direction. I didn't know her, never saw her before that moment, but there had been an air that was both proprietary and sexual in her movements. I saw Paul wink and, in another corner, a knot of junior officer's wives stifled giggles.

Every woman wants a hero, all right—and she'd had mine. I didn't know where or when or how, but she had.

"She doesn't know?" I heard someone ask.

"Sshh! She'll hear you!" someone else hissed.

I didn't say anything that night at the club. After we came home, pleading nausea, I went to bed. About an hour later, Paul slipped between the cool sheets next to me.

"You have fun tonight?" he asked, softly.

"Oh, it was okay." I tried to sound cool. "You know, another squadron beer fest."

"Yeah." He kissed my hair and rolled over. "Well, good night, Kay."

When he thought I was asleep, he slipped out of bed and out the door. As I peaked through the window, I watched him roll his red Porsche down the driveway of our concrete block base house. He cranked the engine, as the car rolled over the curb and, as quietly as he could, he drove down the street to meet his whore.

I sat in the darkened living room, on our blue federal couch, clasping our silver-framed wedding portrait, rubbing my pregnant belly when the key turned in the lock at 4:45 that morning.

Through that long, dark night, I had time to think and to cry. When the tears wouldn't come any more, I knew I wasn't going to get divorced over this little blonde bimbo, whoever she was. My mother's words kept echoing in my head: *"If you do anything to ruin this marriage, there is something seriously wrong with you."* I knew I hadn't done anything wrong, but if I were to come home from Florida as a two-time divorcee, she wouldn't see it that way. But I also wasn't going to let Paul get away with it.

I watched the doorknob turn slowly, as the man who been my hero tried not to make a sound as he stepped inside the door. I hurled the wedding portrait at him. It landed short of its mark, the glass shattering around his tennis shoes. There was a quick gasp, and he stood suddenly straighter.

"Kay, I...."

"So, did you fuck her? Was it better than what you get at home?"

Paul stepped over the broken frame, coming toward me, his muscular arms extended in supplication.

"Baby, I...."

I bolted from the couch and crossed the room, picking up a Waterford bud vase Mother gave us as a wedding present. I clasped the neck of the vase like a baseball bat.

"Answer me!" I screamed, my voice raw and ragged. "Answer me, goddamn it answer me!"

Paul's arms fell limply at his sides.

"I'm sorry, baby…it didn't mean anything…."

"Didn't mean anything? Didn't mean anything?" I swung with all the power in my arms and flung the vase at his head. This time, my aim was better. The vase shattered on the wall just above his head. He ducked, to avoid the flying glass, but made no move toward me.

"Why, Paul? Why?" I screamed, waving my clenched fists. Paul stepped over the broken glass and the ruined portrait and came toward me.

"Don't you touch me! Don't you dare touch me!"

He fell to his knees and folded his thick arms around me, burying his blonde head in my stomach. He smelled of fresh soap, and his hair was damp. He stood in her shower, used her towels to dry himself off, so I wouldn't detect the smell of sex or her perfume. *Maybe she's been in the shower with him….* I cringed at the thought of them playfully covering each other with soap, rubbing their wet, naked bodies against one another.

"Baby, I'm sorry. I don't know what happened. I don't have any excuse," he murmured into my nightgown-covered pregnant belly.

I grabbed a handful of his hair and pulled his head back, forcing him to look at me. There were actual tears in his eyes.

"Tell me you don't love her," I whispered, struck by his contrition.

"I don't, baby, I don't. It was just some crash-and-burn queen…I met her in the bar before. She's got a thing for pilots."

"Tell her go fuck someone else's husband, then." I looked into his eyes.

"It won't happen again, I promise." Tears ran down his cheeks. At that moment, I believed him. I stroked his face.

"Please, Paul, don't break that promise. Whatever you do, don't break that promise."

He stood and took me in his arms. "I promise, baby, I promise," he whispered.

Of course, it happened again… and again. But by that time, I had Andrew. I didn't want to take this gurgling little baby boy away from a father who so clearly adored him, and I wasn't about to listen to Mother tell me how much of the problem was my fault. It would never cross her mind that Paul Armstrong was congenitally unfaithful.

And so, we struggled on together. No one else knew the pain and the tears, the deployments when he left in anger, the hang-up phone calls in the middle of the night, the whispers behind my back that no one thought I heard at the officer's wives club. A lot of wives took the attitude, *What goes TDY stays TDY*, but I had never been able to do that. I heard the line *Gear up and rings off!* more than once.

Every woman wants a hero. Not just me.

It took me years to acquire this mask of the Good Officer's Wife. Soon, though, I found I played my role too well. Like all the citations and awards that hung on our wall, I became an ornament to be seen and paraded about. I thought that's what everyone wanted of me. Left to my own devices, I crashed and burned; wasn't that what Grant Matthews was, one big accident? One big train wreck? I needed Paul, I thought, as my redemption for Grant.

Then it struck me. Why should I make him look good, after all he'd done to me? I had two babies now. Lillian was conceived in second period of infidelity, fighting, and making up just one year after Andrew's birth. I didn't want my daughter's role model to be a woman who tolerated her husband's wholesale whoring. After a while I stopped caring about how it looked and got on with my own life. At Eglin, I started a soup kitchen for indigent veterans who slept on the beaches. At Osan Air Base, in South Korea, I worked at an orphanage for Amer-Asian children. At Langley, on Virginia's Chesapeake Bay, I worked with the mentally ill at Eastern State Hospital.

It's amazing the effect small objects can have on the rest of our lives: one letter, with one Korean postmark, containing one little photograph smiling back at me with those familiar green eyes, shaking all my foundations. The letter contained a handful of Korean bank notes.

I save money for us by house in USA for all three of us, the letter read. The pen strokes were broad and black, despite the poor English.

I knew then that it was over.

But Marcus—why did I always come back to Marcus? He was safe; that was why. He knew me as I really was and never asked me to be anything else.

Yet, until everything was settled, I was still married to Paul. That bound me.

* * *

The doorbell rang, echoing up that god awful presumptuous staircase. Quickly, I threw the kids' clothes into a box.

"Coming!"

Balancing the box on one hip, I threw open the door.

"Darling, must you yell down the stairs like that? It's *so* like a fishwife." My mother, dressed in a glittery cocktail dress, folded her perfectly manicured hands in front of her.

"Mother. Hello."

"I was just coming from one of Lovey's little soirees and saw the lights on, so thought I'd stop by." With a practiced, perfect step, she slipped by me into the foyer.

For a sixty-seven-year-old woman, she was, as always, in perfect shape. Mother's addiction to cosmetic surgery was a poorly kept secret...only she thought no one noticed. Her friends kept an active, gossipy tab on the number of procedures she had done. I knew of one tummy-tuck and a chin job in the last few years; maliciously, I glanced along her carefully coiffed hairline for any telltale pink lines.

"I'm expecting company any minute, Mother."

"Oh, I won't be long. Are the children in bed?"

"No, they're out playing in the backyard."

"Isn't it late for that? My goodness, Kay, I'm not the wicked Witch of the West, I'm your mother! Aren't you going to ask me in for a cup of coffee?"

I sighed and put down the box and signaled for her to follow me into the kitchen. "Come on."

"That's better."

She folded herself gracefully into one of my kitchen chairs, while I fussed through the clutter trying to find a pair of clean spoons.

"I really wish you let me send Novella over to clean for you."

Novella, Mother's live-in Jamaican maid, was one more of her affectations, but easily forgivable. Novella had worked for our family for years, returning to her own home after our dinners were cooked and the kitchen cleaned up.

After Novella's two sons grew up and her husband Clyde died, Mother had invited her to move into a small apartment she built for me above the garage. I refused to live in it, but it was a perfect set up for the two of them. If not for Novella, Mother would be completely alone in that enormous house near the country club.

Novella had given me those intangibles that a mother normally did.

"Now stand straight, Miss Kay. You want the world to notice you when you enter a room," she'd said.

"Remember, Miss Kay, you're a lady. Keep a little bit of mysteriousness about you. Be elegant. Be grand, but remember those who aren't as fortunate as you."

"Miss Kay, remember your manners."

Novella made certain my hair was combed and my clothes were spotless when I left for school. She helped with homework when she could, but most often referred me to my father. Despite her thirty years of being in the US, her voice never lost the lilt of her homeland.

For some unknown reason, Novella, tall and elegant and filled with so much more class than ninety percent of my mother's friends, never called us by our first names. It was always 'Dr. Montgomery' or 'Miss Kay' or 'Mrs. James.'

"I don't think so, Mother. I rather my children learn how to care for themselves."

"It certainly doesn't look like your lesson is sinking in."

My teeth grinding together, I slapped some Oreos on a plate and banged them on the table, along with two mugs.

"Oreos? Are the biscotti I gave you last week gone? They are so delicious and—"

I slammed my hand on the counter. "Mother, why in hell did you stop by, if all you wanted to do was needle me? My house isn't clean enough, I have bad manners, and now I'm a poor hostess. I'm so glad you're here."

"Now, Kay, I only meant…"

The doorbell rang again.

"I know *exactly* what you meant. Excuse me."

"Hey! Ready to go?" Marcus, leaning comfortably against the doorframe, smiled invitingly at me. I wanted to trace the line of his worn lapel up his collar and feel the warmth of his face in my hand. But not now.

"Thank God, it's you. I can't…Mother's here." I dropped my voice to a whisper. "Save me."

"Ah, Mr. Henning, I recognize that voice anywhere." Mother appeared in the foyer, offering her hand like some kind of feudal queen.

"Mrs. James." Marcus shoved his hands in his pockets and nodded.

Mother raised her eyebrows at his snub and folded her perfect hands. "I'm assuming that the *Journal-Gazette* will be present next Thursday at the symphony auction. The proceeds benefit the music scholarship fund at the college."

Marcus shrugged. "I couldn't tell you. I don't have my assignment calendar in front of me."

"And what brings you to my daughter's house this time of the evening?" she asked.

"I have a client who is really down on her luck," I interjected, before they could start throwing barbs at each other. "Marcus brought her some food, and I have a box of the kids' old clothes for her."

"I knew it wouldn't be long before you started this absurd do-gooder behavior again. You're certainly not giving away anything I paid for, are you?"

"What?"

"I mean, really, Kay! You had the opportunity to see the country, the world even! And you spend it with all the downtrodden inferiors you can find! I don't know where you got this Mother Theresa complex of yours."

"I think it's time you left."

"Even Jesus said the poor will always be with us."

"Mother, you and your twisted theology can leave now."

"Well, when you've finished clothing the naked, feeding the hungry, and healing the sick, we'll do lunch. So good to see you again, Mr. Henning."

Mother swished out the door.

"*Damn* her! She knows exactly how to push every button I've got! One of these days, I'm going to throttle her!"

"She's certainly a formidable foe." Marcus loosened his tie and followed me back to the kitchen. "Hey! Oreos. My favorite. Where does she come off with this high-and-mighty act of hers?"

I smiled, as I watched him brush his sandy, brown hair from his eyes and seat himself in a kitchen chair. I don't know what he thought about my looks, but in the years since we seen each other last he kept himself in pretty good shape, despite the fact his hair was a little thinner on top than I remembered. He never had any of the flash or the heroics that accompanied Paul everywhere he went.

Marcus was bandy-legged and thin, not much taller than me, which means just plain short. His undistinguished face was the kind you'd pass on the street without noticing, but his brown eyes…oh, those eyes. They seemed to draw you into his very soul. Maybe that was made him such a good reporter.

I poured us each a cup of coffee and helped myself to a couple cookies. "You know, I never thought about it before. I've just been living with it so long, I don't care where she came from. She's real closed-mouthed about her past, for some reason. I do know that she's an only child. She was working as a medical secretary at the Plummer County Community Hospital, when her parents died in a car crash just before she met Daddy. She used to tell everyone she was from Monterey, California, until one of Daddy's partners' wives, Ellen Nussey, asked her about some people there, and Mother couldn't answer."

"There's no other family? Aunts? Uncles? Cousins?"

"Not that I know of." I washed and dried a couple of coffee mugs, then filled them with hot coffee.

Marcus popped another Oreo into his mouth. "Don't you think that's strange?"

"I never thought about it, I guess. Should I?"

"I sure wonder. I mean, she's *your* mother. I have all kinds of questions. What about what she looked like as a child? Where did she go to college? Did she go?"

The phone rang.

"God, Marcus, you think you were a reporter or something." I winked as I stepped into the hall. Too late…there was a fuzzy click, and the dial tone buzzed in my ear.

"Oh well, if it's important, they'll call back. Probably Mother wanting to patch things up."

Marcus wandered into the living room and sank into a wing chair. "No, she wouldn't be home yet. Come on out here and relax."

"I wish I could." Theatrically, I flopped into the opposite chair.

"You've fought enough of everyone else's battles for one day. It's time to be good to yourself." He sat his coffee mug down and moved toward me.

"If I was good to myself—" I started to say, *I never would have left you.*

"What?"

"Nothing." I closed my mouth and tried to pull my carefully constructed shell up around me.

"I don't mean to make you uncomfortable."

"You don't," I lied. *You make me feel pain, Marcus, pain like I haven't known in years.* Mercifully, the phone rang again. "See? I'll bet you dinner that's Mother right now. She can't stand it when we argue."

I stepped into the hallway and picked up the phone.

"Mrs. Paul Armstrong?" a nasal, Oriental voice intoned.

"This is she."

"Go ahead, Major Armstrong."

Oh God, not now. Emotion, already too close to the surface, caught in my throat, and I began to cough. Marcus jumped up to slap me on the back, but I waved him away.

"Kay, honey, hello! Hey, you oughta see a doctor about that cough. I've been trying to call you for a few days. Where've you been?" Static rose and fell between us in waves, but Paul's smooth confidence cut through the noise.

"Hi!" The words were strained and fake. "I'm…I'm surprised to hear from you."

"Waddaya mean, *surprised*? I'm your husband, hon! You make it sound like I'm the insurance man or something." He was full of easy confidence, the hero I used to know.

"Bad choice of words. I'm sorry." Balancing the receiver on my shoulder, I carried the phone over to the stairway and sat on the second step. Marcus brought me my coffee. As I accepted it, my arm curled around the phone, as if I could prevent one man from sensing the other's presence.

"I can't talk long. This one's on Uncle Sam," Paul said.

"Morale call, huh?" Once a month the Air Force paid for a phone call home for each service member deployed overseas. Morale calls were few and far between and often at very inconvenient times. Needless to say, I hadn't been spending any extra money phoning his on-base apartment. There was too much I didn't want to know.

"Yeah. Sorry I couldn't call earlier. I've just been wrapped up in…."

My hero stumbled. I remembered the envelope with the Korean postmark, the screaming, the accusations, the completely destroyed trust. I bit my lip and pressed my thumb and forefinger against my eyes.

"Well, I've been pretty busy. Lots of flying time, lots of flying."
His voice trailed off again.

Another long, uncomfortable silence. I took a deep breath.

"The kids are outside, right now." I tried to bridge the yawning gap between us. "Want me to get them so you can talk to them?"

"Oh yeah? So you're all alone, huh?"

My breath caught in my throat. "Maybe you ought to call them this weekend. I know they love to hear from you."

"Used to be, you couldn't wait to talk trash in my ear when the kids weren't around. Now you change the subject."

"Used to be I thought I had you all to myself."

Our tenuous bridge caught fire, and the embers fell glowing into the chasm between us.

"I miss you Kay. I miss what we had."

"You should have thought about that a long time ago." I lifted my face to the ceiling to keep the tears from spilling down my cheeks. Marcus walked back into the living room and sat down, the wing chair groaning loudly.

"I wish I could fix things between you and me, make it the way it used to be again." Paul's confidence was gone, replaced with the pleading that marked all of our final days together before he left for his second tour at Osan. "I can't live my life knowing that some little—"

"Paul, please."

"You, of all people should understand that," Anger rose in his voice. "You, Miss Gonna Save The World...."

Static swelled and rolled between us again, drowning his words. That was okay. I had heard them before. I knew what he would say. There was an electronic buzz and, abruptly, the conversation was severed.

I hung up and lay my head down on the receiver. Too much, too much for one night. I wanted to cry, to pound my fists, to let the rage and anger explode. But not now. Not with Marcus here.

His footsteps stopped in front of me, and wearily I lifted my head.

"Things are a little tough between you and the Major, aren't they?"

"That would be awfully convenient for you, wouldn't it?"

"Kay, I didn't come here to argue with you. I want to help." He sat down beside me and tried to pull me close.

I sighed and pushed away. "You want me all for yourself…
It's real obvious," I said. "You've never been good about hiding your
intentions. And yes, my marriage is in trouble—"

"Kay, I—"

"No, don't pretend. Since you think it's so damn important, I'll
tell you. He had an affair the last time we were stationed in Korea,
before we came back to Virginia. She had a little boy. Happy now?"

Marcus was silent for a moment. "So he's back in Korea with
his little geisha?"

"No…and geisha's are Japanese. He's back in Korea to find
his son. She put him in an orphanage and disappeared. He wants to
bring him back here."

"And live in this house?" Marcus was incredulous.

"Gee. That's exactly what my reaction was," I answered
caustically.

Marcus sighed. "I'm sorry he hurt you like this, Kay."

"*You're* sorry he hurt me? *You're* sorry? What kind of crap is
that?"

"I would never do that to you."

The wall around my heart broke and I fell into his warm
embrace. Sobs broke over me in waves; all the pain of the last few
years came rushing out, as I buried my head in his shoulder, and he
held me close.

"I know. I know. I know," I sobbed.

"It's okay," I heard him whisper. "I'm here now. I'm not going
anywhere."

CHAPTER 3

Marian

The voices came more frequently these last few years. I controlled them for so long, but now they were beginning to control me, just like I could no longer control Kay and this silliness she was pursuing. The voices flew out at the most inopportune time, before I could get to my bedroom and the little bottle of comforting capsules.

This morning during breakfast, it was the crash of breaking glass in the kitchen and Novella talking to herself, admonishing her own clumsiness that set them off.

Hold still, honey.

Hold still, honey. This won't hurt.

Don't scream. Someone will hear you. It'll be over soon.

Don't scream, or I'll hit you again.

Don't scream.

I bit into my napkin. *I won't scream,* I promised the voices. *I can't.*

"I'm sorry, Mrs. James." Suddenly Novella's voice was calm and placating behind me.

I snapped to attention.

She sat my grapefruit half down in front of me, placing the pointed grapefruit spoon precisely on my right. Her hair was covered with one of her atrocious flowered turbans, this one covered in massive orange blossoms. The fabric didn't even come close to matching the skirt she had on, but at least she was wearing the white apron I demanded.

It was as if she wanted to constantly remember that god-for-saken island home of hers, even after forty years. She insisted on hanging on to her Jamaican accent as well—God only knows why.

"I turned around and knocked the Pyrex measuring cup right on the floor. I hope I didn't scare you."

I grabbed her big black hand.

"Your nails are dirty."

"It's just coffee grounds."

I pushed it away. "Well, wash them. When you're done, bring me my muffin."

Novella nodded, threw back her shoulders proudly, her face a wall of black stone, and walked silently back to the kitchen. I hated it when she did that.

Alone, I blushed awkwardly, furiously wiping the hand that had clutched hers. I had to regain control before she came back with my breakfast. I stuffed the napkin back onto my lap and tried to eat, but couldn't. My coffee cup rattled against the saucer as I sat it down, its rim christened with coral lipstick.

Novella placed my muffin in front of me. My mind, under my own control again, slipped to Kay. I had a bad feeling about that job she took, always chasing truth, justice and any other rainbow ideal, but seeing Marcus Henning at the door the other night was too much.

"That young woman can do the most irritating things!"

"Who's that?"

"Kay. Why does she persist in following these strange, phil-anthropic urges of hers?"

"They aren't many people like her. You oughta be proud that girl does what she does to help people."

"Really, Novella. I do love her, but she can be such an embarrassment… these lowest common denominators she always dredges up."

Thoughts of a doorbell ringing in the middle of the night nearly fifteen years ago filled my mind. It had been Kay, sobbing on my doorstep, her nose bleeding and her left eye swollen shut. It brought back painful memories I never wanted to remember. I hoped this boy, this Grant Matthews she married on impulse wouldn't do it again. I sent her home, after a phone call to their little apartment had resulted in an apology from him.

The next time, she went straight to the emergency room where God knows how many people had known and worked with her father. They sent her to a battered women's shelter and convinced her to file domestic violence charges – even worse, because every one in town would know that Dr. Montgomery James's daughter lacked any class whatsoever.

"This is what comes of you associating with the lower orders, my dear," I said, when I had picked her up at the shelter. "If you persist in filing these charges, it will destroy your father's good memory here in Jubilant Falls, and God knows what they'll say at the country club."

She protested, but in the end I won out; she didn't file any charges.

The third time, I didn't know anything about it, until my lawyer, Martin Rathke called me and said she filed for divorce, using another lawyer.

That time, Grant blackened both her eyes, broken her nose, and gave her a gash across her cheek that needed to be sutured shut. I paid for a nose job and convinced her to dump her lawyer and use Martin.

Novella looked at me sharply. "What's bothering you?"

"Nothing you need to trouble yourself with."

"You ready for another cup of coffee?"

"*No!* I mean, *no thank you*. That will be all."

"You sure you're okay?"

"That will be all, Novella," I said, clenching my teeth. "I just remembered I have an appointment this morning. Clear this all away."

Once out of her sight, I ran up the stairs and into my bedroom. The plastic amber bottle was in my dressing table drawer. I choked down a capsule without water and fell back on the bed waiting for calm to wash over me.

I hadn't lied about the appointment. There were only four more pills left. I would have to call Ed Nussey this morning and have him give me another prescription. Maybe this time he wouldn't be so insistent about having that lab work done. I didn't have the time, but couldn't live without my pills.

In a few moments, I felt calm and back in control. Carefully, I reapplied my lipstick and headed downstairs.

"Novella, I'm going out."

* * *

"I can't keep giving you these pills, Marian. You've got to be closely monitored on these meds, and I haven't seen you in months." Ed Nussey looked over his desk at me. His black reading glasses sat on his hooked nose and made him look like some silly schoolteacher. His white lab coat hung on his angular build like a sheet, and his stethoscope hung around his turkey-wattled neck like a noose. *Really, Ed,* I thought, *you either need a good plastic surgeon, or it's time to retire.*

"Don't be so foolish, Ed. Monty gave them to me all the time." That much was true. My husband, Montgomery, had insisted on watching me closely, too; but with him, there was comfort in knowing that no one other than he knew what was going on. I couldn't let Ed in. He might tell Ellen, who spread more news that the *Jubilant Falls Journal-Gazette*, and then God knows how far it would go.

Someone is going to find out anyway, a voice told me. *Someone is going to find out the truth about you one of these days.*

"Just write the prescription, and I promise I'll come in next time."

"Marian, you better. This is the last time." Reluctantly, his big-knuckled hand dragged his pen across the prescription pad. "Stop and see the receptionist on your way out for an appointment."

"Of course."

I ran past the receptionist and out the office to the ladies' room down the hall. I choked down another of my remaining capsules, drinking water directly from the faucet. *God, what if someone sees me like this?* I choked in terror and locked myself in a stall.

I can't go on like this forever. I lay my forehead against the cool, gray tile. *This can't continue.*

If the truth were known, they'll come for you. They'll take you back.

Tears coursed down my face, spotting the chrome toilet paper holder. I bit into my purse handle, to quiet my sobs. *No one must ever find me. No one must ever know.*

I had been found once thirty-five years ago, six months after Montgomery and I were married. Montgomery and I had gone for a long weekend to Chicago. I had gone shopping at Marshall Field's for a new fur coat, back when furs were still the mark of taste and class and not the mark of some political incorrectness. I felt a pair of eyes boring into my back and turned to see the woman behind the counter staring.

"My, my, Marian! I just knewed it was you! I though so the minute I laid eyes on...."

"What do you want?" I snapped.

"Why, nothing! It's just such a surprise to see you, of all people, here in Chicago. Ya know, you were quite the story after ya left town."

"What do you want? Money?" I searched through my clutch purse for a spare bill.

"Why, Lordy, no, deary! Ya just wouldn't believe what all's gone on back home since you left," she babbled. "Why don't we get together for a cup of coffee sometime soon? Do you live here in Chicago now? I love to catch ya up on all of it."

"Meet me at the diner on the corner in fifteen minutes." I dropped the silver fox coat in the aisle and walked out.

She was already there when I arrived. I sat quietly, picking nervously at a piece of angel food cake in front of me, offering only minimal information, as she rattled on and on. Finally, she finished her story.

I laid a one hundred-dollar bill on the counter.

"This pays for everything. You can keep whatever is left. Whatever you do, don't tell anyone you saw me here."

I never went to Chicago again. I wouldn't even order out of Marshall Field's catalog.

As time went by, the yoke of my masquerade had worn heavier and heavier on my shoulders. The voices told me I be caught if I went outside. I made Montgomery hire a housekeeper to do the marketing, and I stayed safely hidden away from anyone who might know the truth, until one day Montgomery had told me there were these marvelous little pills that could gave me the courage to go out again. Besides, Montgomery's practice and his stature in the community had grown. I had responsibilities, and I needed to live up to them.

Now, thirty-five years later, as the medicated calm began to reassert itself, I smoothed my hair and fixed my make-up. No one must see through me like that woman once did...or like I did myself.

Confident again, I squared my shoulders. It was time to meet Lovey at the club for lunch.

Dear Lovey. I don't know what I would have done without her in those early years after I married Monty. She helped me through all manner of social occasions, helping to plan menus and parties when Monty's practice was just starting out and making the right impression had been so critical.

Of course making the right impression is still vital, but the waters are more familiar now.

After a while, I became able to handle my social calendar on my own, but I still relied on her friendship.

She taught me everything I needed to know: who was important, who was *nouveau riche* and couldn't be relied on, who gave the most important parties, and what one needed to do to get an invitation.

We were good friends for many reasons, but mainly because she, like me, had not come from the same moneyed background that so many other club members. Of course, I never told her the whole truth. She just knew that my parents were of modest means.

She was the kind of woman I admired, a take-charge kind who really ran the day-to-day operations of McNair Machine Tool to allow her husband David the freedom to pursue whatever whim came to mind that morning. Lovey was the one who did the wheeling and dealing, assuring her husband's associates that deadlines would be met, payments would be made, and products would be superior.

Which of course, they were.

She would swoop down upon McNair Machine Tool once or twice a week, terrorizing the bookkeepers and the clerks, checking their books and their attitudes.

Behind her back, they called her Queen Leona II, but in my mind the real Leona Helmsley was the victim of a vicious press. She built an empire, hadn't she? In her fashion, so did Lovey McNair. I was just fortunate that she asked me along for the ride.

For many years, she badgered Montgomery and me to buy into various schemes; most of them were quick incorporations to take advantage of a lagging real estate market, or booming stock market – quick profit-making set-ups that she put together and liquidated like some people change socks.

Montgomery would have no part of it, but he never said why. He never liked Lovey, so rather than cause an argument, I simply deferred to him when she brought whatever scheme up.

Monty died of a stroke in Kay's junior year of high school. The sale of his share of the medical practice and our other holdings left me very comfortable, if I must say so myself. When a check came from an unknown life insurance policy, I decided it was high time I made a few fiscal decisions on my own. This time when Lovey approached me, I said yes.

After a few years, we built quite a little nest egg. I was a silent partner in all of this, so I really didn't have a voice in how she ran things. Still, there were times when, really, I thought her methods were a bit extreme.

But Lovey always said she really had all the business sense. I couldn't know anything about running it, she said. Maybe that was what made her so successful. I truly admired her business acumen and her razor-sharp ability to see through a situation as it truly was and go right to the heart of a matter, make a sharp decision, and stick to it no matter what. Sometimes, I thought she could be a little heavy-handed, but she always assured me that what she did was in our best interests.

She was already seated when I arrived.

"Sorry to keep you waiting."

"Hello, Marian. I hope your doctor's appointment went well?" Her eyebrows arched.

"Everything's fine. Just had Ed refill my sinus medication."

We both ordered chef salads. As our waiter disappeared into the kitchen, Lovey frowned somberly.

"Something wrong?" I asked.

Lovey shook her head. "A little dust-up with a client."

"Oh?"

"It's been taken care of."

Lovey looked less than reassured.

"Don't worry so much! As long as the checks keep coming!" I teased lightly. This was strange; I never had to reassure Lovey about anything.

"Yes. As long as the checks keep coming." My friend and partner frowned again and lapsed into an uncharacteristic silence.

The veins in my forehead began to throb. "You're beginning to frighten me. What happened?"

The waiter brought our salads, and Lovey's forehead creased deeply as she picked out the green pepper rings.

"One of our clients thought they could get away with not pay-ing this month." Her eyes shot daggers across the table at me. "It's been taken care of."

"Oh dear." I wrung the napkin in my lap and leaned across the table. "How did you fix things?"

"The way I usually do."

My stomach turned over. "However limited our agreement may be, I am a partner in this little venture with you. And I know how you deal with problems." My voice was barely above a whisper.

"Stop it," she hissed. "You don't always know how I fix things...but it won't happen again. Pull yourself together, and don't be such a child."

"I'm not being a child!" I hissed back.

"Everything's a crisis to you lately, Marian. I do wish you would stop."

"No, it's not! And I will not stop until I get some answers from you!"

"Dear heart, these people are not the *crème de la crème* of the Eastern seaboard either." Lovey laughed at her own wit. "It's all they understand. Besides, it's fixed now. "

"How did you fix it, though?"

"I don't want you questioning me. It's my decision on how to handle things."

"You called *him*, didn't you?"

"Marian, you're building mountains from molehills again."

"That Weisenbach woman was a molehill?" I burst out in exasperation. "It took fourteen thousand dollars to fix that...the judge, the chief of police, the arresting officer...."

Lovey slammed her meaty fist down on the table, her voice barely above a whisper. "You're still getting your check once a month, aren't you? Aren't you?"

"Well yes, but I don't think...."

"I have the authority to run the operation as I see fit, and if I see fit to ask a certain employee to perform a certain task, then it will be done. You will *not* question me."

I picked up my folk and tried to eat. I knew I didn't have the ability to run the business like she did, and I knew I was only a silent partner in all this, but I hated it when she made me feel so unworthy. I pushed my plate away, pain constricting my chest.

"I'm—I'm sorry."

"So, how are Andrew and Lillian these days?" Lovey asked, loud enough for everyone around her to hear. "I'm sure you're thrilled to have them living so close to you again."

So the subject was closed. All I wanted was the answer to a few questions. Half of it was my money after all.

"Lovey, just one more question, if you don't mind?"

Lovey's eyes narrowed into heavily made-up slits. Her jaw clenched. "Why don't you go home and lay down. I'll call you later to check on you. Lunch is on me."

"But...I...I...." Lovey's iron glare stopped me in my tracks. "You're right, I'm not feeling well. Thank you."

If only Monty were here to advise me, I thought, picking my way through the luncheon crowd. *Maybe he had been right about her all along.*

* * *

A week later, we were at the social hour, prior to the Plummer County Community Hospital Charity Board meeting. The two of us stood next to the table, which was spread sparsely with hors d'oeuvres, cookies, and weak punch. It was one of those few days where my calm was not medically induced. I had felt so marvelous upon rising that I had skipped my medication all together.

We hadn't seen each other since lunch at the club; my comments that day were swept under the rug, and the waters seemed to be calm between us. Lovey may have run our business with an iron hand, but – thank God – she was still my friend.

"Did I tell you I saw Marcus Henning and Kay having lunch recently?" Lovey viciously skewered a cheese cube with an unnaturally green toothpick.

"Really?" I looked over the foiled tray of store-bought sugar cookies and selected one.

"He made a rather ugly scene, something about that business last year. It was all very embarrassing for Kay, no doubt."

"No doubt."

"He is such a strange character, isn't he? Does he still carry a torch for Kay?"

"I don't know," I replied. "He did stop by her house the other night when I was there."

"Don't you think that's strange?"

"Well, no, I mean, he had just written that lovely article about Kay's new job."

"When I saw them at Hawk's, they seemed to be standing a bit *too* close, if you get my drift. I would nip that in the bud, Marian.

Her husband is serving his country clear across the world and that, well— you know. People will talk."

Cold terror swept through me. *My God, was Kay silly enough to get involved with that rabble again?* He was as much of an idiotic, idealistic do-gooder as she was. And, worse, he had no money, no future, and the manners of a toad.

I broke open a bottle of Dom Perignon and danced a jig in the kitchen the night she confessed she had turned down Marcus's proposal (not in front of her, of course). They had been an off-and-on item, since that first disaster of hers. Thank God she used her head and realized that marriage between them would have been another disaster.

But, what if something was going on between them already? *My God.*

Lovey raised her painted eyebrows and turned to the lithe woman bearing down on us with a stack of folders in her arms. I would have to think about Kay's reputation later.

"Ellen. Ellen Nussey," Lovey cooed. "I didn't see you earlier. I was beginning to think you weren't going to make it."

Ellen Nussey, the president of the Charity Board (and Ed's wife), smiled indulgently. She wore too much Indian turquoise jewelry and gauzy California-style clothing all year long, and her perpetual tan accented a row of somewhat horsy, although perfectly capped, teeth.

Ellen and I had known each other for years. That didn't mean I liked her.

"Don't you know I have been here since two o'clock trying to get these committees straight?" Ellen asked. "Marian, how are you? Card club is at my house this Thursday, correct?"

"Yes, it is." I clenched my teeth.

"Wonderful, I'll see you then. Oh, before I forget," Ellen showed her equine teeth and handed me two folders. "Since you did such a marvelous job on the table decorations for the New Year's Ball last year, I knew you wouldn't even consider saying no for a second year. Mrs. Mazza, Mrs. Waymack, and Mrs. Larghente will be on the committee with you. This is the budget and their phone numbers. The one-hundredth anniversary of the hospital is this year's theme."

"Thank you."

"The other folder is the phone tree. It's your month to contact the other board members."

"Of course." I hated the Charity Board almost as much as I hated Ellen Nussey. However, my position brought with it certain obligations, which I understood and followed to the letter.

Ellen's worthless chatter filled my ears, but I no longer heard her. If only Kay could see *her* obligations. Kay had been terribly closed-mouthed when she returned home with just the children. On the surface, she said it was an unaccompanied tour to Korea; only Paul could go and not the family.

"But you've gone before!" I exclaimed.

"That was different," she said.

End of explanation. Deep down, there was something wrong that she wasn't telling me.

And, if Marcus Henning was sniffing around like a rutting pig again, he might provide a temptation that my daughter certainly didn't need right now. She had a husband with a brilliant military career ahead of him and those two wonderful children. She couldn't throw all that away—I wouldn't let her.

"We could do something about the situation, you know." Lovey laid her broad hand on my arm.

"Pardon me?" I said, shaken from my reverie, answering automatically. "Of course we could. You always know best."

Later, I would wished I paid more attention.

* * *

That's it! Why hadn't I thought of it before! I turned away from my bedroom window, letting the dark, heavy curtain cover the wet, miserable weather outside. All I had to do was affect some kind of reconciliation between Kay and Paul! If I acted quickly, the two of them would be cooing like lovebirds, and Marcus Henning would be out in the cold, away from my daughter. But first, I had to put my plan into action. Confidently, I went down to breakfast.

"Good morning, Novella," I said, as she poured my coffee.

"Morning Mrs. James. I'll be right back with your grapefruit."

"Oh, no need Novella, no need. I'll just take my muffin and some butter and jam in Dr. James's study, if you don't mind."

"Yes ma'am." My maid looked at me strangely. "Anything else?"

"Yes. I have some writing to do this morning in the study and will be using Dr. James's fountain pen. Bring me something to wash the ink off my hands and see that I'm not disturbed."

Novella didn't move.

"Why are you staring at me like that? Go!"

"I've known you for almost thirty years now. This is this first time you want something' different for breakfast since Doctor passed."

"It's not the end of the world. I can change, can't I?" I picked up my cup and saucer with both hands. "I'll be in the study."

I called the room off the foyer Montgomery's study, although I moved there after his death. I made sure it was a replica of the room he *really* used as a study when we lived in our first home off Church Street. Monty's study had been the most masculine room in the house, and I enjoyed being reminded of his presence. Just like our Church Street home, one wall was covered with mahogany bookshelves filled with his medical books and other volumes. Beside the fireplace, an authentic suit of English armor stood beside a black leather sofa. I breathed deeply, inhaling the masculine, leather scent that still filled the room. Montgomery had been my salvation; he had brought me out of the secretarial pool at the county hospital and given me a life I never knew existed. He was also the last one to know the truth about me.

Almost immediately, Novella entered with a tray, carrying a warmed washcloth on a silver salver and my breakfast.

"I may be a while. Bring me the coffee pot, and see that I am not disturbed."

"Yes, ma'am." Novella shook her head, turbaned today in brilliant blues, muttering as she shut the door behind her.

I filled Montgomery's Mont Blanc pen with ink and, dismissing Novella's grumbling, began to write:

Dear Paul,

You know me, I'm such an early bird. I have just begun my Christmas shopping and I like to let you in on a little secret. How would you like...

Perfect! The words flowed as easily as the ink. It took another few minutes to recopy the letter on a page of my best vellum letterhead. Purposefully, I addressed the envelope and, after waiting for the ink to dry, carefully sealed the contents inside. Everything was now in motion. I could relax and enjoy breakfast.

As I ate, I looked across the desk at a picture of my precious grandchildren. Andy was sitting on a child-sized chair, wearing the most adorable little suit, and clasping a plump-cheeked little Lillian, dressed in a red velvet holiday dress, on his lap. Looking like a miniature version of his father, Andy was smiling toward the camera while Lillian smiled at him. It was one of my favorite pictures. Kay had sent the photo in a silver frame as part of my Christmas gifts and I often moved it throughout the house so I could keep my little angels in view.

I loved those children more than anyone could know – it was one of those pure child-like loves, uncomplicated and innocent, unlike the relationship with my own daughter. I felt like it was such a chance to start my life again, to atone for so much, if I could see just one more smile and hear one more childish giggle. An afternoon with Lillian and Andrew was the greatest gift I could receive, and I couldn't let Kay ruin my chances to spend time with those precious, precious darlings by ruining her marriage to Paul.

The phone on the desk rang, just as I finished my last bite. I waited for Novella's discreet knock.

"Excuse me, Mrs. James," she said. "I know you didn't want to be disturbed, but there's a man on the phone. He won't tell me his name, but says he's got to speak to you. You want me to handle it?"

"No thank you. I'll take the call." I knew who it was. Coldly, angrily, I picked up the phone. "What do you want?"

"Mrs. J., how are you?" the voice at the other end of the line oozed menacingly, like a panther circling a wounded gazelle, ready to jump in for the kill.

"I have told you repeatedly I do not want you calling this house. Call Lovey or my lawyers, but never ever call this number again."

"But Mrs. J, I have some information for you."

"Whatever it is, I'm sure they can handle it."

"Not this."

My insides quivered, and I gripped the sides of the desk. He knows. Somehow the secret is out. "I don't know why Lovey insisted that we hire you."

"Because I'm so good at what I do. You of all people should know that."

I shivered.

"I have spoken to your friend and partner," the caller continued. "She told me someone is making a nuisance of himself. I can fix that. I can make sure it doesn't happen ever again."

"What are you talking about?"

"The reporter. It's also possible that your daughter needs to be shown the error of her ways."

"What are you talking about? My daughter hasn't done anything wrong."

"That bitch owes me." There was a slow, hollow click, as the connection was severed.

The hair on the back of my neck stood on end, and air rushed out of my lungs. The receiver fell from my hand, dragging the rest of the phone with it into a noisy pile onto the floor.

"Mrs. James? Mrs. James, you okay?" Novella pounded on the study door.

You can't escape, a voice rang in my head. *Retribution will find you, and it will eat you alive.*

My insides heaved. I wanted to vomit. *Has Kay become involved in any of this? And his threats… was he seriously going to hurt Kay? How was I going to keep her safe? Monitor her every move?* I had to talk to Lovey. Now.

"You okay?" Novella pounded on the door again. "You don't answer me, I'm calling the ambulance!"

I tried to smooth my hair, but my fingers locked at my temples. Tears stung my eyes, and I swayed back and forth, wanting to scream, scared that I would.

"Mrs. James! Mrs. James!" The doorknob rattled.

Be quiet or someone will hear you.

"I'm, I'm fine, Novella."

"Then open this door, so's I can see you."

Purposefully, I replaced the phone on the desk and opened the library door. "See? I'm all in one piece. Are you satisfied, now? See that the phone company has my number changed by the end of the day," I barked. "I'm going over to Kay's."

"Yes, ma'am." Novella barely nodded. "I'll do that."

* * *

Of course, I didn't go to Kay's. I went directly to Lovey's, the Mercedes screeching to a stop in front of the McNair's Tudor home. Putting politeness behind me, I swept up the front steps and into their living room.

"Lovey! Lovey McNair! Come down here right now! This whole situation is getting out of hand!" I clasped the newel post and called authoritatively up the staircase.

"Darling, don't shout. I'm right here."

She emerged from the dining room, wrapped imperiously in a noxious, pink peignoir. Her husband, David, stood behind her in a quilted, maroon smoking jacket, his pipe held effeminately in one hand.

"Damn it, Lovey…" I stopped and recovered my composure. "I am most upset. May I speak to you privately?"

"David, if you don't mind?" she asked.

He shrugged foppishly and returned to the dining room.

Taking me by the elbow, Lovey led me upstairs to the bedroom she occupied. She closed the door and indicated that we both sit on the lush, ruffled bed.

"Now, dear, whatever is troubling you?" Lovey folded her fat hands across her ample bosom.

"Your goon called my house a few minutes ago."

"Oh dear. He wasn't supposed to do that."

"He made threats, Lovey! He threatened that stupid reporter, and he threatened my daughter! What in God's name are you doing? And how dare you think you have the right to interfere with my daughter's life!"

"I'm not doing a thing. Why would I want to bother Kay?"

"You said something to that monster—that disgusting excuse for a human being, and I want to know what it was!"

Lovey's hard eyes met mine. "I simply mentioned that I had seen your daughter having lunch with Marcus Henning and that you were concerned that people would talk."

"What business is it of yours?" I felt the hysterics rise in my throat and struggled to stay in control. "I don't need you to go solve any of my problems for me—and certainly not in the way you solve problems! Of all the people in the entire world to tell that Kay was even back in town!"

"Marian!"

The tone of her voice told me I was treading once more on dangerous ground, but I didn't care. "Someone's going to get killed one of these days, Lovey! Then where will we be?"

"You're blowing things all out of proportion again." Lovey's voice dropped, ominously. "You're watching too many soap operas. No one is going to get murdered."

"I don't watch *any* soap operas, and you know that! He threatened Kay! Whatever you've done, you've dragged my daughter into it, and I won't stand for it!"

"He can be rather unsettled at times, can't he?"

"Unsettled? *Unsettled*? He's unhinged! He's a dangerous maniac!" I screamed. "I want this called off, right now!"

"I haven't called anything *on*, my dear."

"I will not have my daughter's life put in danger or have anyone's—" the word clogged in my throat "—murder on my conscience!"

"You're making this into another one of your dreadful melodramas, Marian. If it will make you happy, I will speak to him this afternoon." With a dismissive wave, she signaled that the conversation was over. She stood and opened the bedroom door. "Shall we?"

At the foot of the stairs, she patted my shoulder. "So nice of you to drop by," she said, loud enough for David to hear. "I do hope I've calmed any fears you have about the New Year's Ball. Do drop by again."

"Call it off, Lovey," I hissed. "Call it off, right now."

"Yes, you too, dear."

Abruptly, she shoved me out onto the porch and slammed the door behind me.

"You can't do this to me, Lovey McNair!" I pounded on the door. "I won't let you do this! Do you year me, Lovey? Do you hear me?"

CHAPTER FOUR

Marcus

I stared up at the Aurora Building, a high-tech honeycomb next door to Hawk's and just a few blocks down from the paper on Detroit Street.

Jess knew the bare bones of what I was doing, but not much more. He wanted me to turn the whole thing over to an attorney, where it rightfully belonged, but I refused.

"Let's give whoever this guy is behind Aurora Development a chance to fix things. Let me go talk to him," I told Jess.

"You're a journalist, not a hired gun," he answered. "You're supposed to be objective. You've got no business getting involved personally."

I shrugged.

Remember Jefferson City. Don't screw this one up too, was what he really was telling me. *You've got too much to lose this time.*

If only I knew how much.

I took a deep breath and opened the heavy glass door.

Inside the lobby, an elderly security guard sat benignly behind a wide round desk, pouring himself a cup of coffee from a large plastic Thermos bottle. A directory hanging beside him proclaimed this as the Aurora Building, listing all the tenants, but none of them specifically was Ludean's landlord.

"Pardon me," I leaned over the security guard's desk. "Can you tell me where the Aurora Development Corporation offices are located?"

"It's all Aurora Development, pal." The guard drained his cup and poured another.

"If I wanted to speak to someone about one of Aurora's rental properties, who would I talk to?"

The guard lowered a fuzzy eyebrow over one eye and glowered. "Residential or office space?"

"Residential."

"Third floor, number three-forty." The other eyebrow lowered suspiciously.

"Thank you." I stepped away from the desk and into the elevator. As the elevator door closed in front of me, the guard was still staring intently at me, speaking quietly into the phone.

Suite 340 lay at the end of a gray hallway muffled with grape carpeting. There was no name on the door. I knocked once. When there was no answer, I went in.

The office consisted of two, possibly three, rooms. The room I stood in was unfurnished, except for a telephone that sat in a corner, swirled in electronic umbilical cords; in the other stood a brass coat tree with an expensive suit jacket hanging on a wooden hanger.

"What can I do for you?"

I turned around to see a beefy, barrel-chested bull of a man, at least six feet tall, coming from the other room. The sleeves of his custom-tailored shirt were rolled halfway up, exposing muscular, grizzly bear arms. His hands looked huge and lethal as he wiped them on a paper towel.

There was something in the face, something I couldn't put my finger on, but I felt we had met before. He recognized me, too; there was a glimmer of recognition in his narrowed black eyes.

"Hello, I'm Marcus Henning, with the *Jubilant Falls Journal-Gazette*."

"I know who you are."

"Oh?"

"From the paper. You're a reporter."

Maybe that was it. I had seen him, or he had seen me at one of those idiot social functions I was forced into covering. Still, he didn't have that practiced air of boredom I had seen so often. There was something feral, something raw. I couldn't figure it out. Ignoring all my instincts, I extended my hand in greeting.

"I need to speak with whomever is in charge of Aurora Development residential rental property."

"That would be me."

"And you are?" Like an old gunslinger, I pulled my notebook from my back pocket.

He opened his mouth, then closed it again. "I work here," he said finally.

"You don't have a name?"

"Not to you." The fuzzy hulk in the fancy shirt balled up the paper towel and tossed it into an empty corner.

"What exactly do you do?"

"I run the place."

"I see. Well then, sir, a woman named Ludean Tate claims to rent from your firm. Is that true?"

The goon cocked his head and thought for a moment. "Yeah. She's a tenant."

"She claims to have contacted you repeatedly about the condition of her apartment and that you or your firm have refused to make repairs."

"Aurora Development insists on keeping their rental properties in excellent condition." A prepackaged PR answer. He knew what I was after.

"I'm surprised to hear that." I wish I could remember where I met this Neanderthal. I flipped a page on my pad and began to read the list of needed repairs. "My investigation of her apartment shows two broken windows, a semi-functioning toilet, peeling paint and wallpaper. That doesn't sound like excellent condition to me."

"Nine times out of ten, it's the tenant that tears those places up like that."

"I see. Do you recall being contacted by Miss Tate to make repairs?"

"I couldn't understand her if she did." He'd talked to her, all right. Otherwise he wouldn't know about her speech impediment.

"That doesn't mean she deserves substandard housing. You know there are also two children residing in that apartment?"

"So?"

"What if that littlest kid decides she's a little hungry and has some paint chips for lunch? What if she's done it three times a week for the last three years? What would happen then? What do you think a steady diet of lead-based paint does to a kid's brain?"

He shrugged.

"It causes brain damage. I guess you won't mind if I take some of those paint chips down to the health department and have them analyzed for lead content then?"

"Listen buddy—" He stuck a hairy finger beneath my nose. "There's no need to make threats here."

"When was the last time the fire inspector came through that place? Or does Aurora Development pay off the local inspectors? Can I assume that repairs will be made, or at least well underway by September first?"

"That's next week! I can't—"

"If you can't get started on them, the *Journal-Gazette* is prepared to run the story on the front page. Do I make myself clear?"

The miscreant stepped back. "I understand."

"Then I can contact Miss Tate and assure her that work will begin immediately?"

"Well, I have to contact my supervisor."

"And who is that?" I poised my pen above my paper.

"It's...ah...." he stopped abruptly. "Somebody who lives out of town."

"Why can't you tell me? What are you hiding?"

He shook his head. "None of your business."

"It won't take much digging for me to find out. Why don't you just save us both a lot of trouble? "

"I've had about all I'm gonna take from you, buddy." He jabbed a thick finger into my tie. "I suggest you get out of this office right now."

"Then repairs will begin on Ludean Tate's apartment as soon as possible?"

"I said get out!"

"In case you or your mysterious supervisor decides to contact me, here's my card."

The ape shredded the card, dropping the confetti on the grape carpet. "If you don't get out of this office," he said, speaking slowly. "You'll never see daylight again!"

"Have a nice day—asshole." I waved and slammed the door behind me.

Hopefully that will do it, I thought, punching the *down* button at the elevator. *I may not have a story if he does, but at least Ludean—*

Pain ripped through my left arm, as I felt it twist up between my shoulder blades; someone grabbed a handful of my thinning hair at the back of my head, and I tasted blood as my face slammed against the elevator button.

"Listen, dick brain." The Neanderthal's voice roared in my ear. "If I were you, I wouldn't mess around here any more. There's more trouble here than you or that hare-lipped little bitch ever thought about. You got me?"

"You sonuvabitch…" I sputtered, against the wall.

"I said—you got me?" My face slammed against the wall again, and stars swam around my left eye.

Suddenly, the elevator chimed, its parting doors my only escape. The Neanderthal pulled me away from the wall and shoved me in. "Don't come back."

* * *

"Oh my God, Marcus, what happened to you?" Jess stood up from behind his computer.

I flopped down in the seat next the city desk, a wet wad of brown industrial-strength paper towels against my face. "I met the landlord from hell."

"Jesus Christ! Is this that welfare mother story you were telling me about? What happened?"

"Yeah. I asked him his name."

Jess turned to the other reporters beginning to assemble around us, barking out orders. "Somebody go get me a photographer! I want this documented! I want the police called! Nobody does this to one of my reporters!"

"Hold on, Jess! No cops. Not yet."

"What? Wait a minute!"

"No, *you* wait a minute! This is my story, and I'll handle it the way I want." Dropping the wet paper towels in the trash, I swiveled in my chair and quickly logged onto the newspaper's computer system, where a newsroom phone message file was kept. "Anybody call from Aurora Development or about Aurora Development?" I asked no one in particular. Scrolling down the green screen, I saw four messages from Ludean and one from Kay. Something must have happened, but Ludean left no number. I waved everyone around me away and dialed Kay's number.

"So, how did it go?" she asked.

"This goon that operates the place wouldn't give me his name, but I think I got through to him." Gingerly, I touched my swollen face.

"You really think so?"

"No doubt. I made an impression." *On the wall.* "Have you heard from Ludean?" I asked, trying to change the subject. "She's called here a couple of times, but didn't leave a number."

"She's not scheduled to come back to the center until next week, unless she walks in."

"You let me know if you heard anything, right?"

"Of course! Marcus, I'm so grateful for all this. I hope she has some good news. What can I do to thank you?"

"Oh, there are a few things that come to mind."

Kay started to speak then stopped, I assume, to put me back in my place.

Quickly, I did it for her. "How about a simple dinner?"

"Much—ah— better suggestion. I'll see if I can get a babysitter for Friday night. How's that?"

"Great. See you then. I better go. I need to get down to Ludean's place and see what she needs. Then, I've got to go down to the clerk of courts."

"OK. See ya Friday." The phone clicked in my ear.

I wouldn't do this for anyone but you, Kay. Or would I? What was my real reason? To salvage a failing ego? Rebuild myself in my best friend's (and boss's) eyes? Remind him that I was the real journalist we both remembered? Or simply to make myself look good in the eyes of the woman I loved?

* * *

Later that afternoon, I knocked on the shoddy door of Ludean's apartment. Her eyes were shining, as she opened the door.

"They were here today!" she crowed triumphantly. "Wait— who did that to you?"

"Never mind. Who was here?" Being around Ludean more made it easier to understand her, I thought.

"The man to fix my apartment! Look!" Her bony finger indicated two new panes of glass in the living room window.

"Did he do anything else? Did he leave his name? A card?"

She shook her head to all three questions, but she was clearly thrilled that at least something had been accomplished. "But he said he'd come back and do the rest real soon!"

"Good. The man that you give your rent money to...did he come with the repair man?"

She shook her head again.

"That's okay. He sure didn't waste any time." So, my visit made a difference. I only hoped that Aurora Development would complete the job. "Ludean, do you happen to know his name?"

She puckered her sallow brow. "It was on 'is desk."

"Desk? What desk? The office was empty when I was there this morning." Damn it, this was getting weird.

Ludean opened her arms wide. "Big brown desk, right inside the door."

"And it's there on the first of the month, when you go to pay your rent?"

"Uh-huh."

That's strange. "Listen, I have to get back to the newsroom. It looks as though things here are on the upswing. If someone doesn't come back in the next week or so to start the rest of the repairs, you let me know."

I wanted to believe that my one confrontation had caused all of this activity, but a niggling voice deep inside said that I had not heard the end of this.

At the clerk of courts office, I learned that Aurora Development was a tangle of dummy corporations that ended with a firm called Land Management Limited. The owners were not listed, just the names of Martin Rathke of Rathke, Fitzsimmons, Wyler and Dean, the prominent legal firm in Jubilant Falls.

A bunch of lawyers wouldn't be so stupid as to be messed up in trash housing, would they? Or is it all a front for someone else?

Rathke, Fitzsimmons had a large staff of fresh, starving young attorneys that handled most of their corporate legal affairs in Jubilant, as well as ninety percent of the civil cases. Privately, Jess and I referred to them as the Thundering Herd. The senior partner Martin Rathke was a large man, resembling not so much your average well-to-do barrister as a remnant from the days of snake oil salesmen and hanging judges.

I remembered our crime reporter John Porter wondering once why Rathke never ran for a judgeship.

"He's got more power right where he is," an old-timer had cryptically answered. I hadn't understood, at the time. I was too busy writing up weddings and engagements. I could use the old guy's knowledge here and now, but he died a few months after his retirement – a heart attack finishing his final fishing trip off the Gulf Coast. Instead, I dropped a quarter into the courthouse pay phone.

"Rathke, Fitzsimmons, Wyler and Dean."

"Martin Rathke, please."

"May I ask who's calling?"

"Marcus Henning, *Jubilant Falls Journal-Gazette*."

"One moment." There was a click, as I was put on hold and music to drill teeth by played in my ear.

Halfway through a string arrangement of "She's Having My Baby," there was another click, and Rathke's oily voice came on the line.

"Good afternoon, Mr. Henning. What can I do for you?"

"Mr. Rathke, can you tell me who the owners are of Land Management Limited, the company behind Aurora Development?"

"Son, that's privileged information. I can't tell you that," he chortled.

"Can you tell me if the people behind Land Management are aware of the condition their tenants live under?"

"I'm sure they are, son. What's this all about?"

"I have spoken with a woman who claims to have repeatedly contacted Aurora Development in regards to repairs on her apartment, and the repairs have not been completed. Do you have any knowledge of this?"

"Why would I? That's an administrative issue for Aurora."

"I spoke to someone there this morning who would not reveal her names or his supervisor's names. Isn't that a little odd?"

"Some people are just uncomfortable dealing with you media types."

"So as far as you know, your clients maintain healthy, safe rental properties for their tenants."

"Absolutely. That's all I have to say." The phone went dead in my ear.

There was no way in hell Rathke would reveal to me without a subpoena who was behind Land Management Ltd. Still, I had Rathke's name. I could run with that. Let him take the heat for his client's mistakes. That's what he's being paid for.

* * *

On Friday, I spent too much money on flowers and too little on wine, but I was as expectant as any hormone-driven teenage boy as I took Kay's front steps two at a time. The August humidity was receding, but sweat still hung in beads across my forehead. The doorbell echoed through the cavernous foyer.

"Oh my God, Marcus, what happened to you!" Kay's eyes shone as she opened the door. Her red hair was loose, and she had a heavy wooden hairbrush in her hand.

"It's nothing. I come bearing gifts, as any proper gentleman caller should."

"Thank you so much! But, who hit you? When? Where?"

"You're welcome. I don't know. A day or so ago. Aurora Development." I tried to keep a straight face, which really wasn't too hard since every time I smiled, my swollen lip felt like it was being stretched across a rack. "I could really use a drink, though."

"My goodness! When did you start being proper?" A mischievous sparkle shot through her eyes, and I began to see her icy demeanor giving way to the old Kay I once knew. "Sure. C'mon in." She led me into the living room and, leaning the wine into the corner of a wing chair, set the flowers in a vase on the mantle.

"There are wine glasses on the kitchen table," she continued. "As you can see, I'm not quite together, so if you'll pour yourself a drink, I'll go upstairs and finish up."

"Where are the kids?"

"At Mother's. She decided to be a real grandmother and keep them overnight."

Kay turned to go. Impulsively, I clasped her warm shoulders and pulled her close, till the smell of her sweet perfume filled my head.

"Mmmm...." Her body relaxed against me, not the reaction I expected. No fight, no protest. Spooked, I quickly kissed the back of her neck and let her go.

"Couldn't help myself," I shrugged, with a crooked smile.

She smiled sadly. "I know." She shook her head (Was it regret? Pity?) and disappeared up the stairs, as my confused silence filled the room.

In a few moments, she was back with her riotous hair pinned carefully in place, a picture of perfect composure. My hand shook as I handed her a glass of wine.

"Did this happen at Aurora Development?" She reached up and touched my eye. I winced and turned away.

"Yes. They weren't the Welcome Wagon. Let's just leave it at that. Why did you say that, before you went upstairs?"

She stepped closer, her upturned face close to mine. "Don't get your hopes up, cowboy. Let's go eat."

I cupped her face in my hands and kissed her again. "I've always loved you, Kay."

Something within her gave way, tears filling her eyes as the barriers between us crumbled. There was no pretense between us, no games. Our years apart were gone instantly, as she stood on her tiptoes to kiss me.

"I love you, too," she whispered. "I've always loved you."

Our lips searched for each other, until they met in perfect union and her tongue slid into my battered mouth mingling the taste of toothpaste and blood together. Time ceased to flow, as sweet memories of her touch came flooding back. She made a small gasp, and her back arched as I pressed her hips against mine, grasping hungry handfuls of the sweet, soft flesh I never thought I touch again. I slid the zipper of her dress down to the small of her back and, as it fell to the floor, found myself sinking to my knees in a primal search down her breasts and taut belly through the satin of her slip. Grasping her buttocks, I buried my face in the small shimmering valley between her thighs. Kay shuddered and moaned.

This time, nothing could come between us. This time, I would never let her go.

We were upstairs, pairing violently in her big four-poster bed, silently, greedily devouring each other as if speech would break the spell. In the hot, sticky darkness, I clung to her until my need for her exploded, her nails drawing lines of blood down my back as the echoes of our satisfaction resounded through the room. She was mine again. The major's wife was mine. As we rolled apart, warmth and exhaustion enveloped me. I couldn't help it.

I fell asleep.

What a pig.

I woke with a jerk, sitting bolt upright in bed.

"Welcome back." Kay caressed my arm with one hand, her eyes half closed.

"God, I'm so sorry. I can't believe I did that."

"C'mon Marcus, it's not like I've never seen this movie before." She sat up and kissed my forehead, her face suffused with an unprotected glow. Curling into my arms, she moved to brush a stray curl out of her eyes. The flash of her wedding ring brought me back to reality.

"I want you to know you're the first married woman I've ever violated," I tried to joke.

"It's not something I make a habit out of either." She sat up.

"Violating married women?"

"Adultery in general."

"What do you suggest we do the next time?"

Kay slid back down into the blankets and back into my arms. "That depends. How many chances do you get in life?"

"This is one more than I ever thought possible."

* * *

Later that night, we called out for Chinese. In her seersucker bathrobe, Kay was an expert at eating with chopsticks, while I silently chased a water chestnut around my plate with my fork.

"Can I ask you a question?" I finally asked.

"Sure."

"When did things go wrong? With you and the Major, I mean."

"He's always bought into that fighter-pilot-as-god thing they fill them with at pilot training. I don't know if he was ever faithful to me. But I finally had enough the day I found out that he had himself a fling the last time we been to Korea and fathered a child."

"You mentioned that before."

"Yeah. There was a letter for Paul with a Korea postmark that I steamed open one day. It had a picture of this little boy and a handful of won—Korean dollars—in it. This woman was sending him the money she saved for the house he promised to buy her here in the States."

"Jesus."

"It was pretty bad. But I known for a while that things weren't right anyway."

"Really?" This from the woman I seen fall so hard for the wild blue yonder.

"I was trying to fit into the mold Paul wanted me in, and it didn't work." Kay fiddled with her chopsticks, refusing to look at me.

"What mold?"

"The perfect officer's wife mold, the one who sacrifices all to help her husband climb that all-important promotion ladder. I was actually shocked when I learned that other wives don't get sucked into the game like I did."

"I know you moved around a lot."

"Oh, I loved the travel!" She looked up, and a smile broke across her face. "I was being strangled to death here in Jubilant. I've seen people and places I never would have any other way! But that's not what I meant."

"What did you mean?"

"It's not the moving, or the willingness to move, but being completely absorbed into his identity. I'm Mrs. Major, Paul's wife, Andrew's mother, Lillian's mother, just like I was here, when I was Marian James's daughter. But I pushed Paul into a mold he didn't fit into either."

"Oh?"

"I was in love with his lifestyle, his rank, and his job. After being beat around by Grant, I wanted a hero."

"I never did fit that bill, did I?"

She reached across the table and took my hand, sadness mirrored in her eyes. "Marcus, I was stupid — just young and stupid. By the time I realized that, I was married to someone who had feet of clay, just like mine."

"So, is it completely over between you two?"

Kay sighed. "Honestly, I don't know. It's all so complicated. I don't want to live every day with a reminder that my husband was unfaithful, but I don't want to be a two-time loser, either."

"How can you say that? That day I saw you in the grocery all those years ago, you looked like the poster child for domestic violence! You even said so yourself!"

"But Marcus, I never failed at anything before either!"

"How can you call getting out of an abusive relationship failure? And trust me, this relationship qualifies as abusive, if he makes a habit of screwing around like you say he does."

"Maybe it's part of that savior complex Mother's always accusing me of having. I don't know. I've got to teach the world to read, I've got to feed the hungry, I've—"

"—got to buy the world a Coke," I sang, sarcastically.

Kay laughed. "No. But you know women who feel they have to somehow change their men once they're married to them."

I nodded.

"I just thought that if I loved Grant enough, or did whatever it was he wanted, he wouldn't beat me. Of course, it didn't work that way. At the shelter, they told me it seldom does. In a way, I did the same thing with Paul. If I were the perfect wife, if I loved him enough, everything would be fine. And it wasn't."

"The major never struck you, did he?"

"No. I was looking for a hero, a romance novel hero. And they simply don't exist."

"What about us? I'm not giving you up this time without a fight."

Kay was silent.

"You said you loved me," I persisted.

"I do, Marcus, I do. I won't lie to you, though. I made a commitment to this man and this marriage, and I have children to think about, too. I need to see this year through, to see what happens."

"I won't push."

"And I can't promise."

"I know."

And so, we began again. Late night phone calls filled with whispered endearments, sweet stolen moments, and the occasional night together when Kay could get her mother to take Andy and Lillian. The ring she still wore on her finger meant that our moments together were borrowed and illicit.

Still, the Major was half a world away and I was here.

***

Things with Ludean's apartment never went any further. Half of this business is about getting lied to; the other half is getting crucified.

On the last day of August, I returned to Suite 340 to pay another visit. Three-dimensional letters now hung on the previously blank door announcing a new occupant, Cardinal Insurance.

Inside, a lissome young blonde with legs I thought would never end puckered her pretty brow, but could remember no one who resembled the goon who rearranged my nearly-healed face.

Likewise, the bushy-browed security officer could recall no one fitting that description occupying that same suite.

"It's been policy for a while now that residential tenants mail their rent payment in," he said, avoiding my eyes. "To a post office box."

"How long? What's the box number?"

The guard studied his black Reeboks. "A while now. I don't know the address."

"What if they have a complaint? What are they supposed to do then?"

The guard shrugged. "I dunno."

The goon and his boiler room operation had vanished into thin air.

Within hours, I had a photographer at Ludean's place and was overrun with other tenants with the same complaints she had. Once again, Rathke refused all comments about Land Management Ltd. or who the stockholders were.

The next morning, I had a banner headline, above the fold: Who's behind Aurora Development? There were pictures of Ludean's wrecked apartment, a photo of a mouse boldly crossing the steps as Priscilla jumped back in fear.

This was it; I was on my way back. Even my co-workers in the newsroom complimented me on the story, stopping by my desk to shake my hand or pat my shoulder.

"God job, old man, good job," Jess grinned on one side of his mouth, as he snapped the paper open in front of him. "I knew you could do it."

CHAPTER 5

Kay

What we were doing was wrong.

Wrong. Wrong. Wrong.

I had a husband to think about; I had two kids. I just couldn't throw it all away over some half-baked idea that I could rekindle an old romance. Somebody had to take the moral high ground here. Just because Paul had affairs throughout our marriage – and fathered a child, for Christ's sake – didn't mean that I had carte blanche to take up with someone. Did it?

I agonized over it, every moment Marcus and I weren't together – and we were together as often as I could work it out. But when we weren't, I sat staring at the photos of Paul and me together, wondering where it was my marriage went wrong.

I had to make my marriage work for the kids, didn't I? I couldn't throw the whole seven years away, simply because he couldn't keep his pants on, could I? And wasn't what I was doing no better than what Paul had done?

I could lose my kids over this if he found out. I could lose the two most precious things in my life, if this got out. Even Mother would turn against me.

"If you do anything to ruin this marriage, there's something wrong with you."

"Kay, you couldn't have done better, even if I chosen him myself."

But he's not a god—he's a man! My mind screamed in answer to Mother's old words. He puts his pants on the same way as any one else. He's wounded me terribly, and I can't forgive him.

Damn that living room wall—all his accomplishments, every shining moment in his illustrious career. It's the door to his ego, the zipper to his fly. For every photograph and every medal, had there been a woman? What about every time he had deployed? And who was it? Meaningless one night stands? Or the wives of his squadron mates? What about this woman who had his child? Had she been his great love? Or had it been a cheap tryst with some "juicy girl" down in Songtan City after too much Korean beer?

The anger ran fire and ice through my veins, and it was then my stolen moments with Marcus seemed as much an act of revenge as an act of grace.

Marcus was my solace, my soul mate. I could share my dreams for the literacy center with him, and he never asked, *But, what about my career?*

I wanted a clinic in there for indigent care; I wanted prenatal classes for pregnant teens, breakfasts and hot lunches through the summer for the kids. I wanted exercise classes for senior citizens, and I wanted midnight basketball leagues for the young teenagers like what Ludean's son, Aaron would soon be– who now roamed the street in search of drugs or sex or violence through all hours of the night.

I wanted the center to become the focal point of the South Side community, a way for them to learn, to grow and make their difference in the world, much as I was trying to do. Not just a place to learn to read.

And Marcus supported that. Within a few weeks, he had put me in touch with every freelance grant-writer and federally-funded agency Jubilant Falls had to offer.

Together, we would make it grow. He promised me. *Just you and me.*

And I believed him. Damn my foolish heart; I believed him.

After Marcus's story ran, the next few days were hectic. Even Jess congratulated him with a dour "Good job."

That night, after the kids were in bed, we held a quiet celebration in the kitchen.

"You deserve some credit in this, too," Marcus said, lifting a champagne glass in a congratulatory toast. "You brought Ludean to me."

"Dear Ludean." The champagne gave me a warm, tingling feeling inside. "A speech therapist called the office today to donate her services for her. The staff said that they help paint the place, and other people – folks who read your story, Marcus – called the center to donate clothes and toys. We've done what we set out to do. We made a difference."

"Not quite yet," he cautioned. "The apartment hasn't been repaired. The city housing authorities told me they'll hold a hearing on the situation tomorrow. My guess is they'll give the company another thirty days to complete repairs, then the courts will take over."

"That old sleaze bag Rathke represented me in my divorce from Grant."

Marcus raised an eyebrow. "Really?"

"At Mother's insistence, of course. He handles all her affairs, too."

"Why doesn't that surprise me?"

"Be nice. She's been very good about watching the kids on our occasional weekends and buying my hokey stories about old college roommates."

"Do you think she knows?"

"We don't go anyplace in town. You park your car two blocks away when you come over. Unless she's having me followed, I don't think she has any idea."

"What about the kids?"

I sighed. "They scare me more than Mother. Both of them love their father so much, it would crush them to find out about everything that's going on."

Marcus twirled the stem of his glass between his fingers. "Will they ever? You told them that we're working together. You think they really buy that?"

"It can't be a secret forever, can it?" I leaned across the table and kissed his cheek.

My lips moved from his cheek to his lips, tasting warm and sweet from the champagne. We stood to embrace; his warm arms wrapped around me, and I felt safe, confident, and strong.

"Oh Kay, you mean so much to me," he whispered into my hair.

I wanted to tell him how much I loved him, how much his love had healed me, but I couldn't. My eyes caught a quick glance of a photo of Paul hanging on the corner of his *I Love Me* wall in the next room, and I was filled with guilt.

Suddenly, there was the sound of screeching tires on the street. Footsteps sounded on front walk. There was a thump and a groan, as someone jumped the iron fence.

"What the hell is that?" Marcus asked, as we pulled from our embrace. We ran to the living room, as the glass from the front window exploded across the floor. Upstairs, I heard Lillian begin to cry, and from Andrew's bedroom at the back of the second floor I heard feet hit the floor.

"Mommy! What's that? What happened?" he called from the top of the stairs, his eyes big with fear.

"Stay upstairs! Don't move!" I shot back.

I moved cautiously into the living room, as Marcus yanked the door open and ran into the front yard. There was the sound of screeching wheels, as the car carrying whoever shattered my window pulled away.

"God damn it! I couldn't get a good look at him, but he was a big guy. I only saw his back," Marcus panted, as he ran back up the steps and into the house. "You gotta call the police! Now!"

Amidst the glass fragments lay a brick with a piece of yellow legal paper wrapped around it fastened with a thick, rubber band. I reached for the brick.

"Don't touch it! You'll disturb the fingerprints." Marcus cried.

Trembling with fear, I ignored him and picked up the brick anyway, pulling off the rubber band and the paper.

In heavy black, felt-tip marker, someone from my past, someone I hoped never to see again, had written, *BITCH, I'M WATCHING YOU. REMEMBER THAT. ALWAYS.*

I knew immediately who sent that evil message. I crumpled the note in my hand and tossed it into the fireplace.

"What are you doing?" Marcus cried.

I took a match from the mantel and lit it, tossing it onto the note. The paper ignited and burned quickly, the glowing cinders sucked up the flue.

"You're destroying evidence! What did that note say?"

I turned to Marcus. "Nothing important—nothing that the police need to know. It would just scare the children and they don't need that."

"Kay, who threatened you?"

"Nobody threatened me. I don't know who that note was directed toward, but it wasn't important."

"Why don't you let the police decide what's important?"

"This is my house. I'll make those decisions."

"Kay, you could be making a big mistake here."

I looked up at the stair landing into my son's terrified eyes. My children didn't know I been married before their father. It had been a small stupid mistake, and there was no need to tell them, even when he left such a cruel calling card. It would only serve to scare them and insert doubt into a situation that was already filled with uncertainty.

How did he know I was back in town? After all these years why did he still hate me so? It didn't make sense, but I wasn't going to scare the hell out of my kids by making it into a bigger deal than it needed to be.

"No, I'm not. Hand me the phone, and I'll call the police. Nobody, but nobody says anything about the note."

* * *

The next day, I had a new pane of glass put in the living room window. Although Marcus wanted to say more, he wisely kept his mouth shut.

The housing authority acted as he had expected: Aurora had thirty days to fix the place, or it would go to the courts. Members of the literacy center staff and others gathered together clothes, food, and cash donations for the family. We wanted to use the cash to repair the plumbing, but felt that doing so would get Aurora development off the hook. So instead we bought food.

As word of the renovation spread, other Aurora tenants began to show up at the literacy center and the newspaper, until Marcus and I were fairly overrun with stories from other south side residents that paralleled Ludean's.

"I can't believe this, Marcus," I said, tossing another stack of letters across my desk at him. "These people have been so brutally treated. It's like they're completely cut off from the rest of the world!"

"What I want to know is why none of them went to the prosecutors? Or the housing authority? It's a fairly routine complaint to file. Why hasn't anyone acted before now?" Marcus thumbed through the stack of letters. "I can't get Rathke to comment on who's behind Land Management Limited. And, from what I can gather without a subpoena, it's a pretty involved tangle of sham corporations from out of state."

"Yes. Who wants to be recognized as a slumlord anyway? We can't fix up everyone of these houses through donations, Marcus."

"I know."

Still, as summer dragged on, we tried. There were clothing drives and canned-good drives from church groups who had read Marcus's story. But after a while, even they fizzled out after no single owner could be found who would claim to own that tangle of buildings.

And, as the August heat continued to swelter, we waited for repairs to be made. Who ever was behind Aurora Development didn't care that this woman and other South Side residents just like her were living in squalor. That disgusted me most of all.

* * *

It was late August, just about a week before school started. I was surprised, when my secretary, Barbara, showed Mother into my office. Clutching her purse tightly under her arm, Mother looked nervously at her surroundings.

The center wasn't the Trump Tower; it had been reincarnated at various times as an elementary school, a settlement house, a Holiness church, and a mattress warehouse. The scars of its many lives showed throughout the interior, and only the surrounding neighborhood poverty made a fresh coat of exterior latex look like urban renewal. I could only hope that I would be here long enough to do some measurable good; I had made such a small start so far.

"Surprise, surprise! What brings you here?" I stepped from behind my battered, metal desk to hug her.

"Be careful, dear. I just had my hair done. Is the Mercedes safe outside?"

"Mother, just because people here are poor doesn't automatically make them thieves, too. Have a seat." I gestured toward a padded, metal chair in front of my desk.

Mother wrinkled her nose in disdain. "I don't think so. How can you stand—"

"Don't start."

"Oh, all right. I only stopped by to take you to lunch. Can you join me? I've got a little surprise for you."

"Sure. I guess so." Surprises from my mother usually didn't involve good things, at least to my way of thinking, but she come down here to see me. How could I say no? Calling out my plans to Barbara, I grabbed my purse and followed Mother out the door.

"There is something very important we need to talk about, Kay," Mother began, as she put the Mercedes in gear and pulled away from the curb.

"Oh?" I held my breath and pretended to arrange the shoulders of my suit jacket. *She knows about Marcus and me.*

"I have been asked by more than one person..." She steered the big car into traffic.

Here it comes.

"And not just Lovey, mind you..."

Shit.

"...whether or not you are going to put the children into Walshingham Academy this fall. I have it on very good authority that they have only a few spots left in their second grade program, and Lillian could start kindergarten there, too. It would give them the very best start on their education."

Air rushed from my lungs, and I began to laugh, mostly from relief, but Mother didn't take it that way.

"Kay, I'm serious! You can't possibly consider placing my grandson in Jubilant Falls public schools!"

"For God sake, the schools here aren't that bad. You didn't have any problem sending me."

"That was before busing and drugs."

"Drugs came in with a court order as well?" I teased, nearly giddy that Marcus and I had not been a topic of country club conversation.

"Kay, be serious. The public schools still provided an education back then. And, besides, Jubilant didn't have any private schools at that time."

"Almost. We just had all the upper-class white kids at my school and all the 'lower orders' as you like to call them going to school down here on the South Side." I shook my head. "No wonder the courts brought in busing."

Mother harrumphed and pulled the Mercedes into Hawk's parking garage. "The Colonial Cafe is all right, I trust? Or is that too far above your egalitarian tastes?"

"It's fine, Mother."

Inside the restaurant, she became oddly silent until the waitress took our order.

"I'll have the diet plate and a cup of coffee, please." Mother slapped her menu closed and glared at me.

"Burger and fries, please." I handed the menu to our waitress. "Mother, what is with you?"

"I think you are doing your children a grave disservice."

"I can't afford private school, not for two kids. Not with Paul's expenses in Korea right now." I remembered my first lunch here with Marcus and felt guilty just saying Paul's name. It had been over a month since I had even spoken to my husband. He had written the kids a few times, and they had answered his letters, but I had never bothered to put pen to paper.

"Do you think for one moment that I was asking you to pay for it?" Mother raised her hands in disgust. "Of course, I would pay the tuition. But if you're set on destroying their education, I can't do anything more."

"Stop it."

"Fine. The conversation is closed."

The waitress came with our lunch, and silently we began to eat.

"So, how is Paul?"

"OK, I guess. I haven't heard."

"Does he anticipate getting orders for Symington, after this little tour?"

"I have no idea where he plans on going after Korea."

"But you'll follow, correct? Just like the good wife that you are?"

Now it was my turn to be sulky. "Yeah, right."

Mother laid her fork down. "Kay, I know that you two are having problems. It's to be expected in any marriage."

"What's your point?"

"The point is life is nothing but problems. Do you think your father and I always had a smooth time of it? Men who intend to make something of themselves often give their wives and family short shrift while they are pursuing their careers."

"This has nothing to do with his career."

Mother ignored me. "Do you think I was always gracious and understanding every time a patient called in the middle of the night? Do you think I smiled politely, every time I had to hold his supper and put you to bed before he even came home?"

"Don't you get righteous with me!" I exploded. "You still don't cook, and Novella tucked me in!"

"That's not important. You simply have to understand that, while your husband is climbing to the top, you're going to have to sit back and wait for him. When he is promoted to general, then you'll be able to enjoy each other."

"Yeah, right!" I hooted derisively. "What about all the time you and Daddy had to enjoy each other? Wasn't it fun finding him dead on the bathroom floor in the middle of the night?" My voice escalated; people were beginning to look at us, but I didn't care. "The man worked himself to death—and for what? That mausoleum you call a house? That Mercedes? Yeah, he's enjoying everything, six foot under."

"Lower your voice. There's no need for this," Mother's voiced dropped to an ominous whisper. "I don't know what the problem is between you and Paul, but I do know this much—you better work it out, before any more gossip about you and that nosy reporter gets back to me."

"What's that supposed to mean?" I clenched my napkin in my lap.

"I don't know and I don't want to know what's going on. But while you're righting the world's wrongs, I suggest you preserve your own wedding vows and make sure that your children are cared for in the best possible way—by making sure they get the best education Jubilant Falls has to offer. If this gets ugly, you'll at least have Walshingham Academy on your side. I'm doing this for your own good, Kay."

"You like to think everything you do is for my own good, don't you? I want to know who told you. It was that old battleaxe friend of yours, Lovey, wasn't it?"

Mother froze, and an odd, hunted look came across her face.

"No. It wasn't Lovey."

"Then who? I think I have a right to know who's spreading these lies about me." God, I hope I sounded convincingly pious.

"I can't tell you."

"Oh, for God sake. It's not like it's national security or anything. What if something like that got back to the literacy center board?"

"You'd probably lose yet another do-gooder job. But that's not important." Mother sipped her coffee, gazing over the rim of her cup like a grand duchess. "It's beyond me why you've got a business degree, but you insist on behaving like some government social worker. The important thing is making sure that my grandchildren aren't being shuttled between divorced parents. Or worse, that I only get to see them during summer break because their mother was behaving like a whore and lost custody."

I leaned across my plate, twisting my napkin in my lap. She'd hit the bull's eye, and she knew it.

"Alright. I'll take the kids to Walshingham Academy first thing tomorrow," I agreed. "I'll even let you and your filthy money pay for it all, because appearances are so goddamn important to you."

"I'm only thinking of the children, something you haven't done since Lovey saw you here with that weasel of a reporter."

"So it was she." Mother didn't answer, but I had all the confirmation I needed. "And you've got the nerve to believe her above your own daughter! You won't ask me if it's true—you just assume it is. You don't care if I'm having problems in my marriage. Just patch it up, don't let anybody see what goes on behind closed doors."

Mother paled and put her perfectly manicured hand to her throat. I rolled my eyes.

"Oh don't be so puritanical. Just once in my life I like to know that I can come to my mother when I'm having problems and get a little support. That's all I've ever wanted from you. and you know what? I've never gotten it. Never in all my years have you supported anything I wanted to do!"

Mother exploded. "And you've made such lovely decisions my dear! The kind any mother would be proud to hold up to her friends." Her voice moved up a bitter octave. "'Mother, this is Grant Matthews. We got married last night. Mother, I'm calling you from the emergency room. Grant broke my nose. Mother, I'm at the emergency room again and this time they're stitching up my face. Mother, I need money for a divorce lawyer....' Can you see why I'm concerned about how everything looks? You insist on sinking to the lowest level Kay, and this time you're not going to do it! Not if your actions will cost me my grandchildren! I'll do anything I can to stop this foolishness of yours."

The silence stretched uncomfortably across the table. As if to break it, the waitress approached our table, smacking her gum.

"Ya'll are finished here, now?" she asked, reaching for my plate. "Is this separate checks, or how we gonna do this?"

"We're finished now," I said, glaring at Mother. "We're really finished." I stood and threw my napkin on the table, then fished around in my purse for a ten-dollar bill. "I'll find my own way back to the office, thank you," I said, slapping it on the table. I turned to go.

"Kay, wait! You don't understand. It's for your own good!" Mother reached for me, as I stepped away.

"You really, really believe that, don't you?" I stopped.

"Yes, Kay. Yes I do."

"Then that's your mistake this time, isn't it?"

I turned on my heel and walked away.

* * *

But I was so happy with Marcus! Our relationship was a sweet, safe cocoon, swaddled in all the buffers that romance brings. The years between us had evaporated, and as time passed I realized that my decision to come back to Jubilant Falls was the best I ever made.

It was too good to last.

In mid-December, I waited with the kids in front of the airport's plate-glass window. My stomach churned in guilt, dread, and horror as the small commuter plane rolled across the tarmac. That morning, a telegram came announcing that Paul would be coming home for Christmas:

Kay— Will arrive in Jubilant 16:25 local time. On leave until 15 Jan. Merry Christmas! Paul.

There hadn't been time for the answer I wanted to send: "Don't bother!" Instead, I stood awaiting his arrival, mute and guilty.

"Daddy! Daddy! Look, Mommy, there's Daddy!"

Involuntarily, I sucked in my breath as Paul disembarked from the plane and walked to the gate, two bags of gifts in his hands. He was dressed in tight jeans, his broad shoulders nearly bursting the seams of the brown, leather aviator's jacket. No wonder everyone thought he was a hero; every inch of him looked the part.

I smiled appropriately, as he came through the gate and stood stiffly as he hugged me, the shopping bags banging between my shoulder blades.

"God, it's good to be home, Kay." Paul's lips moved dangerously close to mine, and a deep, familiar need crashed against a deeper scar of betrayal somewhere deep inside me. I turned my head quickly, offering only my cheek for his kiss.

His green eyes hardened for a moment, then clouded over with hurt.

"Let's go get Daddy's luggage!" I called out brightly, leading the procession to the baggage claim carousel. Andy, still in his Walshingham school uniform, and Lil chattered excitedly behind me with their father.

We spoke very little to each other in the car. We couldn't even if we had wanted to; the children's babble would have prohibited anything deeper than "How was your flight?" or "Was the food any good?" Lillian stood in the back seat with her arms around her Daddy's neck, with Andy seated firmly on Paul's other side, trying to out-shout his sister as they filled their father in on what had happened during the last six months.

I kept my stiff smile plastered across my face, saying as little as I could. How could Mother ask me to live up to my vows with a betrayer, a cheat, and a liar like Paul? I hated the sight of him, but until we were alone no one else would ever know.

That night, we lay side by side in that old cannonball bed, staring silently at the cold moonlight tracing across the ceiling the naked branches of the oak outside the window. Paul rolled over and embraced me, kissing my neck. His hand slid to my breast, and his powerful leg eased over mine. His erection pressed against my thigh, and I felt sick.

"Mmmmm. I've missed this," he purred into my neck.

"Stop it." I pulled the covers up to my shoulders and turned away.

"What is this? Punishment?"

"I was under the impression that you weren't coming home for another three weeks and then only for a few days. That was our agreement."

"I had an opportunity to come home, so I took it. Jesus, I thought you be happy to see me."

"You guessed wrong."

Paul was silent for a moment. "What's his name?"

My reply wasn't convincing or quick enough even for me. "What's whose name?"

"The other guy."

"What other guy?"

"You're a very poor liar, Kay. You always have been. I had two letters from you in the last five months, you hardly talked to me on the phone the last time I called, and now that I'm home you're cutting me off cold. What else could it be?"

"Are you sleeping with her?"

"Jesus, Kay, don't be ridiculous. I don't even know where she is. If I knew—"

"You'd be out of here so fast, we'd never know you even came home, wouldn't you?" All the wounds that I thought were healed tore open again, and I knew how damaged I had been six months ago. It had been Marcus's love that kept me going, nothing else. I thought of him sleeping alone in his odd little apartment, and the pain around my heart grew.

"So, who is it?" Paul repeated his question.

"Go to sleep. We've got to go out and get a Christmas tree tomorrow morning." I rolled back to face him. "Mother wants us to have dinner with her, too. I'll thank you to put a good face over all this."

The bed springs moaned in protest, as Paul turned toward the window. I rolled over, too, tears beginning to pool in the corners of my eyes. The damage had been already done before he came home, I reminded myself. This whole thing is all his fault.

* * *

At the Christmas tree lot early the next day, I stood apart from Paul and the kids as they bartered over a blue spruce. It was ungodly cold. It took a long time, though, for the numbness in my fingers to match the numbness in my head.

This marriage was dead. I could see that now. Like a hit-and-run accident, all that was left was to push the dead carcass out of the roadway and get on with our lives.

Suddenly, I wanted to hear Marcus's voice, to feel his warm arms wrap around me, enveloping me with his love.

I blew on my hands. I had to talk to Marcus. The 7-Eleven across the street had a pay phone inside. Paul wouldn't follow me. After last night he was too angry even if he didn't show it, and, besides, he wouldn't leave the kids. I could get away with it. I shoved my hands into my pockets and slogged through the snow.

Once inside, I felt the store's warmth begin to seep through my heavy coat and listened as the quarter clanked through the phone. Marcus answered on the first ring.

"Hello?" His voice was tense and expectant.

"Hi honey. It's me."

"God, I miss you."

In the glaring fluorescent lights, amid the double cola Slurpees and the stack of two-day-old *Wall Street Journals*, I felt the security of his love. I didn't belong with that big dumb jet-jockey; I belonged with Marcus. I knew I could never return to Paul. The man who truly loved me, who would stand by me through all that lay ahead of me, never traveled at Mach two and never, ever would betray me.

"I miss you, too. I can't live like this any longer, Marcus. I'm going to tell him about us."

"If you think that's the right thing to do." I heard him exhale heavily. "I'll be here, Kay, if you need me." Softly he hung up the phone.

Across the street, Paul had the tree strapped to the top of the Porsche and was looking around for me. Andy and Lil were jumping around in excitement. I hung up the phone, quickly bought four cups of hot chocolate, and returned to my family.

"Just checking in at work," I said lightly, passing the Styrofoam cups around.

Paul shot a sideways glance at me. "Oh, really?"

"You used that excuse for years. Why can't I?" I shot back.

"Because maybe I really was checking in."

"And maybe you weren't."

He sighed. "Let's go home."

"What's left of it."

Paul set the tree up near the front window, placing the Christmas angel he bought in Munich on top, as I watched from the couch.

As the children decorated, I realized nearly every ornament was a milepost in our marriage: glazed sand dollars on gold cord from two years in Florida with Eglin's 33rd Tactical Fighter Wing; pewter colonial pineapples from Williamsburg, Virginia, when we were stationed nearby at Langley Air Force Base and assigned to the 1st TFW. There were wooden snowflakes from Germany and brightly colored miniature Korean ladies. *This family has a history*, they seemed to say. *Can you let that go?*

"Look, Mommy! Daddy brought us home some new pretties for the tree!" Lillian held up two handfuls of miniature, paper fans.

I laughed nervously and hugged her chubby little body. "Where's your brother?" I asked.

"He's upstairs, wrapping a Christmas present." Paul answered, turning his face from me. "In his last letter, he asked me to get you something from Korea. I hope you like it."

"I'm sure I will." How artificial it all sounded; what nice, polite conversation! Is this what leads to a civilized divorce? Two people simply splitting up the joint property and amicably going their own way? At his last pre-Christmas deployment, his homecoming had been a wonderful evening spent cuddling on the couch with the warm haze of wine and blinking tree lights washing over us. Now, the relationship was irrevocably fractured, and we had both come painfully to that realization.

"Glass of wine, Paul?" The best of Marian's upbringing came to the surface. One must always provide adequate refreshments for one's guests, even when married to them.

"Sure." He followed me back to the kitchen. I pulled a bottle of chilled Chardonnay out of the refrigerator.

"Kay, about what happened...."

"Last night, or our little exchange of pleasantries at the tree lot?" Studiously, I rummaged through a drawer to find my corkscrew, deliberately banging the kitchen utensils against each other as I searched.

"Well, both." Paul's voice was awkward and strained. "It looks like we've pretty much come to the end of our road together, doesn't it?"

I stopped rattling utensils.

"I had hopes that when I came home, there was a chance we could work things out. I know what I did was wrong, Kay. I just hoped you could finally forgive me." Paul reached across and, with his index finger, traced the blue vein across the back of my hand. "Especially when your mother sent me that ticket."

"My mother brought you here?" That blackmailing conversation at Hawk's cafeteria came back: *Don't let anything more about you and that nosy reporter get back to me.* She probably thought she could engineer some sort of make-up between us.

"Damn her!" I exploded. "She won't do anything nice for someone, unless she gets something out of it, too!"

"You didn't know?"

"Hell no, I didn't know!"

"I got this letter from her saying how much you and the kids wanted to see me over the holidays, but were afraid to ask that I come home early. She said that you didn't have a whole lot of money, trying to pay for private school and all...."

"That bitch forked over the tuition for Andrew and Lillian. I wanted to send them to the public schools, but that wasn't good enough for her!"

"Honey, she was just trying to make it a Christmas gift to us." Paul covered my hand with his.

I pulled away, meeting his gaze squarely. "Well, she certainly made some big assumptions there, didn't she?"

"Don't, Kay. Your mother only meant the best for us, I'm sure."

"Why do you think she's some helpless little widow with only good deeds in her heart? She knew we were having problems, and she just thought she stick her surgically altered nose in."

"There, see? She only had our best interests in mind."

"Sure she did."

"I'll only stay until New Year's Day, then I'll go back." The death knell had begun to sound for our marriage. Fearfully, I met his gaze.

"Paul, I'm so sorry." I reached forward to touch him but it was suddenly artificial, wrong. My hand fell limply on the counter top.

"No, I'm sorry. All I ask is that you give me lots of time in the summer to see the kids."

"Sure."

"And the car... just keep it 'til I get back."

"No. It wouldn't be right." I thought of Marcus sitting on the passenger side and blushed. "I can take it wherever you want me to for storage, then buy my own car."

"Throttle back, Kay. Keep it. I'll agree to whatever you want, within reason. Have your lawyer draw up a separation agreement, and I'll sign it. We can finalize the divorce when I get back." He turned and headed down the hallway.

"Please." Instinctively, I reached out to touch him one more time, to remember all the good times we had, all the wonderful things we had done together.

"No, Kay. I made a serious mistake, and now I have to pay for it."

So this was why divorce could be more painful than death. Even when it would be finalized, we would still be tied to each other through the children. In spite of it all, we would still have contact.

Abruptly, I had a vision of Paul coming to get the children for summer visitation in the years ahead, slowly stepping up the front steps of this awful house (God, would I still be living here?) as I stood on the porch, pasty-faced and smiling, with the children in front of me like a barricade, while Marcus, Paul's replacement, stood behind me.

Oh, my God.

"Paul."

"Yes?"

"Do you want to tell the kids now?"

"No. Let's not spoil this last Christmas together."

"When?"

"When everything is settled." Without a word, he turned on his heel with military precision and returned to the living room. My hands shook, as I tried to pour the wine into my glass, slopping it onto the counter and the floor. Impatiently, I grabbed the dishrag and got down on my hands and knees to wipe the spill. Salty tears ran down my cheeks, mixing with the wine on the floor. My hair fell forward into the puddle, and somewhere in the depths of my soul I heard my heart break.

* * *

We tried to make it as wonderful a Christmas as we could, but it was like granting one wish to a dying man who didn't have any idea how soon the end was coming. No matter how warm and wonderful we tried to make the holiday, we knew it was our final one together, and that was sad.

Mother spent Christmas Day with us. We tried valiantly to look as if nothing were wrong between us, but I sat too stiffly beside Paul; the kisses and touches we affected had the quality of a bad, high school play.

Paul brought Mother and me each a brightly colored silk kimono robe, and the kids each got a jacket with an Oriental dragon on the back and *KOREA* in ornate script written between the shoulder blades. Both jackets had patches from Paul's 51st Tactical Fighter Wing, sewn on the shoulder.

There were too many toys for the children and too much food to eat, but beneath the surface the discomfort at putting on such a performance never left. By nine o'clock that night, I found myself saucing up my eggnog a little more than everyone else to keep myself steady; my voice was a little over-loud and my laughter too forced.

At 10 p.m., after the children were asleep and Mother had departed, I came out of the kitchen to find Paul's pillow and an old blanket folded up on the corner of the couch.

"What are you doing?"

"C'mon Kay, We've lied to everyone all day long. Let's not do it any more." Paul sat down and pulled his shoes off. "I'll just sleep down here."

The next day, not six hours after Mother came by and picked up the kids, leaving some frivolous gourmet lunch for us ("Just to inspire a little romance for you love birds," she winked.), Paul was packing to leave. After the children came back, we went back to the airport to say good-bye to him. We held each other tightly in a final, sad embrace, knowing that the next time we saw each other it would be in court, that everything we had together was now finished. My actions as well as his had led to the demise of our marriage, and nothing would revive it.

"We had a lot of good times together, Kay," he whispered in my ear. "I'm sorry. I don't blame you at all."

Sobs filled my throat. "Oh, Paul...."

"United Flight 478 now boarding through gate 23 from Chicago, with service to San Francisco and Los Angeles!" A disembodied female voice floated through the corridor. "All passengers..."

"This is it, I guess." Paul held me at arm's length. "Remember me kindly."

Andrew and Lillian began to cry. Paul hugged them both tightly, tears cresting in his eyes. "Be good for Mommy now," he rasped. "Bye-bye." Playfully saluting Andrew, he turned to board his plane.

* * *

"Mo-o-om-m-e-e!" Lillian's small voice rang out in the darkness.

Why do children's cries for help sound so blood curdling in the middle of the night? I rolled over and switched on the bedside lamp. Marcus, my love, had arrived and departed after the children had gone to sleep; my eyes couldn't have been closed for more than ten minutes. Maybe not—it was 2:36 a.m. God, I hate digital clocks. Whatever happened to *about* 2:30 or *a little past* 2:30? The red numbers shone definitively in my face, as I struggled to come awake.

"What is it, Lil?" I managed to call back.

Lil's sleeper-covered feet hit the hardwood floor. She came running into my room, sliding in between my blankets before I could stop her.

"Lil, honey…you're all wet!"

"Mommy, I pee-peed my bed."

Damn it. Now I have to strip both beds. Since Paul's return to Osan two weeks ago, Lillian began to wet the bed again. I knew his abrupt arrival and departure was the cause.

"Come on, sweetie." I took her hand and led her to the bathroom. I sat on the edge of the claw-footed bathtub, trying to rub the stupor out of my eyes and peel the urine-soaked sleeper off her. Once the tub was full, I plopped Lillian into the water with her bathtub toys and went to change the sheets.

Just as I was tucking the fitted sheet around my own mattress, the phone rang. It was 2:43 a.m.

I suppose every military wife lives with the fear of that phone call, secure only in the insecurity that active duty brings. I had often wondered what I would do or how I would react when my phone call came, but each time dismissed it as an unlikely possibility. Paul was simply too good a pilot. Our marriage was beyond hope, but Paul's flying ability brooked no criticism. I prayed for a wrong number, as I picked up the phone.

"Hello?"

"Mrs. Paul Armstrong?" A man's deep voice asked.

"Yes?"

"Mrs. Armstrong, this is Chaplain McBroom at Symington Air Force Base. I'm sorry to call at such a late hour, but I'm afraid there's been an accident. We just received word."

"Paul?" I sank onto the cold, fresh bed sheet, too stunned to react.

"Yes ma'am. We'll be right over."

The receiver dropped heavily from my hand back onto its cradle. What now? What do I need to do? I don't want to meet Chaplain McBroom at the door without someone here with me. Whatever he was going to tell me, I didn't want to acknowledge it alone. The chaplain had a half-hour drive from Symington to Jubilant Falls. There would be enough time for Mother to get here. I picked up the phone again and began to dial.

At the other end of the line, the phone clicked.

"Mother?"

"You have reached the James residence. At the tone, please leave your name, particularly your telephone number…."

Damn it.

"… and the time and date of your call." *Beep.*

"Mother, this is Kay." I spoke as flatly as her taped message. "It's about three in the morning. Something's happened to Paul. The chaplain's coming up from Symington. I think it's serious."

"Mommy! I'm getting all pruney!"

Lillian! How could I have forgotten her? I pulled her out of the tub and rapidly rubbed her pink, little body down with a towel.

"Who called on the teffelone?" The word tripped off her tongue.

"Nobody, sweetheart." There was no need to alarm her, until I knew the whole story.

"Then why did you call Grandma?"

Little pitchers and their big ears, I thought.

"Don't worry about it, Lil. Let's get you a dry sleeper and tucked back into that nice, clean bed."

All too soon, I was back at my own bedside, staring at the phone. The alarm clock's digital numbers flooded blood red across the nightstand: 2:59. Chaplain McBroom would be here in fifteen minutes. I picked up the receiver again. There was only one person left to call, the one who had always been there when I needed someone to lean on.

"Hullo?"

"Marcus, it's me, Kay. There's been an accident."

"What, the kids?" He was instantly alert.

"Paul. The chaplain's on his way over now."

"It's okay. I'll be right there." The phone clicked sharply. It was 3:02.

Quickly, I found a flannel robe in the closet and slipped it over my shoulders. The dark mahogany stair steps were cold beneath my feet as I found my way downstairs. Instinctively, I felt my way down the black hallway to the kitchen, blinded in the sudden light as I flipped the switch. Before anyone could arrive, I poured a shot of Canadian Mist into a coffee mug and sat down at the kitchen table.

Maybe Paul wasn't dead. Maybe he was only hurt. Just two weeks ago he had said, "Remember me kindly." Could he have known? Had he carried some weird premonition of disaster in the back of his head? My God, how could we have torn each other apart like we did?

I should have been more forgiving of him and that woman's mysterious little child. All the scenes, all the broken trust. We had torn each other apart through the years and gladly. Now, Paul could very well be dead.

The doorbell chimed, eerily echoing through the downstairs. I took a generous gulp from my mug and went to answer the door.

It was 3:13.

"Mrs. Armstrong." Chaplain McBroom stepped inside and took both my hands in his. Behind him stood a first lieutenant, awkwardly shifting from one foot to another. "I regret to inform you that your husband, Major Paul Dennison Armstrong, died as a result of an aircraft accident this morning at Osan Air Base."

My sobs filled the room, the odd keening wail of a wounded animal. It reverberated off the walls and rattled the French doors into the living room, leaving unseen prints of bloody agony where it touched the staircase, bouncing off the wallpaper and against the second story ceilings as the lamenting sound faded. With it went all hope of forgiveness and atonement; it was recognition that the opportunity for Paul and me to make peace with each other was gone.

"Did he burn?" I heard myself ask through the haze of tears. "Did he burn? I don't want him to burn."

Chaplain McBroom led me into the living room and helped me into a wingback chair.

"From what information we have now," he said slowly, "Major Armstrong reported hydraulic failure in his landing gear on approach and tried to abort the landing. We don't have all the information yet. I don't know if emergency measures failed, or what exactly happened, but the plane landed nose-first and exploded on impact. He never had time to eject."

I gripped the chaplain's arms, digging my fingernails into his coat, fighting against the image of yellow fire trucks racing with screaming sirens to the end of the runway, of water cannons dousing the burning remains of Paul's F-15, of the blackened purple ooze that had once been my husband, my hero.

"It couldn't have been pilot error," I whispered. "It couldn't have been. Something must have happened."

The doorbell chimed again. It was Mother, hastily dressed in Etienne Aigner boots, a pair of slacks, and a sweatshirt trimmed with Battenberg lace cutouts. Even in a crisis, she never failed to look perfect. Behind her stood Marcus, his face red with emotion and cold.

"Darling, what has happened? Is everything all right?" Mother stepped inside the door. "That reporter came pounding on my door a few minutes ago and said that Paul had been in an accident. I got your message from the machine then, and he brought me right over."

My eyes swept to Marcus, still standing outside on the porch, a wrinkled trench coat over flannel shirt and jeans, his sockless feet inside snow-caked running shoes.

"Thank you so much." I whispered.

"What happened?" he asked.

"Paul's dead. His plane crashed. Please, Marcus, it's cold. Come inside."

"No. This is a time for you and your family. This is not a time for me to be here. If you need me, I'll be out here on the porch." He smiled wanly and shoved his hands deep into the pockets of his worn trench coat.

"If you insist."

"I insist."

I closed the door, softly. Mother had, in the meantime, introduced herself to Chaplain McBroom and stoically received the news of Paul's death. I found myself in her awkward embrace, something that had not occurred since daddy's funeral.

So now we're both widows, I thought.

"Darling, I am so sorry." Mother's hands rubbed across my back. "Whatever can I do for you?"

Before I could answer, she took charge.

"Chaplain, please tell that man on the front porch to go home. He's not needed."

* * *

We buried Paul in Arlington Cemetery. He had grown up in Washington D.C.; his parents were buried in nearby Arlington, and after all Paul deserved a hero's burial. To the children and Mother, he was a hero for dying in service to his country; in my mind, it was atonement for rushing to judgment. I clutched the folded flag tightly to my chest to deaden the roar of the jets, as the three silhouettes crossed the Potomac in a missing man flyover shadowing the never-ending rows of identical, white headstones.

Andrew, ever his father's son, sat stoically, his green eyes never flinching, never filling in any show of emotion, staring at the gray casket. Lillian, only five years old, would probably never remember much about her Daddy. She sat swinging her legs on Grandma James's lap, wondering aloud why everyone was crying. Andrew would remember every action, every gesture, every word.

As the limousine snaked back across Memorial Bridge, into the District toward the funeral home, I laid my head against the cold window glass and pressed my lips against the folded flag still clutched tightly in my arms.

"Mommy," Andrew asked in a clear voice. "What happens now?"

"God only knows, sweetheart. God only knows."

CHAPTER 6

Marcus

My God. He's dead. The major is dead.

I paced up and down the porch that early morning, shivering as snow slid into my shoes. Irritably, I kicked the porch rail, showering the wet powder out from between the tread of my Nikes into the bushes.

Shit. Why didn't I take the time to put socks on?

Because she called you.

Because she needed you.

And now you're standing here in your friggin' bare feet, waiting like a damn dog. Things are gonna change now, aren't they? You got what you wanted, didn't you?

She's free now.

She's yours now.

So what is it? What are you so scared of?

This isn't right. A man is dead, and I'm a vulture, circling around and waiting for his body to get cold, so I can slip in right next to his wife at night.

You scum-sucking bastard.

"What is it, Mr. Henning?" Marian James poked her head out the door.

"Hmm?"

"I said what is it? Why are you making all that noise?"

"What noise? Oh, that. Just cleaning out my shoes."

She raised her patrician eyebrows. "I see."

"How's Kay?"

"How do you think?"

"Look, can't we just bury the hatchet for once and think about her?"

"It seems to me you've been doing enough thinking about her, Mr. Henning." Without a sound she closed the door. Inside, Kay must have told the children the news. I heard the kids' voices raise in keening wails through the window glass.

She's yours now, man.

Nothing in your way any more.

* * *

"Put it bottom-right on page one, then jump it inside," Jess said, scrolling Paul Armstrong's obituary down his computer screen, dictating to the copy desk how the story should be played.

"Jesus Christ, Jess." I came to work the next day feeling like I been on a three-day drunk.

"It's a story, whether you like it or not, Mark." Jess looked at me. "As director of the literacy center, she's a prominent member of the community, and her husband died. If he had a heart attack on the ninth hole of the golf course, it would be page three, but it would still be news. The fact that he bounced off the end of a runway in Korea makes it better. Ted—" Jess pushed a button, sending the obit electronically across the newsroom and craned his neck over his computer screen to catch the eye of a copy editor. "Put a thirty-four-point head on that."

The copy editor spoke with a pencil in the corner of his mouth. "*Lit-center exec's husband dead in plane crash*?" he asked.

"That's fine."

"Jess, can't we soft-pedal this a little bit?"

"It's news, Mark. Don't you listen?"

"Jesus Christ. Don't you ever think about the families you write about?"

Jess jumped up from his seat and grabbed me by the battered lapels of my corduroy sports coat. "I don't know what's going on between you and Kay Armstrong, and I don't think I want to know," he said. "But I sure seem to remember that she had you wrapped around her finger, before she dumped you like a hot rock to marry Mr. Flyboy. Now Flyboy's dead, and, as far as I'm concerned, it's news. If you've got a problem with that, I suggest you go to welding school, because you don't belong in this business." He released me abruptly, nearly sending me across the top of an empty desk.

"Sheee-it," whispered a sportswriter, as I stumbled word-lessly out of the newsroom.

When I got home, there was a message from Jess on my machine. "Hey, Mark, I'm sorry about what happened. You've got some comp time coming, and I know this whole thing has you shaken up pretty badly. Why don't you just take the rest of the week off, okay?"

How considerate of him. Automatically, I reached for the bot-tle of scotch beneath the kitchen sink and chased the dregs of this morning's coffee from my mug with lukewarm water. All I wanted was oblivion.

* * *

The first time Kay and I met for dinner those many years ago, the scar above her eye she had gotten from the beating Grant Matthews had given her was still pink, but the bruises around her eyes had gone. She looked radiant in a turquoise sequined dress, with her red curls cascading around her face like a halo as she stood beside the maitre d'.

"My dear Mrs. Matthews." I took her hand.

"No, it's Kay James again. I took back my maiden name. I'm starting again."

"Good for you." I folded her arm in mine and, together, we followed the waiter to our table.

I don't remember what we ordered. I don't even remember what we did after we ate. I just remember having felt a tremendous connection with this red-headed fireball in front of me. We shared so much: a belief in humanity's ability to rise above itself if only given the right help, the need to give back to those less fortunate, and a passion to change our world for the better.

Somewhere along about midnight, we ended up sitting on a park bench along Shanahan's Creek, watching the moon cast fluid silver ribbons across the water. Kay had pulled off her shoes and tucked her feet beneath her.

"What a wonderful night," she said, tossing back her head. "The moon and the stars, they're so beautiful."

"Like you."

"Speak to me, sweet lips," she laughed, cynically.

"No, I really mean it."

"Sure you do."

"Can I see you again?"

Smiling, she cocked her head and looked at me. "I *suppose*."

"You suppose? Can't you come up with something a little more, oh, I don't know, *feeling*?"

She laughed that laugh of hers, lively, full, and deep-throated, and laid her head on my shoulder. "Honestly, I've never met anyone like you, Marcus Henning. I don't know what to think of you."

"Just think of me, that's all I ask."

"And if I do?"

"I'll die a happy man."

She laughed again, and drew her face to mine. "Then, I'd be honored to see you again," she whispered, and kissed me.

That was the beginning. We saw each other every night that week. I spent a king's ransom on fancy restaurants, movies, and gifts like flowers, candy, and stuffed animals. She accepted each gift with polished politeness.

Then I gave her a music box that played *Lara's Theme* from *Dr. Zhivago*. We had just returned to her North End apartment from another dinner at another fancy restaurant. We were seated on her flowery, feminine couch; it was late and, I'll admit, I had hopes of not waking up alone.

There was frigid silence, as she tore off the silver paper.

"You'll do anything to get in my pants, won't you?" she said.

"What the hell is that supposed to mean? I found something nice that I thought you like, and I bought it for you." I was flabber-gasted.

"Nobody ever buys me anything, without an ulterior motive." She closed the box, as tears began to roll down her cheeks. "I thought you were different."

I reached over and touched her shoulder. "Why is that?"

"Until I met you, I never thought anybody could like me for me," Kay began. "When I first saw you at that dance, I thought you were just like any other man there. The country club crowd my mother runs with are all such fakes, and my mother's the worst of the whole crowd. Then, when I saw you at the grocery store, and I was so, so ugly, all those stitches and those bruises …"

"You've never been ugly to me."

"And you still wanted to go out with me. My heart just burst right then. I thought here's somebody who wants me for me, not just for my mother's money or my looks, because, God knows, I certainly didn't have any then. And then, this whole week…"

"I've been doing everything wrong," I finished the sentence. Gently, I leaned over and kissed her cheek. "I'm sorry. I didn't realize."

"Anytime Mother wanted something from me, she bought me something first. She's always been so cold and so distant, and it got worse after Daddy died. The only real mother I ever had was Novella. Novella's the only person who ever really loved me. "

"Who's Novella?"

"Our maid."

So even rich families abuse their children…just in different ways.

"You don't know what it was like, wanting nothing but a normal life, wanting nothing but Ward and June Cleaver, or *Father Knows Best*…I wanted parents who were real, who didn't spend Christmas and Thanksgiving in the Bahamas, who didn't have the hired help drop me off at school while all the other kids pointed and stared."

"Lower middle class life ain't perfect either, sweetie."

"But don't you see? What I wanted was a *connection*. I wanted my parents to notice me for the person I was, not whose genes I happened to be carrying around, or whose name hung at the end of mine. All my life I've heard "That's Kay James, Doctor Montgomery James's daughter." I wanted to be a part of something that was real, and I knew what went on at my house wasn't real."

"How did you end up married to that goon I saw you with?"

"I thought I was pregnant. We panicked, ran off and got married. A few weeks later, I found out I wasn't. You know, the first time Grant beat me up he blacked my eye. The second time, he broke my nose."

"Oh my God, Kay."

"Mother paid for a nose job, on the condition that I not go to the police about it. She didn't want my name showing up in the *Journal-Gazette's* police blotter," Kay smiled crookedly. "The next time it happened, he broke my arm, and I made up a story about falling down the steps. But finally, it got so bad I went to the battered women's shelter, and they helped me find a lawyer, who Mother, of course, didn't approve of. It hadn't been a week after the divorce, when I saw you at the grocery."

"Are you still scared of him? Do you think he'll come back and bother you again?"

"Mother says he won't."

"I won't let him hurt you, Kay. I won't let anyone hurt you ever again."

Kay wrapped her arms around my waist and laid her head on my chest. "You don't know how much I want to believe that, Marcus."

"Anything you want, I'd do for you."

"Don't say that."

I kissed the top of her head. "I've never known a woman who could be won by saying you wouldn't do anything she asked."

"No, I didn't say that," Her red hair had shone with the light, as she shook her head and, smiling, pushed away from me. "Don't do what I expect."

God knows I tried not to. With enough testosterone backed up in my cranium to blow the back of my head clean off, I kissed her check politely at the door and went home.

Back at my apartment, angry and frustrated, I pulled a beer out of the refrigerator. *This better be worth it,* I thought. Savagely, I twisted the top off the bottle and tossed the cap into a corner.

So underneath it all, beneath the fire and the sarcasm, beneath the veneer she put around herself was a little girl who needed to be loved for what she was, not what she had. But, God, aren't we all looking for that? I wanted her to love me because of whom I believed I could be, not what I had proved myself to be.

At least the scars of my failures didn't show as obviously on my face as hers did. Who could strike a face like that?

That night, I fished my TV remote from beneath the stack of old newspapers on my coffee table and begun surfing through the channels, settling on some spaghetti western. It would have been just a matter of waiting her out, getting her to trust me, winning her over; she certainly had me caught.

There was a knock on my door. *What the hell?* "Who is it?" I called from the couch.

"Marcus, it's me."

I threw open the door, and there stood Kay in her sequined dress, holding a bottle of champagne in one hand and her silver shoes in the other. Without a word, I took her in my arms and kissed her, tasting the sweetness of her lips, lingering over a curl above her eye, scattering kisses across the soft curve beneath her chin.

"Can we take this inside?" she whispered.

"Of course."

"I'm trusting you with my heart, Marcus. Please remember that."

"Always. Always. Always."

Drunk or sober, the thought of that night still sends chills down my spine. I still remember watching her as she slept on my pillow. Between that night nearly ten years ago when I first held her in my arms and the first time she beckoned me upstairs this summer, there had been too many mistakes and too many missed opportunities. I had pursued her relentlessly, confident in my love and in hers.

Now, with the major's death, reality came crowding in.

She was free again.

And I was terrified.

What was it that terrified me? I poured another shot of booze into my coffee mug and slugged it down.

I had lived all these years wanting an image, a dream. What I waited on, what I staked my hopes on wasn't real; even what we had built these past six months wasn't real.

Looking back, I saw that Andrew and Lillian had been kept completely away from me. Except for that first meeting on the front porch and the night someone broke her window, I never saw her kids.

There were the few late nights when I could slip over after Andrew and Lillian were in bed for a few stolen moments, but I wanted more than anything to wake up next to her in the morning, to see those beautiful blue eyes look across the pillows and hear her murmur "Good morning."

"We can't let the kids see us together," she said, after more than one whispered late night visit. And maybe the clandestine way we met added to the mystique – the lunches at the dark Colonial Café, the late night visits when I park my car a block or more away and then skulk through the gentrified streets and slip down the alley behind her house and up to the back door.

It made our stolen times together more delicious.

Who could blame Kay? I had agreed, thinking it was best for the kids.

Now, I saw it was really the best for me.

Without those two kids around, I could stay inside this dream I had about Kay, this seven-year-old image of a woman whose daily life I really didn't know. I knew about her work, of course, because of Ludean Tate. I didn't know what happened when she came in the door after work. I wasn't there when she picked up the kids, or fixed their supper, or helped them with their homework, or put them to bed at eight o'clock. I wasn't really a part of her life, until Andy and Lil were tucked in their beds, or away at Grandma James' for the weekend. I never wiped noses, or settled spats. Andy never came to me with a question about his science homework and Lillian never showed me pictures she'd colored in kindergarten.

Suddenly, Kay wasn't a long-held romantic dream any more; she was a package deal.

I would be a father—a stepfather, really, but a father just the same. Andrew and Lillian Armstrong would look to me for everything they had looked to the major for, would want from me all those things that kids wanted from their father.

Father. I would be their father, responsible for every aspect of their lives. Like my father had been…*"I'll have no pansy-ass fairy writers in this house…you understand that, boy?"*

I had spent a lifetime living up to his conviction that I, with my regal name and outlandish dreams, would never escape my working-man's background, would never amount to anything more that a puddle of warm spit.

I felt his hard, calloused hands squeeze my face again, like they had so many years ago. "You understand that, boy?"

Yes, now I understood. I could be stepping in for a man, who – except in his behavior to his wife – had been more than I ever could be: a hero, a god in the eyes of his country and family. How could I replace that? Who could, except John Wayne?

But more than that, I looked back at the damage my father did to me and knew I couldn't even risk doing that to Kay's children. An eerie mantle of complete responsibility hung invisibly on my shoulders, pushing down against my lungs, forcing air out in a long, slow heave.

The whole thing could turn into a real nightmare. I heard more than one story about stepchildren who made marriages collapse, or made life a living hell. Even as adults, children from first marriages had done more damage to the second marriage until love splintered and died.

A lawyer friend once told me that, when a woman had to choose between a boyfriend and her children, the kids always lost. But when it came to choosing between the second husband and the kids from the first marriage, the husband always lost. Always. There was a tie there deeper and more primal than anything on earth, a mother protecting her babies.

What if that happened to me? To us? What if Andrew and Lillian Armstrong hated my guts? Was I up to it? Was the love I felt for Kay worth the possible assault from the major's children? What if I didn't like them? What if they were spoiled little brats, destructive little shits that worked every minute of every day trying to come between me and Kay. I couldn't stand it.

You're making all these assumptions on the grounds she even marry you, I told myself sternly.

She said "No" before. She might say it again.

Would she?

Could I take that chance?

What other choice did I have?

* * *

In the meantime, as my uncertainty over Kay and her children grew, my star began to rise in the newsroom, thanks to Ludean Tate's situation, which was dragging slowly through the courts. The story had bounced its way through the newsroom.

After I did the first story, I handed it off to Addison McIntyre, our city government reporter. A short, stocky woman in her mid-forties who smoked too many cigarettes and worked more hours than I thought humanly possible, she was whispered to be Jess's successor in the likely event he moved on to a bigger paper. She was more than competent; she was driven. Addison had come into journalism when having a *girl* in the newsroom was a rarity. Sometimes I wondered if her short brown hair, her bitten, nicotine-stained nails, and her colorful use of expletives were an effort to blend in with the boys or just a facet of her own rough-cut personality. She lived in Jubilant all her life; her dad was a former state trooper, and knew everybody who was anybody.

It was also no secret Jess harbored dreams of sitting in Ben Bradlee's chair at the Washington *Post* one day. We even joked he slept with a picture of the *Post's* famed editor emeritus under his pillow at night. Like so many of the folks who started here and moved on to bigger and better things, Jess one day would do the same.

Addison was more than likely his successor and we all knew it.

She had followed the story through the city housing author-ity's investigation, and then our cops and courts reporter John Porter was slated to pick up the story when the trial began later in Febru-ary in Municipal Court. Once Aurora had refused to comply, attorney Martin Rathke continued to delay and obfuscate and had probably perjured himself.

We hadn't put it on the wire yet, so it still remained a local story. Surprisingly, the television stations from the next town hadn't stayed on it beyond the day my first story had splashed across the front page. And the story involved more than just Ludean now. We had some fifteen tenants who come forward and whose complaints had been verified.

I was covering fluff less and less frequently; many of the silly events I spent days covering were farmed off to stringers or part-timers. I was working my way back from failure, and, damn, it felt good.

It was late January, when John, Addison, Jess, and I sat in the paper's conference room with copies of our Aurora Development stories spread around us.

"We've got one month before this thing goes to trial, and we really need to keep this story on the front burner in everybody's mind." Jess inhaled on his cigar and exhaled toward the ceiling. "What would it take to really dig into the ownership of Aurora Devel-opment?"

"A trip to Wilmington, Delaware, where the original incorpo-ration documents are filed," I said, spinning my pencil between my fingers on the table's shiny surface. "Aurora is owned by something real nebulous called Land Management Limited that's tied into another corporation and another and so on. All of them are what's called a Delaware Business Trust, which is like a corporation, but with more privacy for the owners. I don't think that whoever is behind Land Management Limited is local, but you never can tell. Delaware's got one of the most widely used corporate laws in the country. You can be anywhere in the world and file as a Delaware corporation."

"Like the old man would pay for that, the way advertising rev-enues have dropped," Addison nodded towards the back wall, where a painting of our publisher, J. Watterman Whitelaw, hung; it had been painted sometime in the mid-sixties, when he taken over the place from his father.

"But why would somebody from out of state come to Jubilant Falls to be a sleazy landlord?" Porter looked up from doodling on his notepad.

About medium height with thinning-but-curly hair, Porter had the dimpled cheeks, cool, gray eyes, and devilish arch to his eyebrows that women found irresistible…or at least that was the rumor. Unfortunately, Porter was proof that even the best writers could go stale if left on the same beat too long. He could make a story shine when he wanted to. These days, that happened less and less and I had some real fears he ignored some of the big clues that might be found at the Plummer County Courthouse because he was more interested in romancing the municipal court judge's secretary.

"That doesn't make good sense," Porter shrugged his shoulders, like a vulture adjusting his wings.

"But most people don't work so hard to hide the fact they've got a bunch of rental property, either," I countered.

"How about this…" Jess leaned forward. "How about the three of you profile every one of the complainants? One or two a week, until the trial starts…"

"And Rathke will subpoena us up one side and down the other, claiming we poisoned the jury pool, if it ever goes to trial," Porter replied.

Jess frowned. "I haven't been at a newspaper yet where a motion like that ever been granted."

"Anyway, it's going to be the same story over and over again," I said. "'I used to work at Traeburn Tractor. I got laid off. I lost my house.'"

"That's a possibility." Jess furrowed his brows together in thought. "We need to find out who's at the bottom of Aurora Development and put together a story that just sums the whole thing. Here, let's do this…three of you put together a story that will go on Sunday's front page and on the wire. Porter, I want you to dig through court records and see if there's ever been any other complaints filed against Aurora, anything you can find, no matter how small or insignificant. I want it in a sidebar. I'll put a call into the AP bureau chief in Delaware, promise him the story if he can dig anything up."

"It's worth a try," Porter shrugged.

"Get going then, folks," Jess stood up, and we gathered the newspapers together and began to file out. "Marcus, wait…" he laid a hand on my shoulder. "I need to talk to you." He shut the door behind Addison and Porter.

"Everything okay?" I asked.

"The old man wanted me to tell you what a good job you've been doing," he said, smiling proudly. "I have to say, this has been the biggest story to hit us in a long, long time, and you've been on it like a pro, a real pro. I know things have been tough professionally and personally for you for a while...."

"Don't remind me."

"Well, the old man wants you doing less of the lifestyle stuff; says we need to be more competitive in the investigative stuff...."

"No shit?" I could hardly believe what I was hearing.

Jess nodded. "He's seriously thinking of establishing a special projects editor, kind of an investigative thing, you know. And he mentioned your name."

"What kind of special projects? It sounds great, but how much investigative journalism can you do in Plummer County?"

"Some of the things he specifically mentioned were looking at the living conditions of the migrant workers that are coming into the area, welfare reform, that kind of thing. He thinks you can do it...and I have to agree with him."

"Thanks."

"Now, nothing is definite right now.."

"Oh, I understand." The fact that somebody realized I wasn't a total journalistic failure was enough for right now.

"I just wanted to let you in on what was going on."

"Sure. Hey, thanks for believing in me."

Jess opened the conference room door. "Everything except your taste in women, Marcus. I never doubted you for a minute." He slapped me on the back and we walked back into the newsroom.

The three of us spent the afternoon putting the story together. Jess sent the photographer, Pat Robinette, out to get a few shots of Ludean's place. We held the story, waiting for the Delaware AP reporter to call us back.

Three days later, he did.

"No can do, my man," the reporter said. "Whoever filed this baby filed it under seal."

"So what's all the secrecy for, then?" I asked Jess, after I hung up.

"Who knows? Somebody somewhere feels they've really got something to hide."

* * *

"Marcus, this is hardly the place for kids. This is pure, first-date territory." Anxiously holding Andrew and Lillian by their hands, Kay looked around the palm-filled dark interior of Jubilant Falls' poshest restaurant, the Emmett House Inn. It was the Friday after we ran the preview story on the hearing and, feeling confident after hearing my publisher's compliments, I decided that it was time to introduce myself to Andrew and Lillian. Kay warned that it might not be a good time just yet, barely a month after their father's death, but I was determined not to let this seven-year-old boy and this nearly five-year-old little girl come between their mother and me.

If I could win the approval of my publisher, how hard could a dinner with these kids be, anyway?

"Well, isn't this almost like a first date?" I turned and smoothed my hair in one of the restaurant's many gilt-framed mirrors. *Here I am,* I wanted to say, *a man so deeply in love with these kids' mother that I spend a weeks wages just to win them over.*

"Well, yes, but..."

"I want to make a good first impression, that's all. So, Andrew, how do you like school."

The boy looked at me sullenly. "Fine."

"I color, play dollies..." Lillian began to tick off her kindergarten curriculum on her fingers.

"You don't go to a real school. You go to a baby school." Andrew leaned around Kay and stuck out his tongue.

"Mommy! Andy called me a baby!" Lillian squealed.

"Stop it you two. That's enough. Marcus is being very nice to us, by taking us out to dinner. The least you two can do is be nice to each other."

"How many in your party, sir?" The maitre d' sniffed imperiously, sensing the impending disaster. "Do you have reservations?"

"Four. The reservations are under Henning."

"Ah, yes. Follow me, please."

He seated us in a circular booth in an even darker back corner of the dark restaurant. Two enormous oriental vases filled with palm fronds hid us from the other diners.

"Why is this place so dark, Mommy? Don't they have lights?" Lillian asked, moving along the chintz upholstery on her knees. Finding a seat, she picked up her fork and began a singsong rhythm against the empty water goblet . "I wanna win-dow. I wanna window. Window window window."

"Lil, please don't do that." Kay took the fork from her and tried to divert her attention. "What sounds good for supper? They have all kinds of wonderful things here, honey."

"This place is stupid. They don't have any cheeseburgers," Andrew interjected loudly. "Mom, I want a cheeseburger."

"Mommy, I can't see over the table when I sit on my butt." Lillian moved to stand on the expensive upholstery, but Kay caught her by the hand and made her sit still.

"When the waitress comes, we'll get you a booster seat."

"Can we get cheeseburgers, Mom?" Andy asked. "I'm not eating anything but cheeseburgers."

"I like nuggets. You like nuggets, Marcus? Daddy like nuggets. He's dead." Lillian began to wiggle back and forth in her seat.

"Lillian!" Kay held a finger to her lips.

"I'm not eating anything but cheeseburgers," Andrew repeated.

"Andrew, I'm not saying it again. They don't have cheeseburgers. They have grilled cheese or chicken legs or a small plate of spaghetti. You can choose one of those."

"I don't want those." Andrew's lower lip poked out, and he folded his small arms across his chest.

"My God, is every meal like this, Kay?" I asked, pulling the candles, the salt and peppershakers, and the sugar bowl from Lillian's ever-growing grasp.

"Not if you carry your own tray to your seat, and there's a free prize with your Happy Meal."

"What's that supposed to mean?"

"Look around, Marcus. How many other children to you see here?" Kay asked gently.

"Honestly?"

"Honestly." She patted my thigh reassuringly.

"I haven't seen so many geriatric diners, since lunch time at the Happy Times Retirement Home."

Kay laughed. "Exactly. This is the kind of place where parents come to remind themselves that they're still adults, and they can make sentences that are longer than four words."

"I wanna window. Window window window." Lillian began her sing-song again, this time tapping on the goblet with her fingernails.

"Lillian is stupid. Stupid stupid stupid," chorused Andrew in some sort of manic, choral put-down.

"Window window window!"

"Stupid stupid stupid!"

My nerves jangled with each repetition, but it never fazed Kay, who calmly read her menu as if she were in the silence of a graveyard.

"Window window window!"

"Stupid stupid stupid!"

The rhythm and the tempo picked up. Andrew added to the din by pounding on the table with his fists, the sound echoing through my head like the beginning of a migraine.

"Window window window!"

"Stupid stupid stupid!"

"Window window window!"

"Stupid stupid stupid!"

"Enough!" Kay clamped her hands across the children's mouths. Silence fell throughout the restaurant, as the diners turned to stare at the circus in our corner.

"Excuse us," she said, smiling weakly. Several diners shot nasty looks our direction, before returning to their meals.

Andrew looked at me and grinned, as if to say *I'm going to run you off, if it's the last thing I do tonight. We have a family already and you're not welcome here.*

A waitress hurried to the table. "How are you folks doing, tonight?" Before we could answer, she rushed on. "Are you all ready to order?"

"I want a cheeseburger." Andrew crossed his arms defensively.

"Andrew, they don't have cheeseburgers," Kay snapped. "You'll have to choose something else."

"Mommy, fries?" Lillian asked.

"No fries, honey. They have—"

"Squid!" Andrew yelled out. "Mom! They've got squid! That is so gross!! Order the squid, Lillian!"

"Andrew!"

Once again, diners were laying down their forks to stare at us. I couldn't believe the scene these kids were making. All of my fears were coming true; these were little animals, little beasts intent on making me look like a fool. What was I doing thinking I could form a family with these little toads?

"Mommy, I have to pee." Lillian squirmed dangerously in her seat. "Moo-o-o-ommy."

"Maybe I should come back in a few moments." The waitress began to step away.

"No! Wait!" I grabbed her wrist. Through clenched teeth, I placed our order. "Give us four of the largest slices of chocolate cake you've got. With ice cream. I want two large cups of Irish coffee and two glasses of milk. Now."

"Yes, sir."

"Marcus, these kids can't just have cake and milk for dinner!"

"The milk isn't for them, the Irish coffee is! We'll eat the cake, then go to McDonald's."

Kay laughed. "Now you're getting the idea!"

"Mo-o-om-m-my! I'm gonna pee-pee my pants!"

"Hang on, Lillian. We'll be right back, guys." With a flourish, Kay grabbed her daughter and fled to the ladies' room.

Andrew and I stared uncomfortably at each other. The waitress brought the four slices of cake and the drinks, and – silently – he and I began to eat.

"I don't like you," he said, finally.

"I can tell. But you don't know me very well, Andy," I replied. "Maybe if you got to know me a little better."

"I don't want to."

"Well, I'm planning on being around for a while. You know I think your mother's a pretty special lady."

"I hate you."

"You're not giving me much of a chance here, Andrew."

"I don't care. I hate you."

This is going to be a real uphill battle, I thought, taking a sip of my Irish coffee. I know less than I thought about children. Any ideas about treating Kay's children as miniature adults who could be reasoned with was vanishing into thin air, but I had to give it one more try.

"What if I told you I loved your mother very much? What if I said I like to marry your mother some day?"

Fire and rage lit up the boy's eyes.

"No! You're not my dad! You'll never be my dad!" He picked up his glass of milk and tossed the contents in my face. "I hate you! I hate you! I hate you!" he screamed, each sentence was a wailing crescendo. "You're not my daddy, and you never will be!"

Kay came around the corner with Lillian, and Andrew threw himself on the floor, kicking and pounding his fists. "You're not gonna ever be my daddy! Never! Never! Never!" he screamed.

In the corner of my eye, I saw the maitre d' coming toward our table. People were pointing and staring at us, in well-deserved disgust.

"Andrew stand up! Stop this behavior right now!" Kay yanked the boy up by the arms. "I have never been so embarrassed in all my life!"

"I hate him! I hate him! I hate him!"

"Andrew, stop it!"

"No! You can't make me!"

"Marcus, I'm terribly sorry, but I think I better take the kids home in a cab." Quickly, she gathered her purse together and, pulling Andrew by the arm, left me to ponder what life would be like with my future stepchildren.

CHAPTER 7

Kay

I took no perverse pleasure in noting that Paul's will had not been changed before he died, that everything reverted to me and not some other woman. The hardest thing to do was to pack up his stuff. His commander, Col. Thorwald, took leave and brought his personal belongings back.

Col. Thorwald stood ramrod straight in my entryway, a huge box covered in brown paper and masking tape at his feet, but there was no mistaking the pain that filled his craggy face. I thought his graying hair made him look a little older than his forty-seven years, especially when twenty-five of those years had been spent in the cockpit of one fighter plane or another. He was wearing his blue uniform with the leather fighter pilot jacket, twisting his flight cap in his hands.

"He was a good man," Thorwald said, as we hugged briefly.

"I know."

"We're still looking into the hydraulic failure that caused the accident. I want you to know that this will not be blamed on pilot error."

I nodded. "Good."

Thorwald shifted from one foot to the other. "Kay, we all knew why Bear came to Korea. It was pretty much an open secret that he was looking for that little boy."

"You knew?"

"Everybody did. He was obsessed about finding that kid. It couldn't have made things very easy for you."

I sighed. "No, it didn't. When he was home at Christmas, we decided to split up. I was to file everything, and then we finalize it before he went on to his next assignment."

"I'm sorry to hear that. I don't know why he behaved like that, when he had somebody like you at home."

"I never understood it either, Colonel." *But I'll bet you never sat down with him and said that,* I thought.

"You let me know if there's anything I can do."

"I'm fine."

He nodded and, placing his flight cap on his head, saluted.

"Take care," he said, and he was gone.

I sat on the floor beside the box, folding my legs beneath me. What was in here? How much of the man remained?

I tore the brown paper off the box and opened the cardboard flaps. I picked up each shirt, each pair of pants and smelled it, hoping for one final scent of the man, but someone had washed them before packing them. Who? His Korean lover? Another female officer? All I smelled was soap and dryer sheets.

His own personal collection of knickknacks broke my heart. There was a picture of the kids and me together at Virginia Beach that had been in his locker; a picture of a signpost in front of the on-base officers' quarters he lived in, with arrows pointing to cities in all directions: Moscow (3,627 miles), Mifflin, PA (6,866 miles), Mount Holly, NJ (6,964 miles), Pyongyang (131 miles); the Myung Jin bus schedule; a small American flag; a box of cheap Korean souvenirs for the kids; and a few tattered paperbacks, westerns by Louis L'Amour. Nothing to indicate he was anything but the perfect officer, the perfect gentleman, the perfect family man.

Quietly, I closed the box and took it up to the attic. Later, I would pack up the *I Love Me* wall and the photograph of him kneeling on the wing on his plane at Eglin. Scrapbooks and mementos of our life together, hidden in the corners of the attic for the year he would have stayed at Osan, held memories I could only thumb through and wish they had been different.

How many women had he slept with over the length of our marriage? Had I known about all of them, could I have been as forgiving as I wanted to be now? I looked at our wedding portrait: a young officer beaming with all the promise that his future in the military held and his blushing bride crossing under an arch of sabers as they exited the church. This picture was once my favorite, because we were looking into each other's eyes with complete trust, bound to each other for what would only be a love-filled and glorious life. It had been the one I had thrown at him at Eglin – he had it repaired and bought another silver frame to put it in.

At Langley Air Force Base when things went sour, I took it from the wall above the couch in our living room, saying my pupils were red from the camera flash and it ruined the whole effect. It wasn't the light in my eyes, it was the tears. But Paul knew what I was saying.

The trust was gone.

Everything else had been stored here in Jubilant Falls, in anticipation of our next move – or mine.

Was this what it all boiled down to? A collection of personal effects and a stack of clean laundry no one else would ever wear? Maybe someday I could go through them with the children, but not now. For now, they would be relegated to the attic with the remainder of Paul's life. One day, I would pull out the leather flight jacket and the tall green flight suit tailored to accommodate his muscular shoulders and his tiny waist and tell the children about their daddy, when he could be the hero again.

I had hated him so much then and regretted that hate so much now. I had hated everything he did to me, but not what he stood for. Maybe that meant I wasn't such a bad military wife after all. My heart still skipped a beat when the jets from nearby Symington Air Base went overhead, but I never knew if it was in fear or excited anticipation. I had been looking for a hero and found Paul; something inside me still believed in the myth, just not the man. Had I been wrong to do that?

In the end, only the I Love Me wall remained.

Work was a chore, but in the end, it drowned me, too.

Finally, a bad case of bursitis forced me into a short leave of absence, keeping me on the couch with hot and cold packs to reduce the pain in my shoulder and, now and then, a bit of Scotch to reduce the pain in my heart.

Sometimes it hurt even to see Marcus.

Andrew treated him horribly, but who could blame the kid, really? Here was this man who was not his father coming around the house, paying attention to his mother.

Things had changed, since that disastrous dinner at the Emmett House Inn. I'd warned Marcus it was all wrong. Little kids don't appreciate that kind of place, and it was too soon for them to accept another man in their mother's life.

And things were changing with Marcus and me, too, especially since that brick came sailing through the window.

The whole situation and my refusal to share it with Marcus became very wearing on the two of us.

But especially since Paul's death.

Now that we didn't have to hide, now that he could come over any time day or night, Marcus became very tentative with me, leaving some space between us that often left me feeling more adrift than Paul's death. I don't know if it was just to give me space to grieve, or if it was what was going on at the newspaper, but there was an estrangement, a distance right when I needed him most.

Certainly Ludean Tate's story was ongoing. Despite my absence from the office, she was never far from my thoughts. When Marcus's first story ran, the municipal housing authority had been quick to act. Aurora Development had thirty days to get repairs going. Nothing was ever done. As more and more tenants came forward with many of the same complaints, Rathke asked for – and got – extensions on that original thirty days.

After a while, the housing authority got fed up and turned the final extension request down, then turned the case over to the courts. Still, Marcus felt defeated.

"He's paying somebody off somewhere. He's got to be." Flopping down in one of my kitchen chairs one evening after work, Marcus rubbed his hands over his afternoon stubble.

"Why do you say that?" I sat a stoneware mug in front of him and poured him a cup of coffee, then sat across from him.

"The scope of these repairs would put anybody else behind bars, like that." Marcus snapped his fingers. "But there's some connection somewhere, some small town political schmoozing somewhere that I can't put my finger on. You know, we had the AP do some digging in Delaware where the incorporation documents are filed. And we couldn't find out who's behind Aurora. I don't think that the owners of Aurora Development are from out of state. I think they're local, and whoever set this corporation up knew enough about what was going on to make a paper trail that leads anybody who's looking in the wrong direction. Somebody, somewhere in this town has connections to this company, and Rathke's covering them up."

"You'll find them. I know you will."

"I don't know anymore, Kay. I just don't know."

"Why don't you stay for supper, and we can talk about it some more." I cupped my hands over his.

"No, I don't think so. Not tonight."

The kitchen door slammed, as the kids came charging into the house, tracking muddy snow across my linoleum.

"Ma, Lillian says she's going to hit me with a snowball in the face!" Andrew bellowed. He stopped short and stared at Marcus. "Oh, it's you."

"Andrew, that's rude. Say hello to Marcus nicely."

"Andy's a chicken! Andy's a chicken!" taunted Lillian, in the background. "Hi, Marcus!"

"Hi, Diamond Lil." he smiled at her. "Hi, Andrew."

Andrew remained sullen and silent. Lillian squealed, the door slammed again, and the two barreled back out into the snow before I could catch them.

"Doggone that little bugger. One out of two isn't bad. Do you want to stay for supper?"

Marcus stared into his coffee cup. "No, I think I'll go grab some fast food and head back to the newsroom. Maybe if I go through my notes again, I'll see something I hadn't seen before." He rose and swallowed the last gulp of coffee. "See you later, my dear."

"Marcus, just give him time. He'll come around." I wrapped my arms around him confidently.

"I hope so." He kissed me on my forehead, but there was no mistaking the doubt in his voice.

* * *

I have never doubted the ability of small things to make a huge difference in someone's life. A few days later, a small yellow envelope with a Korean postmark arrived at the house, forwarded just two days after Paul's death. It was a letter from one of the nun's at St. Vincent's Orphanage in Songtan City. I volunteered there, when we were stationed at Osan the first time, but something told me this letter was more than just a note to keep in touch or beg for donations. With quivering hands, I tore through the envelope and began to read:

Dear Major Armstrong:

Enclosed are the final papers needed to complete the birth certificate forms. With them, we can then move on to the U.S. Embassy in Seoul, where he can be declared a U.S. citizen.

As you know, Koreans do not have birth certificates. Instead, there are long genealogical records for each family. As an Amer-Asian because his father is a GI, your son would be denied an education, a future or even a past.

I was deeply grateful when I finally met you last month. Your efforts to locate your son and bring him back to the U.S. with you have truly been the main topic of conversation here at St. Vincent's. I have seen too many GI's go as far as locating the children they father, but then either in fear or arrogance they never go through with their plans to support their babies.

Your wife is an exceptional woman; I remember her when she volunteered here several years ago, and she was well loved by both the staff and the children.

But this shows her as the child of God she truly is. Even if the child had not been of another race and culture, which certainly plays a part, few wives would open their hearts and homes to the children of their husband's sin. Those words seem harsh, Major, but there is forgiveness from God in your actions to give this little boy a home. May God bless you both, for your love of this little boy.

While I certainly do not condone adulterous acts, I understand probably better than most of the other sisters here why a service man far from home seeks refuge in the arms of a woman. You see, I lost my younger brother in Vietnam in 1970. The few letters home that he sent spoke of the stench of battle, the loneliness, the tropical heat, and his search for something that would obliterate the ugliness and horror his 19-year-old eyes could not shut out.

After his death, there was a child born of this search, a little boy like your son. His mother was tortured, raped, and killed by the Communists when Saigon fell, and the child, then five years old, disappeared into the refugee camps of Cambodia. My family back home in Boston instituted a fruitless search; either typhoid or the Khmer Rouge had killed him.

By taking little Paul into your home, you will be preventing the waste of another innocent life. His green eyes clearly mark him as an Amer-Asian. If your son was to remain in this country, he could be guaranteed nothing: no name, no future, no past, and as time goes by, no citizenship, no education, and no job. If you had not been determined to find this small child, he would have nothing to look forward to but a life of crime, drugs, and an early death.

Little Paul is an exceptional child. In the last 15 months that he has been with us at St. Vincent's, I have seen a tranquility and peace in his little face—he's nearly four now. He's like no other child I have ever known. Oh, he's stubborn at times, but by and large he possesses a calmness very few children can claim. Every afternoon, before his nap, I sit watching him play with his blocks in the day room, patiently stacking one atop the other until exhaustion sets in, and he comes to me rubbing his sleepy eyes as he lays his head in my lap.

I look forward to meeting you after the holidays, but it will be a bittersweet meeting. I'll miss rocking him, Major. I'll miss the sweet baby smell of him and the soft sigh of deep contented sleep that he makes when he rolls over in his crib.

But for the grace of God, this little boy could have been my brother's child. Knowing that you will give him the love and care he so richly deserves makes it a little easier to let him go, but I will still miss him as I miss the nephew I never knew.

May God keep you, and may his blessing be forever with you-

Sister Michael Mary

In the last fold of the letter, there was a small photograph. It was PJ, smiling into the camera from the lap of an elderly nun. The picture wasn't very much different from the one I had seen before. He was just a little older now. His eyes were still green, just like Paul's, and his dark brown hair, cut like a bowl atop his head, was streaked with blonde. Across the back was written *Paul Pak, age 4, and Sister Agnes.* Carefully, I folded the letter and slipped it back into its envelope. The morning sun had begun to filter through the kitchen curtains, falling onto the counter tops and the small table, where I sat too astounded to think or speak, even in this empty room.

Oh, God. So this nun thought I was wonderful to take this little boy into my home. I laid my head on the kitchen table, as guilt rushed over me.

Yeah, I'm wonderful. I'm so wonderful I could vomit.

"Mommy?"

It was Andrew. What if the situation were a little different, and it had been Andrew that I had been forced to give up? I would want someone to care for him as this nun was now caring for PJ. If I were dead, I would want someone, any member of my family—even my spouse— to provide for Andrew. I would want them to take Andy into their homes and love him like I had been unable to.

It was clear in my mind now: I had to bring PJ here to the States. I had to bring PJ home.

"Mommy, why are you crying?"

I stood and drew my son to me. "Andy, what would you say to having a little brother?"

"Are you crying because you're going to have a baby?"

"No honey, I'm not going to have a baby." I steered him to the dinette. "Sit down, honey. I want to tell you a story."

***

I wrote back to Sister Michael Mary later that same day, telling her of Paul's death and my own decision to bring the boy here where he really belonged. The children were thrilled about having a little brother, particularly one who was already big enough to play with. As Andrew told Lillian, "Not just a tiny one who cries and messes in his diapers all the time. This is a real boy."

Marcus hadn't planned on coming over that night, but soon after dinner the telephone rang. Andrew jumped to answer it.

"Hello, Mr. Marcus." The excitement that had filled his voice all day suddenly disappeared. "Yeah, she's here. Did you want to talk to her?" He was very somber for a moment. I gestured to the food in my mouth and indicated I needed a little time to chew and swallow.

"Mom's got her mouth full. I'll talk to you for a minute, I guess, if you want." The boy's eyes narrowed. "Did you know we're going to have baby?"

I snatched the receiver from him, gulping down my food. "Marcus, hi! Hello!"

"What is he talking about, Kay?"

"Hey, at least he's talking to you."

There was an uncomfortable silence.

"You're not pregnant are you?"

"God, no!" I had to laugh, but Marcus didn't share the humor. Another uncomfortable silence hung between us.

"You've decided about the Major's boy, haven't you?"

"Yes, I have."

He didn't respond.

"Marcus, I need to talk to you face to face about this. I have to show you this letter and PJ's picture."

"Kay, you know how I feel about you."

"And I love you, too. But this little boy needs a home."

"This is what you really want?"

"This is what I really want."

He sighed. "You shouldn't have told the kids so soon. I'm sure that there are piles of paperwork to be done. It might take years."

"Paul had paternity tests done before he died, and most of the paperwork to get him an American birth certificate was already completed when the accident occurred. Once Paul is listed on his birth certificate, he's already considered an American citizen. Half of what we need to do is done."

He sighed again.

"Please come by. We need to talk about this."

"I can't. One of our copy editors called in sick, and I'm working on some stuff at home tonight—that post-modern artist who lectured at the college yesterday. We got a bunch of great photos, and Jess wants a feature."

"Tomorrow, then? I want you to see this letter I got today."

"I'll try."

"Okay." I hung up. The gap between us was widening. Could I stand it, if the distance grew even more after my decision? I brushed my hand across my eyes to erase those thoughts, and turned to finish my meal. Well, if he had problems with the whole thing, they were exactly that – his problems. I didn't want to lose him, but bringing PJ home was something I knew I had to do.

* * *

It was a cold Saturday in March; Mother and I spent the afternoon wandering the Jubilant Falls Mall with the children as a last-resort means to entertain them. The city had been blanketed with six inches of late winter snow, closing everything from the Literacy Center to the city's public and private schools. We had all been prisoner to the white stuff, and an afternoon at the mall had seemed to be an excellent escape. Mother enjoyed her afternoon with the children, and for once our conversation was relaxed and easy.

Pulling the Mercedes into her cavernous garage, Mother spoke to the children before she answered me. "Novella will have hot chocolate and pastry for good little boys and girls. Take all the goodies Grandma bought you into the house, and we'll be right in."

The children squealed with delight and ran into the kitchen.

"I understand that Andrew put on quite a performance recently."

"What do you mean?"

"At the Emmett House Inn, about a month ago." Gazing into the rear-view mirror, Mother patted her perfectly coiffed hair.

"Oh, God. How did you find out that? No don't tell me. I don't want to hear it."

"Ellen Nussey was there with Ed and Lovey McNair. She saw the whole thing."

"I told Marcus that I didn't think it was the best place to take the kids." We stepped from the car and into the kitchen. Andrew and Lillian sat at the breakfast bar, where Novella took all her meals, their legs swinging from the high stools and their upper lips masked in chocolate and whipped-cream mustaches. I stopped quickly to wipe their faces. Mother breezed past us, dropping her packages, purse, and coat on the dining room table.

"Kay, Novella will take care of them," she said, as she pulled off her gloves. "Come in here."

"I think Grandma's mad at you, Mommy." Lillian nodded her head knowingly at me.

"What else is new?"

"Lillian, would you like some more whipped cream in that cocoa?" Novella interjected. "Go speak with your mother, Miss Kay. We're fine here."

I followed Mother, as she pushed through the dining room double doors into the living room and swung around to face me.

"All right, go ahead. Take your best shot," I crossed my arms defensively. "Tell me why my children behaved so badly and how it all reflects on your standing in the community."

"If they weren't so traumatized over meeting their mother's lover, I suppose they might have behaved a little better."

"*What*?"

"From what Ellen and Lovey told me..."

"Now, there's a couple of real reliable sources. You're going to jump on me on the basis of what two old hens say they saw a month ago in a restaurant? It must not have been so horrible that they had to wait thirty days to tell you."

"That's not important. What matters is what kind of garbage are you subjecting my grandchildren to?"

"I don't think there's anybody in this whole world who knows how to get to me the way you do, Mother," I said. I took a seat on the couch, trying to contain my indignation as I leafed through a magazine. "The whole thing was Marcus's idea, and it ended badly. Okay? Can you stop trying to run my life now?"

"Why do you think it was appropriate to go along with this little scheme of his?"

"Because he wanted to meet my children, Mother. I've been very careful about them seeing him."

"As careful as you were about keeping your wedding vows, I see."

I struggled to keep my composure. "Mother, I'm going to say this just once. You have held me responsible for everything that went wrong in my marriage to Paul, and it's not fair. I'm tired of your judging every move I make, and I'm tired of you trying to control my life."

"Don't you talk like that to me!" Mother shot back. "Paul Armstrong was the best thing that ever happened to you, Kay, and you ruined the whole thing with your tawdry little affair with that horrible reporter!"

"That horrible reporter is the best thing that ever happened to me," I corrected her. "I'll have you know Mr. Wonderful couldn't stay faithful to me if his life depended on it!"

"I find that hard to believe."

I took a deep breath to calm myself down. "Mother, this may be hard for you to believe, but it's true. Paul was sleeping with a Korean woman just before Lillian was born." I walked into the dining room and pulled PJ's photograph from my purse. "Look at this!" I shoved the snapshot of the green-eyed, Korean toddler in front of her face. "You can't tell me this child is anything but Paul Armstrong's son."

Mother's jaw dropped. "I don't believe it."

"It's true. That's the reason he went back to Korea without me."

"Well," Mother recovered her composure. "At least he didn't flaunt it in front of the whole town, like you have."

"He didn't have to flaunt his conquests. Everyone in the squadron knew about them. I just know that he had more than one."

"You don't have to bring that little half-breed here to Jubilant Falls."

"Would you want your grandchild living in an orphanage?"

"That's not my grandchild."

"He's Paul's son, so that makes him my stepson, and if I adopt him like I want to, he'll be just as much a grandson to you as Andrew is."

"You can't be serious." Mother rolled her eyes.

"I can." I slipped PJ's picture back into my purse.

"Oh, for God's sake, Kay, have you lost all common sense? You have no money to support your two children, three if you count this, this—" Mother waved her hand, dismissively. "—this little bastard. And then you take up with this nobody, who is such a loser even your own children can sense it!"

"Mother, why do you hate Marcus so much? He may not have money or any of those connections you think are so important, but he's a good, decent man. I don't know what our plans are for the future, but I know that this relationship will work. Just tell me what it is you don't like about him."

She was silent for a moment. "That's not important."

"Yes it is!"

"Kay, you don't know how destructive this man is!"

"Oh please! Now you're getting melodramatic!"

"No I'm not. If there was anything I could do to end this tawdry romance of yours, I would." There was an eerie fire in Mother's eyes. "I do anything, I pay anything to see that man wiped off the face of this earth."

"And I wouldn't put it past you, either. So maybe it would be better if we just didn't speak at all." I walked into the living room and began to gather my belongings together. "Andrew! Lillian! We're leaving!"

"No, Kay, please!"

"Sorry Mother, I'm closing the door. This time, for good."

* * *

That door stayed closed, for nearly two weeks. There was no way I was going to let that old woman run my life any longer. I was my own person, and she didn't have any right to say anything to me.

Then one evening, the phone rang. I pulled away from Marcus and the mindless detective show we were watching and stepped into the foyer.

"Miss Kay?" it was Novella.

"Novella! Is everything okay? Are you and mother all right?"

"Well, I'm fine, Miss Kay, but it's your mother."

"What is it? Is she sick?"

"She's sick only from not seeing you and those children." Novella's Jamaican accent made words which would have been an accusation in anyone else's mouth sound lyrical.

"Oh, for Christ sake, Novella. What are you trying to do? Mend fences?"

"Now, now Miss Kay, you can't take her so seriously."

"I have to take her seriously when she says she'll break up Marcus and me if it's the last thing she does. She wants to run my life, Novella! You, of all people, should know how she is!"

"Miss Kay, please," she cajoled, her Jamaican accent thick and full. "Just one afternoon with her. I'll fix a nice tea for both of you. All you have to do is bury the hatchet. You don't have to spend every waking moment with her. You don't have to agree with the way she lives her life. She just loves you and those children so much, and it's just broke her heart to not see you and your family."

"I'm not ready to bury the hatchet with that woman."

Novella took a deep breath and came at me again from another direction. "When Major Paul died after Christmas, didn't you feel like you had something left to say to him? Didn't you want to tell him you loved him one more time, or apologize for something mean you once said?"

"If only you knew all I wanted to say to that man," I said softly.

"See? That's what I mean, Miss Kay. Supposing your mother dies tomorrow. You know for a fact at her age it could happen. Do you want to live the rest of your life knowing you had the chance to patch things up, and you didn't take it?"

She had me there.

"All right," I said. "You make the arrangements. I'll be there."

"How 'bout tomorrow afternoon at four o'clock?"

"Why do I feel I've just been conned?"

"You won't regret it, Miss Kay. I swear you won't."

I hung up the phone and sat back down next to Marcus.

"Who was that?" he asked.

"Novella."

"This late? I hope everything is fine at Marian's castle keep?" He drew me next to him and kissed the top of my head. It had been a tender, though tentative, evening. He seemed to be making some headway with the kids, and as long as I didn't bring up PJ we seemed to be back on an even keel.

"Yes. She wants mother and me to patch things up, so we're having tea tomorrow."

"What brought that on?"

"The old 'What if she dies tomorrow and you two never made up?' speech."

"I see." Marcus held me close. "What if I died tomorrow?"

"Why are you asking that?"

"Death, or the threat of death, seems to be a big motivator for you right now. You want to bring Paul's kid back to the states; you're going to make up with Maid Marian. What would you do, if I suddenly bought the farm?"

I thought for a moment. "The same thing I regret right now, turning down your proposal eight years ago. I should have married you then."

"What if I asked you right now. Would you turn me down again?"

"Would you accept PJ into the family?"

He was silent.

"I see," I said softly. "I can't say yes if you won't accept PJ."

The wall between us went back up. Bored by the television and disgusted with Marcus, I eventually fell asleep. When I woke up a few hours later with only the blue light of the television glowing through the room, I was alone. The gap between us had become a chasm. Long, deep and unending, it threatened to engulf us as much as it separated us.

How strange that one little boy could have so much power over three people. One now dead had brought him into the world, and two still living couldn't agree to give him the home he deserved.

* * *

"Miss Kay, I am so pleased you agreed to this."

The next afternoon, Novella opened the front door and ushered the children and me into what Mother called Daddy's study where she had covered the wide partner's desk with a linen tablecloth. There were piles of scones; tea sandwiches made of cucumber, smoked salmon and watercress, each with the crusts removed and cut in dainty squares, petit fours, and chocolate cake. An angel food cake sat on a silver platter next to a large, silver bowl of whipped cream. Beside it was a smaller crystal bowl of jam and an enormous strawberry Bavarian. The coffee and teapots towered over the food, in the antique serving set my Grandmother James had given my mother as a wedding gift. Even the antique sucrier had been resurrected, filled with soft, powdered sugar.

"Wow! Look at all that food!" Andrew reached for a sandwich.

"Andrew, you just keep your fingers out of there. You and Lillian have a plate back in the kitchen. Right now, your mama and your grandma need to talk."

"My God, Novella, who else is coming? The Joint Chiefs of Staff? The Pope?"

Novella smiled; there was no other cook like her in Mother's closed social circle, and she knew it. "No, just you and Mrs. James. Sit down. I'll get her, once I settle these two." Novella herded the children out the door, closing it with a gentle click behind her. I made myself comfortable and waited in one of the leather armchairs she had pulled close to the desk.

I'll bet I haven't been in this room for years, I thought. The study was always Daddy's domain, and mother had struggled to maintain it, all these years after his death. Daddy did all his after-hours business in his study, meeting with the other partners in his medical practice, his lawyers, or accountants. I knew I was in trouble when Daddy summoned me to the study, and calmly shut the door behind me.

Daddy had been gone so long, since my junior year of high school, that some days I had trouble remembering his face.

Poor Mother, I thought, suddenly astounded. *Novella was right—I'm all Mother has. It's no wonder she's so manipulative. For a woman with everything, she really has so little in her life. Except for that old cow Lovey McNair, she has to hoard every emotional tie she makes.*

What was she like as a child, I wonder? She never talked about it. Come to think about it, her entire side of the family was never discussed, except to say she was an only child and after she graduated from high school they died in a car wreck. Was she wealthy? I knew she had been a medical secretary when she met Daddy during his residency at the county hospital. But was it a job just to keep a wealthy young woman busy till she found a husband, or did she need to support herself? Had she married into money, or did she have any of her own?

Why was it all such a secret?

The heavy door opened, and Mother in gray flannel slacks and a white cashmere sweater entered the room. She twisted her pearl necklace through her fingers, nervously. Her cheeks were hollow, and she had applied too much rouge to cover her colorless skin.

"Hello, Kay," she said apprehensively. "I'm so glad you came."

A rush of feeling brought me to my feet. We were two adults now, two women who had lost their husbands, not parent and child eternally bickering. I walked quickly across the room to take her hands in mine. This woman was as adrift in this big house as PJ was in Songtan. In our argument, I had cut her off from the things that meant the most to her, and she had suffered. I couldn't do that any longer. She would make me crazy; she would attempt to impose her values over mine, but she was still my mother, my only mother, just like Paul was Andrew and Lillian's only father. Once she was gone, there would be no other. Despite her faults, she was still family.

"Mother, I'm glad I came too," I hugged her. She pulled back rigidly from me, quickly masking a startled look and becoming the Dreaded Social Maven I abhorred.

That's okay, overlook it, I told myself. *She's all the family you've got. You need each other.*

"I do hope we can put all this unfortunate business behind us now." Mother took a lace handkerchief from her pocket and carefully blotted her lipstick. "It has been so difficult for me."

My heart filled with pity. "These last months haven't been easy for any of us."

"Well, do sit down, darling. I'll ring Novella to serve us."

"That's not necessary Mother. We can do it ourselves."

Mother was unsure. "Well, if that's what you want."

"It is." I picked up one of the Minton plates Novella had set out, the beautiful Crown Darby colors shining amidst all the food. "I haven't seen this stuff in years, Mother. I forgot how elegant everything was. What can I get you?"

"Well, I suppose just one cucumber sandwich and some tea."

"No pastry? No cake?"

"No, darling, I don't think so."

"There's enough food here to feed the Atlantic Fleet. You sure you don't want anything else?" I poured the tea and handed it, along with the single sandwich, to her, then began to generously fill my own plate. "I might just call this dinner, there's so much here. I'm sure the kids are having a wonderful time in the kitchen."

Mother raised her eyebrows over her teacup, as I heaped a spoonful of whipped cream over my angel food cake.

"My goodness Kay, you're eating like you hadn't seen food in a week."

"I just forgot how good a cook Novella is," I smiled at her. "Mother, you know you never told me what you were like as a little girl. Isn't that strange? I mean, all these years we've been so at odds with each other that we never took the time to really sit down and get to know each other."

"If you intend on walking down the aisle with Marcus Henning, you best watch your figure my dear. The older you get, the harder it is to take that extra weight off. And any man who steal one man's wife wouldn't think twice about doing it again with somebody younger and prettier."

My jaw clenched. *Just let it go,* I reminded myself.

"My, that hit a nerve. You haven't done anything as stupid as get married again without telling me, have you?"

She's baiting you, I told myself. *Trying to goad you into an argument. Don't take her seriously; she's just a lonely old lady.*

"No, I haven't Mother. If I do we'll certainly invite you."

"I hope not. You've been married twice now. With your track record, you would think you learn to not do it again." Mother's words trailed off as she sipped her teacup daintily.

"Mother, would you shut up? You're going to drive me to drink!"

She hunched over her solitary sandwich. "I didn't mean to ruin our reconciliation," she said plaintively.

I took a deep breath and smoothed my skirt, trying to concentrate on keeping my promise to Novella to make peace with Mother. "That's okay. Let's talk about something else."

"Yes. Tell me what you have been doing with yourself."

"Working mostly. Until everything in Paul's estate gets settled, things are kind of tight."

"Are you in any financial difficulty, my dear?"

"Not really. I mean, we're not starving," I took a bite of a salmon sandwich. "There's plenty of food, and the kids' shoes still fit, but there's nothing for extras right now."

Mother was silent for a few moments. "Darling, may I make a suggestion?"

"Before you do, I want to say something." I raised both hands. "I do not need any suggestions on how to run my life. I'm an adult. I would appreciate it if you would keep your comments about how I choose to live my life to yourself. Would you tell Lovey what to do?"

"But Kay, you don't know about Lovey…" she bit her lip and was silent a moment. "If that's what you like. I just have one little idea…please, hear me out." Without waiting for my reply, Mother plowed on. "This is something I've been planning to do for quite a while, since you and Paul were first married. In fact, I was going to give it to you for your tenth wedding anniversary, but you and he would have obviously split up long before that."

"Mother!"

"I'm sorry." She moved to the desk and pulled a folder from the bottom drawer. "I am prepared to offer you half of my stock in a little venture Lovey and I have had going for years. We call it Marlov Enterprises. That would give you twenty-five percent ownership in the company and even partial ownership in the house you live in. It's a sure thing, Kay. There aren't many of these in life. You be a fool to let it pass."

"I don't know…" If I took this from her, I be right back where I started…under her thumb. But, then, I'd also have more than my paycheck, Paul's Air Force survivor benefits, and the Social Security check I get for the kids.

"Please Kay, take it as a gift." Mother handed me the folder.

"Let me show this to Marcus."

"No! Absolutely not!" she cried out in sudden terror, snatching the papers from my lap. "This is none of his business!"

"Mother, it's not that big a deal! What could it hurt to show it to him?" I stood to take the folder from her hands, but Mother clutched it tighter and backed into the corner, her eyes wild with fear.

"No! No! This is a personal gift, Kay, and I really don't want you to share it! How would you feel, if neighbors were to read your journal or see your tax returns? Some things are meant to be private! Promise me, Kay, promise me!"

"Okay, okay, I won't show it to him, if it will make you feel better." Carefully, I took the folder from her once more. If she been on the window ledge, I don't doubt she have jumped. "I think I should talk to someone about it, though, for my own peace of mind."

"Talk to Mr. Rathke." Mother smoothed her hair and sat back down to pour herself some tea; the spout chimed unsteadily against her cup. "Mr. Rathke has always handled all of the family's legal affairs. Your father trusted him implicitly. He's honest, he's respected."

"Okay, okay, I'll go to Rathke, and I won't show it to Marcus."

"Thank you. Now, if you don't mind, I like to see my grandchildren." Mother, still ashen, went to the door and rang the dainty bell she kept on the table in the foyer. "Novella, if you would bring Andrew and Lillian into the study please?"

Jeez, she sure lost it there for a minute, I thought, helping myself to another cucumber sandwich. I suppose, if it kept the peace between us, I'd tell her I'd keep it under my hat.

Lillian and Andrew came running to embrace their grandmother. Behind them, Novella beamed at me. At the very least, I had made peace with my mother and, after all, wasn't that my whole reason for coming?

During the drive home, I began to rethink my promise. Why should I keep anything at all from Marcus, even if she asked me to? Didn't keeping secrets destroy my relationship with Paul? What frightened her so much that one sentence made her freeze like a deer facing oncoming headlights? Marcus could give me a different slant on this than Rathke could. Rathke, the old slime ball, would only give me Mother's sales pitch all over again: what a good thing it was, why I should take it, think about the children, blah, blah, blah. With all the stuff about Aurora Development and Ludean Tate going on, I'm not sure I trusted old Marty Rathke any more.

I pulled the Porsche into the gravel driveway behind the house and helped Lillian unbuckle her seat belt.

Mother's reaction was extreme, even disturbed. But without knowing any more about her how could I say that for sure? She cut me off like she had something to hide, when I asked her about her childhood. What was this God-awful secret? I had to talk to somebody about it, and Marcus was all I had right now.

"So, how did it go with Maid Marian this afternoon?" Marcus was at the dining room table, surrounded by papers, having let himself in with his own key. Andrew eyed him suspiciously, and Lillian stopped to kiss him briefly on the cheek as they moved past him and upstairs to their rooms.

"Well enough. She promised to keep out of my life. I promised to stay in hers. What's all this?"

"I'm just going through some of this old Aurora stuff. The trial starts next week."

"Anything happen today?" I asked, as I laid my coat and mother's folder across the kitchen table.

"Nothing worth a story. Tenants are paying rent into an escrow account, that's about it."

"Go for the pocketbook, and their hearts and minds will follow?" I sat down on his lap and kissed him.

"Something like that."

"Wonderful! Maybe we'll have this all settled soon! Something happened this afternoon I need to talk to you about."

"Your mother?"

"Well, suppose someone told you something, or, say, was going to give you something, but wanted it to be kept secret. What would you do? I mean, if there was something strange about it, something you didn't feel good about?"

"As a reporter, I could consider it off the record, if it were perfectly clear beforehand that it was not to be used in a story. As a friend, I take it to my grave. Why?"

I hedged. "If the giver became totally irrational? Totally loony?"

"Kay, unless I know the whole story, I don't know what I do."

"Mother gave me something tonight, something she didn't want me to share with you at all, something she became absolutely paranoid about when I suggested that I show it to you." I slipped into the chair beside him and held his hand across the table.

"That's no surprise that she wouldn't want me to have a part in it. She hates my guts. What did she give you?"

"Well, that's the thing. I promised I wouldn't tell." I laughed nervously. "She wanted to give it to me as a gift. She got all bent out of shape, when I mentioned that things were a little tight until Paul's estate gets settled."

"So it's money. Why would she not want you to tell me she gave you money?"

"Well, sorta. But she didn't want you to know about it at all, like you would sell it to the Russians or something."

"Then don't tell me."

"But it was her goofiness when I mentioned your name! She really hates you, you know? She backed into the corner, like you were going to attack her or something. I'm really worried about her now, Marcus."

He sighed in exasperation. "You're gonna have to tell me now…you have no choice."

Quickly I went into the kitchen and grabbed the folder. "It's stock…twenty-five percent ownership in this company Mother and Lovey own." I sat back down at the dining room table. "She grabbed it away from me, when I told her I wanted you to look at it before I accepted it. I'm not in a position where I can turn down a great deal of money, even if it comes from my mother." I slid it across the table to him. "I would just feel better if you look at it."

Marcus read down the first page, knitting his eyebrows together studiously. He turned the page and whistled softly and quietly.

"What is it?" I asked. "What's wrong?"

"Oh my God." His voice was a whisper. "Seven months I've been looking, and here it is, right under my nose."

"What? What's right under your nose?"

Marcus slapped the folder closed. "You cannot accept this stock."

"Why not?"

"Just trust me. It's evil, and it's wrong."

"So is sleeping with a married woman, but that didn't stop you."

"This is not the same thing."

"Sure it is. Tell me what's so bad about Mother's company."

"Marlov Enterprises isn't just two little old ladies getting together to manage some properties for extra bridge money. It's the parent of another company whose business practices are less than honorable."

"So are thousands of other businesses all over this country! But if you were offered a quarter ownership in a money-making venture outright, wouldn't you take it? This is supposed to be a good thing, Marcus!"

"This ain't AT&T, honey."

"This is just a land-owning venture, Mother said. If I took this stock, I have something to call my own. I'll own part of my house! What can be so dishonest about owning a little rental property?"

"Nothing, but you just don't want a part of this."

"And if I do?"

"Then you become eligible for a free, contempt of court citation or ninety days in the county jail for your failure to repair seventy-five houses on the East side of Jubilant Falls."

"What?" I felt like I had been punched in the chest. "You can't be serious, can you?"

"I can't believe it myself. Marlov Enterprises is the parent company behind Land Management Limited, which owns Aurora Development. This is what we've been searching for, Kay! Your mother and Lovey McNair, of all people, are the biggest slumlords in Jubilant Falls."

"There is no way my mother could have known about all this!"

"She had to. Now you know why you weren't supposed to show this to me."

"Marcus wait." I flipped through the papers. "See here? It says here that Mother was signed on as a 'limited' partner. She just provided the working capital and let Lovey run it herself."

"That's fine. She is still an owner, and according to an interview Porter did with the prosecuting attorney today, anybody associated with Aurora Development is liable. Your mother is in as deep as it gets, regardless."

I couldn't believe what I was hearing from him. My mother? A slumlord? A member of my family is the reason why Ludean Tate and who knows how many other people are living in squalor?

"I don't believe you Marcus," was all I could say aloud.

"Are you going to accept the stock?"

"Are you going to keep what I told you in confidence?"

"That depends."

"On what?"

"What you decide to do. Whatever that decision is, it's still a story. It's just a matter now of who writes it. If you accept the stock, the paper has to do something. Because of our relationship, I can't write the story."

"Well, isn't that moralistic? But either way, running my mother down as the biggest slumlord in town is still a story, right?"

"It's her signature on those papers, isn't it?"

"Don't hand me any more of your sanctimonious crap, Marcus Henning. I don't need it. I showed you something in confidence, as a friend, Marcus, as a friend!"

"C'mon Kay, grow up. How would it look, if I suddenly backed off? I be committing professional suicide, and I know who the owners are now. I know where to find them—I know these documents exist. This isn't against you, Kay. If you take this stock, this makes you a party to the legal action. You will be as responsible as your mother for the conditions Ludean Tate has been living under all these years — at least in the eyes of the courts."

"Get out of here right now."

"This isn't any gift to ensure your financial security. Your mother has an ulterior motive. This is a means to make me back off the story."

"You need to leave," I repeated.

"If that's what you want."

I stomped into the kitchen to search for a wineglass. The front door closed with a soft click.

Thank God he's out of here, I thought. *Who does he think he is? This wasn't Watergate, for Christ sake. This was a little old lady trying to make a little money for her retirement, a nest egg—that's all. Right? There was no way she could have known about Lovey McNair—no way! That old battleaxe was about as evil as they come—snotty, convinced of her own superiority, and intent on making sure others knew it. She conned my mother. She had to have!*

I found a bottle of chardonnay in the fridge and poured myself a glass. I sat down at the kitchen table and took a sip.

No, Marcus was right, I admitted to myself. It was more than that. Aurora Development had enormous holdings throughout the city, and I knew full well what they had left undone in Ludean's apartment. But it was such a massive organization! There had to be people up and down the chain of command who were responsible for this kind of thing. What about that awful man who gave Marcus that awful black eye and busted lip? Mother certainly didn't know anything about that, did she? Of course not—she was too wrapped up in her bridge and her hospital charity board functions to know how some monkey in the organizational tree behaved. She couldn't have. Could she?

The thought of that brick sailing through my window so many months ago circled at the edges of my memory. Was that event and the assault on Marcus connected? It couldn't be…

I swirled the wine in my glass and looked back into the dining room.

That son of a bitch.

The folder was gone.

CHAPTER 8

Marcus

My heart was pounding in my ears, as I ran up the granite steps to the front door of the newspaper. The Land Management Limited documents were held tightly in my fist. The old yellowed walls of the *Journal-Gazette* building looked eerie at night, the naked light bulbs suspended from the hallway ceiling like corpses at a hanging.

I found myself praying for a security guard, although the only person I really had to fear was Kay. The newspaper's management liked the idea of having their editorial staff on display at street level, as if we were some discount dog-and-pony show for passing pedestrians. Jess had often requested that we either move upstairs, where classified advertising was, or get a guard, but no dice.

At the top of the stairs, I slipped my key into the front door lock and pushed it open with my shoulder, quickly snapping the lock closed behind me. Exhausted, I dropped everything onto the top of the city desk's computer terminal and flopped into Jess's chair.

My God, I thought, pulling the papers down in front of me and flipping through the pages, *I can't believe its Marian James and that pouter pigeon McNair who are behind all this. What am I going to do now? Call Jess. Jess has got to know about this.*

I picked up the receiver and punched the auto dialer for Jess's home number.

"Hoffman residence." Jess picked up after the first ring.

"It's me, Marcus. Can you come down here to the newsroom? Right away?"

"Can it wait until tomorrow? Rebecca's got another earache, and we're waiting for the pediatrician to call us back." Jess sounded peeved; I heard his little daughter crying in the background.

"How about this: I just found out who's behind Aurora Development."

Jess whistled long and low. "No shit?"

"Such command of the language. You ought to be an editor."

"And you ought to be a reporter. I'll be right down." Jess hung up sharply.

The phone rang again.

"Yeah, Jess?"

"You son of a bitch!" It was Kay. "You lying, dirty thief! If you don't bring those papers right back here, I'm coming down there and getting them myself!"

"You'll get them back, I promise."

"After you've slapped it all over the front page!"

"What do you want me to do? Apologize? This is what we've been working toward for almost a year now, Kay! This is the story that will expose all the wrongdoing for all those people living in those firetraps all over Jubilant's South Side."

"This is also my mother! *You can't do this Marcus.*"

"And you can't deny that you don't want this settled for Ludean's sake and for everybody else whose come forward on this. This is wrong, Kay, whether your mother knew it or not doesn't matter. Her name is on the papers, along with Lovey McNair's. She had the responsibility to know what was going on, to know how her tenants were living."

"I want those papers back."

"You'll get them first thing in the morning."

"*Now*, Marcus."

"Then come and get them." I slammed the phone down and ran to the Xerox machine in the morgue, a room a little larger than a closet, but smaller than the men's room down the hall, where past issues of the *Journal-Gazette*– and therefore 'dead' in journalistic terms –were stored in tall, black-bound books. There was enough time for me to copy everything, before she arrived.

The phone rang again. I set the copier on automatic feed and dashed back into the newsroom.

It was Jess.

"I'm ready to walk out the door. Give me ten minutes. But tell me who it is."

"Kay's mother. Marian James."

Jess was silent for a moment. "Okay. Be right there." The phone clicked again in my ear. Kay would be here any minute. I ran back into the morgue.

Damn it! Who set the copier on letter size and not legal size paper? Every page was too short, cutting off Marian's and McNair's signatures. I pushed another button and began feeding the documents through again. *Come on, come on, COME ON! Why can't this thing work any faster?*

I heard footsteps on the stairs, and the doorknob to the newspaper rattled.

"Marcus Henning, you dirty bastard! You let me in!" Kay's voice, ragged and hoarse, echoed through Jubilant's empty streets.

The last copy slid out into the receiving tray, and quickly I shoved the originals back into their file folder.

"Let me in, damn it!" Kay had moved to the sidewalk and was pounding on the frosted glass. "Open this damn door!"

I turned the deadbolt and, as she burst through the door, grabbed her by the arm with one hand.

"Kay, stop it. You're turning you back on every one of those poor slobs who walk through your literacy center door every day. You can't protect your mother from what she's done. She and Lovey McNair are responsible for this, and they need to be called into account."

"Let go of me! I can't believe you would say that to me!" Kay snatched the folder from my hand and flipped through the file. "These aren't in the same order-you've made copies. Copies that you'll use to slander her all over the front page!"

"Articles of incorporation are hardly slander, Kay."

"Why, Marcus, why?" Tears began to roll down her cheeks. "I don't know what you have planned, but you can't involve my mother!" With a jerk, she twisted herself free and ran toward the copy machine.

"Kay, NO!" She grabbed the pile of papers atop the copier and tore them in two, then in two again, and again. I watched helplessly, as she took each ragged piece and wrathfully covered the floor with confetti.

"There. You're not getting any further with this story. It's over, do you understand me?" She glared at me in triumphant rage.

"You're selling out a lot of people, if you do this, Kay. Of all the things you've done in your life, I never, ever thought you sell out to anything."

"I won't sell out my family. I'm learning how valuable family can be now, Marcus, despite all their faults and all their wrongs."

"Letting little kids eat paint chips filled with lead off the walls is valuable? Letting families live with the stench of shit because they can't get their landlord to fix the john is just a fault? Kay, you're not the woman I knew."

"Maybe I'm not. Maybe I've never been, but you're not going to drag my mother through the mud with this story!"

"I can always have the legal department subpoena them from you or your mother, now that I know where they're at. The people have a right to know."

"Don't you spout free press platitudes to me! I want my house key back. You go through with this story, and we're through."

Sadly, I pulled my key ring from my pocket and slid her key off. Eight years I had waited for her—just like I had waited for a story like this to put my career back on track. Did I have to lose one to gain the other?

"Don't do this Kay. I love you."

"That's *your* problem. If you have anything left at the house, it will be on the porch tomorrow morning. I've got to get back to my kids."

Sobbing now, Kay turned and ran, pushing past Jess as he came through the newsroom door.

" What's she doing here? What's all this?" he asked, surveying the paper-strewn floor.

"Our hard evidence." I sank against the wall in despair. "Deeds to all the houses Aurora owns through Land Management Limited, letters about how they handle tenant disputes, articles of incorporation signed by James and McNair, everything. Kay just ripped it all up."

"What's this?" Jess walked back to the morgue and pulled another stack of papers from the rack beneath the copier. "Isn't that what this is?"

"My God, she got the wrong copies! The fist time I ran the originals through, they were on the wrong size paper! She destroyed the wrong copies!"

"Talk about luck!" Jess crowed, as he flipped quickly through the documents. "We're on our way, old man. We've finally got this thing licked. Those two old biddies will be in jail, before they know what hit them!"

"And all it cost me was Kay." I flopped into my chair and turned on the computer screen in front of me.

"This is the news business, Mark. I've told you that before."

"But would you do a story on your mother-in-law, if you knew she was involved in illegal activity?"

"No, I have to have another reporter do the story, because I be too close to it. But I wouldn't kill the story."

"Then maybe you ought to write this one, Jess. Suddenly this victory seems awfully hollow."

"What are you talking about, Marcus?"

"Conflict of interest. You said so yourself. Marian James is Kay's mother."

"And from what I saw here just now, the apple doesn't fall very far from the tree, does it?"

I grabbed him by the collar. Eye to bloodshot eye, I could smell the tobacco on his breath. "Listen Jess, I know you never liked her, but that's none of your business."

"It is when I see one of my best writers dragging his butt around here like a whipped dog because some broad has him over a barrel!" Jess shoved me away and straightened his collar. "This is the biggest story this paper has had since I've been editor, and you want me to kill it over for a woman? Need I remind you that I bailed your ass out once before? And here I was, ready to talk you up to Watt, let him make you our investigative projects editor. But then some broad whines a little, cries a little, and you want to call it all off? You're not dropping this story, because I won't let you. Besides, it sounds as if you and Kay are through."

I sank back into my chair. "Maybe so."

"Forget about her, Marcus. You deserve better. We've been friends forever, and I've hated to see her yank you around the way she has." He reached over and patted me on the shoulder.

"It's not that easy."

"Don't hand me that." The hard-edged editor took over again. "I'm going to call legal first thing tomorrow morning and tell them what we've got. I want you to get a quote out of Ludean, and I want you there when these two bitches are arrested. Now go home and get some sleep."

"Jess, I can't do this story."

"Then you better learn how, because you don't have any choice. Get out of here."

Leaving Kay's confetti on the morgue floor, I returned home to a night of fitful sleep. Jess was wrong. There was no way I could remain on this story. My involvement with Kay, even if it was now over, was too powerful a conflict of interest. But to lose her again was gut wrenching.

What would I have done in her shoes? How easy would it be to turn in my parents? Could I? The most illegal thing my father ever did was to buy a little corn liquor every now and again from the bootleggers in those southern Ohio hills. If I wanted to turn him in to the feds, I have also had to turn in every one of the people on our grubby little street.

But this was different. This was massive wrongdoing…massive: a systematic endeavor to deprive human beings of decent housing simply because they were who they were.

But what about Kay? How could she suddenly want to protect this woman? I couldn't understand that. Was it the major's death? Was it her cockamamie idea to bring that Korean kid over here? Maybe it was simply that, as her nuclear family was imploding, she was just trying to shore up everything that was left. But did the cost have to be so high? Or was it only my expectations? Either way, I knew when this story ran in tomorrow's afternoon edition – and it will – Kay will be lost to me forever.

* * *

As the sun crept over the horizon, I left the twisted bed sheets behind and drove through Jubilant Falls' empty streets to Kay's to retrieve my stuff. My belongings, mostly a few pieces of clothing, disposable razors, and an extra toothbrush, weren't sitting on the porch. Maybe she had been bluffing. Lights were on in the kitchen. I took my chances and rang the bell.

She looked like death. Her eyes were swollen, and she was wearing the same jeans and white Oxford blouse she had worn last night. Her hair hung in her eyes, and a faint odor of wine hung on her breath.

I stepped inside and took her in my arms, brushing the copper strands from her face.

"I tr-tr-tried to call her last night and have her explain it all t-t-to me," Kay wept into my shirt. Her heaving sobs made it hard for her to talk. "She went into hys-hys-hysterics, screaming that I broken my promise, that I wasn't worth trusting, that the deal was off. "

"How much have you had to drink?"

"I don't know. What does it matter?" Dry, racking sobs convulsed her slim frame, and she held me close. "I can't lose you again, Marcus. I don't have anyone else."

"What did your mother say?"

"Oh it was awful…I was a cheap slut, a whore, I killed Paul just the same as if I shot him."

"Ssshhh. She's a sick woman, Kay, and she needs help." I wrapped my arms around her. "I thought I lost you forever."

"About last night," Kay whispered hesitantly. "I looked over the deeds for the property that Land Management Limited owns. Ludean's house was one of them."

"From what I saw, they own every house within a three-block radius of the literacy center," I said. "Except for this one and a few others, they're all dumps."

"Mother can't know what Lovey dragged her into."

"For her sake, I hope not." I thought of Ludean's apartment; she was raising two children in three rooms that would fit easily into Kay's dining room. Marian had to know. How could she be that ignorant? And how could Kay be so bent on suddenly putting her mother in a good light? I seen enough of Marian James' insensitivity and wanton cruelty to know she had no good side."

"You're going to go after Mother, aren't you?"

"It's going to get ugly, Kay. I can't tell you much else."

"Why not?"

"Some things require a leap of faith."

Kay pulled away from my embrace and sat down on the stairs, resting her elbows on her knees and letting her hands hang limply between her legs. She leaned her wet cheek against the wallpaper. "Marcus, why has everything between us gotten so difficult lately?"

"What do you mean?"

"It's not the same anymore. There's a wall between us now, and I can't break it down." Kay shrugged in confusion. "And it all started with PJ."

"No it didn't, Kay." I couldn't tell her that it started a long time before the major's bastard son ever came into the picture.

It started that night on her porch, the night the major died. I couldn't tell her that I was terrified to be a stepfather to two kids, let alone three. That I realized how little I really knew about her life, and that I was terrified I might not ever fit into it.

"You're tired," I said. "We've both had a hard night. Why don't you get some sleep, and I'll come by tonight. We'll take the kids and go out to dinner, or something."

"Then it does have something to do with PJ!"

"That's not so, Kay."

"Then tell me why everything has gotten so tough lately? Are we going to survive all this pressure?"

I sat down beside her on the stairs and hung my head in my hands.

"Sometimes I wonder," I sighed. "The truth is, it's not really PJ. It's the major. He's everywhere I look, when I'm with you. He's in the shadows of the bedroom, the faces of your kids, in every word you speak and every day you were away from me. The truth is, right now I'm scared of looking at Andrew and Lil and having them call me Dad. My father is a mechanic, for Christ's sake. He's got grease under his fingernails that never comes out, even on Sundays when they go to church, and a son who's never lived up to what he thinks he oughta be. And on Saturday night, my dad likes a little bit of clear liquid happiness out of a Mason jar that he buys from some hillbilly in the sticks. He made my life a living hell. Andy and Lillian's Daddy is a hero in the eyes of everybody on the entire planet. He saves the world twice a day before breakfast, and there's no goddamn way I can live up to that. Then to have one more miniature Major Dad looking at me day in and day out—it's more than I can take, Kay."

"Give it time—give us time. I know it will work out."

"And what if it doesn't?"

"It will, Marcus. We've been through too much to give up on everything now. Going to get PJ in Korea is something I have to do, to make peace with Paul's memory. We had a bad marriage, and we treated each other just as badly."

"I say he had more points on his side of life's great piss-off scoreboard than you do."

Kay smiled briefly. "But letting this little boy's life go down the toilet because of who did what to whom is wrong. And I know that you and I can work through this. We just have to give it time."

For a moment, I almost believed her.

"What about your mother and Aurora Development?"

"My mother couldn't have known about that."

"But don't you see? She *should* have made it her business to know! You're denying everything that Aurora Development had ever been or done! That company's sole purpose was to wring every penny they could out of the poor in this town. And after all your well-meaning speeches about wanting to bring prenatal classes and midnight basketball leagues into the area, I can't believe what I'm hearing!"

"I just can't believe that she would let this happen!"

"And I can't believe you want to bring some little bastard who caused you so much anguish into your home!"

There. I said it.

"But you don't know how it is for those Amer-Asian kids, Marcus. When Paul and I were in Korea, I learned those kids don't have anything. They don't have a future and they don't have a past."

"So send twenty bucks a month to Save The Children! I can't believe that you're worrying about a kid you've never seen that's half a world away, when you're the cure for so many kids right here in your own home town!"

"Marcus, please *listen* to me!"

"No, Kay, you listen to me. Have you ever had a rat crawl between the sheets with you at night? Has Andrew? Has Lillian?"

She winced and turned away.

"Have you ever had to live without adequate plumbing? Can you imagine living with the smell of shit, day in and day out? You've always had everything handed to you. How does it feel knowing that what you had came at the expense of Ludean Tate and her kids? That fancy car your mother drives, her fancy house and even Novella's salary are paid for by the tenants of Aurora Development. This is not any of your half-cocked idealism. It's not watching the major trailing glory in a fighter jet. It's not deciding to patch up a dead man's memory or doing good deeds to bolster your own ego, Kay. This is real life."

"Marcus, look at us!" Kay reached for me, tears running down her face, pleading for something I couldn't give any more. "What's happening to us?"

I leaned back on my elbows on the step behind me, suddenly tired of the fight. "I don't know."

"Why does it have to always be so complicated?" She was begging now, but we both knew we had stepped beyond the point of no return. Like the flame blown out on a match, there was nothing left but the embers. I couldn't fight with her anymore. I couldn't let Ludean and her children and every other tenant that paid their rent to that Neanderthal goon in the empty office continue to live like animals. I had to do what was right.

There was no way anything could ever work between us.

"Kay, even when we first met, it's never been easy. I fastened my heart on something I couldn't have and hung with it like a pit bull, but even a pit bull gets tired. I have loved you for over eight years, and each time I have you in my life, it never seems to work. Why is that Kay? Why?"

Kay laid her face against the garish entryway wallpaper and sobbed. "I don't know. I don't know. I don't know."

"Jess and his wife never seem to go through these twisted machinations. Why do we?" I stood and brushed off my pants. "I can't live like this anymore, Kay. I'm letting go."

* * *

"Is this going to take very long?"

An hour later, I met Ludean at her home. She was sitting on the front porch with Aaron and Priscilla, waiting for me and the photographer, Pat Robinette. My ears still could not get used to her clear speech, accustomed as I was to translating any semblance of recognizable sound during our previous conversations.

I shook my head. "We've found out who is behind Aurora Development. We need to take a few shots of your apartment, Ludean. Then we'll sit down and talk, and I'll ask you a few questions. I need to ask you again what's been repaired and what hasn't since the housing commission ordered repairs, that kind of thing."

The children were clean and scrubbed. I recognized Priscilla's little dress as one of the hand-me-downs from Lillian. Ludean's cheap, black blouse hung on her bony shoulders like a shroud, and her denim skirt had a three-corner tear near the hem that had been repaired with an ironed-on patch. As we entered the building, she leaned forward to help Priscilla up the stairs, and the ribs in her back looked like rungs on a ladder.

Wordlessly, Robinette stepped through the apartment, snapping pictures of peeling paint, the rotten boards beneath the peeling kitchen linoleum, and all the other horrors that lived with Ludean and her family. He paused in front of the one window that had been repaired after my nasty confrontation with that Neanderthal down at the office. The aluminum frame still shone, and brand-name stickers were still on the glass.

"It took me thirty days and a busted lip to get that window in here," I said. "There used to be jagged glass and cardboard there. That's the only repair they ever made on the place."

Pat whipped a telephoto lens from his camera bag and focused on an unlikely prism, created by the double-paned glass that danced across the worn linoleum.

Jess was right— I couldn't get off this story. I couldn't let this woman down. Ludean was struggling too hard to make a better life and I owed her my loyalty. If Kay chose to dump her commitment to making things right in Jubilant Falls to protect the women who created this cesspool, then Kay wasn't the woman I thought she was.

Maybe if I said it long enough, I'll believe it.

"Got it," the photographer said.

"Good. Ludean, I want you to start at the beginning. Tell me the whole story again."

* * *

That afternoon, the story ran with my byline alone. Banner headline. Above the fold.

"You're back on track, old man," Jess slapped me on my shoulders and handed me one of his rancid cigars. "Legal is backing us up, too. They're meeting with the prosecutor this afternoon. I want you there, Marcus, when they bring those women in on contempt of court charges—at least that's what legal is assuming they'll be charged with. This is primo stuff, guy. Primo!"

"Thanks." I let Jess bask in the glory of the upcoming *Ohio v. Aurora Development*. Why wasn't the woman who brought me this story, the woman who believed only I could make it right, standing by my side? And why wasn't I celebrating the fact that this story had rescued me from a life of covering poetry readings and social calendar events? No surprise, that I really wanted no part of it. What I thought would be a triumphant ride through Persepolis was tearing my guts up, costing me the woman that I loved. Christ, why did it have to be so difficult? I didn't have the guts that Jess had, or the slimy willingness to make deals of Martin Rathke. All I wanted was justice. Not power. Not glory. Justice.

How naive can you get?

I tossed the cold dregs of my morning coffee from a Styrofoam cup into the trash. "I gotta get out of here."

"And where shall I tell your clamoring public they can find you?" Jess poured himself a cup of coffee from a metal Thermos bottle.

"In hell."

"Hey, buddy, what's wrong? You did a great job here! You should celebrate!"

"You know goddamn good and well what's wrong. It's not worth it to me, Jess. It's just not worth it. This is the last story I write for the *Journal-Gazette*."

Jess jumped up and stopped me in the doorway. "Not so fast, Bright Eyes. You've got one more story to cover for me! You owe—"

Behind him, I saw the door open and a Louisville Slugger poised, seemingly, to send one deep into left field.

"Jess! Look out!"

The bat seemed to swing in slow motion, making contact with Jess's left cheekbone and jaw, a sickening crunch of wood against bone, as a dark ski-masked hulk filled the newsroom doorway. There were screams; Jess's body, jerky and loose, swung like a marionette on a stick, his left arm in front of his gory skull for protection. The bat came down again on his outstretched arm, sending Jess's body against me. Blood, teeth, and tissue left their mark on my shirt, as he slid to the floor, his eyes fixed and glassy.

The hulk turned his attention to me, roaring like an animal as he raised his bat again to strike. I leaped over the city desk, as the Slugger came down on a computer, and taking Jess's Thermos by the handle tossed the hot coffee in the attacker's face.

He screamed in pain, reeling backward across the newsroom floor in an attempt to escape. I had one chance to catch him; both hands on the Thermos handle now, I was running on pure adrenalin. I followed him in his backward stagger and swung as hard as I could.

There was thud, as the metal bottom struck his temple, and he fell to the ground, unconscious. Quickly, I stripped off the wet ski mask.

It was the goon from Aurora Development.

* * *

You gotta pull through this, Jess. Don't die on me buddy. Don't die.

I stood helplessly at the door of the emergency room as the paramedics ran past with Jess on a gurney.

Thick layers of bloodstained gauze covered the left side of his face. His left arm was splinted, and his breathing came in wet, gurgling gasps. Drops of blood hung on the inside of the transparent oxygen mask over his mouth and nose.

"He's going to make it, right?" I grabbed a paramedic by the shirt.

"You need to sign him in. That's the best thing you can do right now." He yanked my hand from his sleeve and disappeared behind the swinging doors at the end of the hall.

"Where the hell do I do that?" I yelled.

"Sir, there is no need for that." I turned to see a tall, raw-boned nurse standing behind a white counter. "We have other patients here."

The electronic doors parted, and Jess's wife, Carol, along with a burly police detective, ran through the door.

"Marcus!" She hugged me briefly. "How is he?"

Before I could answer, the detective extended his hand.

"Marcus Henning? I'm Detective Mike Berrocco of the Jubilant Falls Police Department. While Mrs. Hoffman fills out the paperwork, I need to speak to you for a moment. Julie..." The nurse behind the counter looked up and smiled familiarly at the cop. "Toss me the keys to the conference room over here, will ya?"

"Sure, Mike."

Berrocco deftly caught the keys and ushered me down the hall to an adjacent room; a single table and five chairs were the only furnishings. Berrocco swept a ragged array of dog-eared and coverless magazines to a corner of the table and slapped a notebook down in front of him.

"You got some pretty big brass ones, Mr. Henning," he smiled, trying to put me at ease. He slipped out of his jacket and rolled up his sleeves. "Our suspect is probably going to need five or six stitches himself."

"How's everyone else down at the paper?"

"A little shaken up, but that's understandable. I've got a couple patrolmen taking statements down there." Berrocco pulled a pipe from his jacket, tamping down the tobacco inside with his thumb.

"Is that why you called me in here?"

"No, Mr. Henning," Berrocco casually lit his pipe, sucking loudly on the stem until the embers glowed. "No. Does the name Grant Matthews mean anything to you?"

"Oh my God, yes! His ex-wife and I, we're—we used to—" My heart constricted, within my chest.

"I get the idea. Was it a nasty divorce? Big custody battle, or property settlement?"

"No, nothing like that."

"You weren't named in the divorce? No adultery, no hanky-panky while she was married?"

Not this marriage, I wanted to say. "They were only married a couple years, but he was charged with domestic violence at least once. She and I didn't get together until after everything was final. Why?"

"He's the man who assaulted Mr. Hoffman."

Suddenly, three images came together in my head: the goon who slammed me up against the elevator doors at Aurora Development, the unconscious face of Jess's assailant, and – a lifetime ago – at a country club dance, the image of a man glaring at a beautiful redhead who held silver shoes in one hand and a glass of champagne in another.

"That doesn't make any sense! Why would he be after Jess?"

"Hey, the newspaper sometimes writes stories people don't like." Berrocco shrugged. "Down at the cop shop, we understand that. Tell me what happened."

"I was ready to walk off my job. Jess was trying to stop me. This guy came up behind Jess and just swung."

"Anything else?"

I was silent for a moment. "Yes. I had one other run-in with the man you say is Grant Matthews. About six months ago, on a story." Briefly, I told him Ludean's story and my encounter with Matthews at the Aurora Development office, how he was the head goon in charge of collecting rents for Marian James and Lovey McNair. Finally, I told him about Marian's relationship to Kay, her offer of stock in Aurora Development following the major's death, and how the *Journal-Gazette* got hold of the documents for today's story.

"What was the nature of your relationship with Marian James?"

"She hated me. She couldn't stand it that I was seeing her daughter."

"This may seem a little bit far-fetched, but is it possible that Grant Matthews' attack on Hoffman was a hit meant for you?"

Oh, God. I thought of the brick through Kay's living room window, and the room began to swim. No wonder she didn't want to tell the police! I lay my head down on the table, wanting to vomit.

"Mr. Henning, if Mr. Hoffman dies, Matthews could be looking at murder charges. These two old ladies you're telling me about could be charged with conspiracy to commit murder. Will you come down to the station and ID this guy? It sounds like we've got enough to keep the prosecuting attorney busy on this one for quite a while."

Why was this happening? Why did Matthews even have a job with Aurora Development, considering that he beat the hell out of the owner's daughter? Why would she reward him? Why didn't it make any sense?

At the station, Berrocco showed me into a small room with a one-way mirror, where we could observe Matthews being interrogated by two plain clothes detectives. Still handcuffed and with a white bandage covering the side of his head where doctors had sewn up his head wound, Matthews was trying to sign a piece of paper in front of him. Once he had, the two detectives stepped out of the room. Looking around his surroundings like a caged baboon, he raised his handcuffed wrists to scratch his face. The black hair on the back of his knuckles triggered memories of meeting elevator doors up close and personal.

"That's our suspect, Mr. Henning. Can you identify him?"

Before I could answer, one of the plainclothes cops stuck his head in the door. "Hey, Mike, this guy has just confessed to everything, and it's one hell of a story. 'Course, his lawyer is on the phone screaming duress, but you know how that goes," the cop shrugged.

"Oh, yeah?"

"Yeah. He says it was a hit, meant for another guy. Claims two little old ladies wanted it done."

"Who?" I whirled around.

"Who's this?" The cop jabbed his thumb in my direction.

"I'm the other guy."

Berrocco nodded.

"The suspect claims it was two women named Marian James and Lovey McNair, who ordered the hit because of a story you were doing. They both wanted you off, but one of them wanted to also make you stop seeing her daughter, this guy's ex-wife."

* * *

This time, the big-city television stations wanted a piece of my story. Remote trucks from all three networks were right behind the two squad cars, as they pulled into the jail with Marian and Lovey. By that time, Martin Rathke was waiting to meet them there, along with some lacquer-haired TV news babe.

Marian was horrified, twisting her wrists against the handcuffs and cowering against the side of the escorting policewoman as photographers and cameramen closed in.

"Cower, you bitch," I hissed under my breath. "Cower and hope that I don't get hold of you before anyone else does."

Only McNair held her head high, whispering to Rathke as he fell in step beside her.

"Mrs. James, are you responsible for the condition of the apartments on East Grand?" The TV reporter stuck the microphone in Marian's face.

Rathke jumped in front of his client and shoved the microphone away. "Mrs. James and Mrs. McNair have no comment, at this time."

"Are you aware—" the reporter shoved her microphone at Marian again.

"I said no *comment!*" Rathke shoved her, knocking her against her cameraman and onto the hard cement. Rathke grabbed Marian by one arm, McNair by the other, and swept into the jail.

The reporter got up, dusted off her very attractive behind, and looked straight into the camera. "Did you get that Gordon? Are we rolling? Okay," she launched into her script. "There you have it ladies and gentlemen. Two of Jubilant Falls' best-known philanthropists, charged with contempt of court for allegedly ignoring a court order and who police are now saying are responsible..."

I turned away in disgust. Jess was right. I didn't have guts for this business.

CHAPTER 9

Marian

Ellen Nussey was at the house when I was arrested.

I was standing before the mirror in the foyer, adjusting my scarf when the bell rang, ready to drive to one of the Cincinnati malls for a day of shopping, a little reward for myself. Despite that terrible scene with Kay over our investment property, I knew she would see the stock gift for what it was: security for her and her children. I felt calmed and self-possessed all day, thinking how wonderful my plan had been working. I was protecting everyone's interests and providing for my daughter's financial stability. No doubt about it.

Kay said that awful Marcus Henning was threatening to do a story exposing everything, but I didn't see anything. Come to think of it, I didn't see the newspaper yesterday afternoon at all.

"Novella, did we get a newspaper yesterday?"

The door chimes sounded before she could answer, their sonorous tones echoing around me.

"Novella, the door, please." I searched through the bottom of my handbag for a lipstick.

Novella appeared from the dining room, her feather duster tucked under her arm. She glared at me, as she opened the wide, front door.

"Mrs. James, Mrs. Nussey is here to see you."

I turned around again.

"Marian, I do hope you don't mind this intrusion." Ellen blew gracefully through my door, her gauzy skirt flowing behind her and her thoroughbred smile pasted perfectly in place. A heavy turquoise necklace lay on her artificially browned neck. "I was just in the neighborhood, and I simply couldn't pass by your house without telling you that I don't think I can make it to card club next Tuesday." Ellen fingered the turquoise stones, as if to call my attention to them. Ellen's ludicrous presumption of some kind of California casual lifestyle here in Ohio turned my stomach.

"It's not anything serious, is it?" I feigned concern. Most likely it was Ellen's youngest brat, Jameson. Nearly as old as Kay, he was still living at home, at least when he was sober. Jamie, as Ellen cloyingly referred to him, was always doing some sort of damage, to himself or his parents' property, or other peoples' property. He had been in and out of rehab all his life. I was convinced it was Ellen's inability to control her son; she claimed he had a *chemical imbalance.*

"No, heaven's no. Jamie—" Ellen smiled insipidly. "—is bringing his children home for a short visit. Since he's been sober, the courts are allowing supervised visitation again. We just got word today."

Wonderful. The drug-abusing hoodlum bringing home his little bastards from the last slut he lived with outside of marriage, I thought. *Let's have a celebration. Seems to be all the rage these days.*

"Have you found someone to replace you?" I snapped the clasp on my purse. I didn't need to hear anymore about this illustrious brat. "We can't play without a fourth."

"Well, I was wondering if you knew anyone? Maybe Kay?"

"Kay doesn't play bridge."

Ellen's gaze wandered to the living room window. "Why, there's a police car pulling up your drive!"

"What? I wonder what's going on!" Two policemen stepped from the squad car and headed up the walk. "What could they want?"

"You know, it's funny how things run through your head at times like this, isn't it?" Ellen began to babble in fear, fingering the turquoise necklace nervously. "I was just thinking, *What could that boy have done now?* But, of course, no one knows where I am. So the police couldn't know to come looking for me here, unless they were looking for my car and—"

The doorbell rang again, cutting her short.

"Novella!"

"No, no, I'm closer." Ellen jumped for the door knob. "It probably really is about Jamie, anyway. Oh, I had such hopes of seeing my grandchildren today. Yes?"

Two policemen, one tall and lanky, the other squat and muscular, stood side by side on the stoop. "Mrs. Marian James?" The tall policeman asked, his Adam's apple bobbing.

Ellen sighed, visibly relieved. "Oh my, no, I'm not Mrs. James. Please come in. I do hope it's nothing serious. Marian?"

My stomach sank to my feet, and my hands went numb. *They've found you. After all these years, you've been hunted down like the demon you are, and they've found you.* I straightened my shoulders and held my head high. "Yes, officers? What can I help you with?"

"Are you Marian James?"

"Yes, I am."

"Ma'am, we have a warrant for your arrest."

"What?"

"Yes ma'am. You've been charged with conspiracy in the attempted murder of Jesse Foster Hoffman."

Jesse Hoffman? The editor of the newspaper? My mind reeled with the impossibility of it. The voices always said they would find me. I have done terrible things, awful frightful things that would ruin everything I have ever worked so hard for. I deserved to be sent away forever for that.

But *Jess Hoffman*?

"You must be joking." Ellen's nervous laugh echoed through the entryway. "Mrs. James isn't a murderer, much less a conspirator. This must be some sick joke."

"No mistake, ma'am."

"I didn't—couldn't kill Jess Hoffman!" I stammered. I started to say, "I killed…." then stopped.

It struck me: the confrontation with Lovey before Christmas. Lovey's plan to get Marcus Henning had not been called off. I needed to see Martin Rathke. Martin could get this fixed. Martin had gotten me out of scrapes before, quietly, and usually with a minimum of cash. This would certainly take more, but I had to protect my secret. If only Montgomery was still alive, none of this would ever have happened.

"Ma'am, if you'll cooperate with us, we'll let you walk to the squad car without cuffs."

"I certainly will *not!*" I stood straighter and looked the flatfoot right in the eye. "I don't know you, young man, but I know your boss, and he certainly would not allow this gross miscarriage of justice to be perpetrated on someone of my standing in the community."

"Have it your way, ma'am."

The short, squat officer grabbed my wrist and spun me around sharply, slapping handcuffs on me. He pulled a laminated card from his shirt pocket and began to read. "You have the right to remain silent. Anything you say can, and will, be used against you in a court of law. You have the right to an attorney. If you cannot afford an attorney, one will be appointed for you."

I managed to gather myself together to present an imperious front, although I was shaking inside. "I demand that you remove these handcuffs! This is some sort of sick joke, some kind of perverse crank, and I demand that you release me this instant!"

"C'mon grandma, cut the act. We're going downtown." The muscular cop grabbed my arm and pulled me out the door.

"Ellen! Have Novella call Kay and Martin Rathke! Immediately!" I called out, as the policeman laid his heavy hand on my head and pushed me down into the cruiser's back seat. The car door slammed shut as Novella and Ellen stood slack-jawed at my front door. The car backed down the drive and into the street. I fell against the seat cushions in despair. What was going on? Why hadn't Lovey listened to me?

My God, all of this in front of Ellen Nussey; she is to the Jubilant Falls Country Club what CNN is to the nation. I'll never be able to show my face again. I'm ruined! Martin, yes, Martin will fix this! He's got to! This has all got to be one big mistake. I never knew any specific details, so they can't make anything stick. I got a thinly veiled threat over the phone, and I went right to Lovey with it. Yes. That's it. I had nothing to do with this. Nothing at all. Grant Matthews was responsible for all of this. Grant Matthews and Lovey McNair; it was all their doing, not mine. How could I ever get myself out of this mess? This is all one big mistake. One horrible mistake. Martin will see to it that everything gets ironed out.

The cruiser slowed down. Oh God, don't let me be seen by anyone I know. I lowered my head in mortification.

"Looks like they've got the other one," the shorter cop said, pointing.

I looked up to see the McNair's Tudor monstrosity to my left.

There, in front of the house, was another black-and-white police cruiser. I snapped to attention as the front door opened and two officers escorted an undaunted and imperious Lovey McNair to the squad car.

Editor Jess Hoffman. Had that vile reporter Marcus Henning been the target? Had he been injured? If he had, could it be tied to me?

Why hadn't I said anything to Kay? The more you know, the more it can be tied to you, Lovey had said. I really had known everything and done nothing about it. A silly letter, that theatrical conversation in Lovey's bedroom. If only Montgomery was still alive! Yes, Monty could have fixed it. He would have made sure all the charges were dropped, made sure everything was smoothed over with a minimum of fuss. But he wasn't; he was dead. Paul Armstrong was dead, too. Had my scheme to reconcile Kay and Paul succeeded, this would never have happened. And my parents, my parents. I loved my mother so much. I had to do it, though. I had to do it.

Why did everyone I love have to die?

Ma, no! It's not your fault...it's all mine! He told me it was! Said I made him...no Ma, put the gun....

The police car slowed almost to a stop, long enough for me to watch Lovey regally survey her realm as she stepped into the police car. Her gaze extended to the street, blinking in sudden confusion as she recognized me. Suddenly, she lost her footing on her slate steps and stumbled. The two police officers on either side of her caught her before she fell and slid her bulky frame into the back seat. I turned my head away in shame.

My cruiser accelerated gently, moving the car back into the line of traffic as the tall, thin driver picked up the radio microphone. "Dispatch, eleven-oh-one."

"Eleven-oh-one, ten-two." The dispatcher's voice crackled, in response.

"We're ten-nineteen, ETA ten minutes, with a ten-fifteen, one Marian James. "

"Eleven-oh-one at oh-nine-forty-five hours."

Montgomery would have never allowed this to happen.

Arriving downtown at the police station, I was photographed, fingerprinted and searched by a big lesbian-looking deputy, who patted me down in an all-too-familiar way. Afterwards, she led me down the hall to a plain, gray, cinder-block room. It was empty, except for a small, medical examining table.

"All females charged with felonies have to submit to a body cavity search, before being placed in a cell," she said flatly.

"What? You must be joking!"

"You heard me." The deputy folded her arms and stood beside the door. "The doc will be in here in a minute. Take off everything from the waste down, and get up on the table."

"Can't I have some privacy?" I pleaded.

"No, ma'am."

I cringed and turned my back, old familiar feelings of being hunted and trapped rising from deep inside me. Behind me, the door opened and closed. I heard the snap of a rubber glove. "What are you doing?" I asked.

"Relax, honey. This won't take long." A man's gruff voice, raspy from too many cigarettes, filled the room.

Someone nearby started screaming. I felt myself drift to the ceiling, free and child-like. *Who was that lady on the floor? Ma, can you tell me? Why was she making all that noise? Why was she all curled up in the corner like that? Ma? Ma?*

* * *

Everybody turned out for the funeral in that scrappy little West Virginia coal town where even Mr. Roosevelt's New Deal couldn't reach. One by one, the mourners filed past my brothers and me at the churchyard gate, shaking our hands in turn, congratulating us on what a wonderful service it had been. How wonderful and how sad. Such a nice woman, your mother, they all told my brothers. No one spoke to me, though, sixteen years old and painfully self-conscious in my borrowed, ill-fitting, black dress and the pair of heavy brogans that had belonged to my brothers. Each person who passed looked at me as if I were some animal at the zoo, awkwardly taking my hand as if I would give him or her a disease, or something. Numb and alone, I heard my brothers respond with nods and thank yous. Only the pastor looked me in the eye.

"Time will heal your wounds, Marian. Pray to God, and he will heal your heart."

I hung my head in shame. Only he knew the truth, that Ma had shot herself with Pa's big pistol when I told her what he been doin' to me while she worked third shift at the cannery down the road.

"Thank you, Rev'rund. I'm sure she'll be just fine in a few days." My oldest brother Conrad, tall and lanky like Ma had been, looked so funny in Pa's best suit, his muscles bulging through the shoulders of the jacket, his sleeves rolled up to cover the shortness of the sleeves. Pa would have worn it, if he'd be sober enough to come. Since he hadn't, it was up to Conrad to stand up for him, and he done it real good.

The pastor laid his hand briefly on Conrad's shoulder and walked back into the white, frame church.

My other brothers, Jarred and Otis, older than me by two and three years, stood sulkily beside Conrad in the dirt road flecked with coal dust as the last of the mourners filed out. Jarred pointed down the road at a clump of women, gray as the coal town that surrounded them, standing together and whispering.

"Ole bitches. Ole two-faced bitches." He picked up a rock, ready to heave it at the group.

"Stop it, damn it," Conrad yanked the rock away from Jarred. "Just ignore 'em."

"Why you hafta tell?" Jarred turned on me. "If you o' just kept your mouth shut, we still have her. She still be alive, if it wasn't for you!"

"Shut up, Jar...you doesn't know what you're talkin' 'bout!" Otis grabbed his shirtsleeves, swinging my brother around to face him. "You ain't laid there, night after night, hearin' what I heard!"

"We all heard it, Otis. We all heard it." Conrad, always the peacemaker, yanked my brothers apart with his strong hands. "I don't recollect either of you-uns ever doin' anything 'bout it either, so just shut up."

"He coulda killed all of us, Con, and you know it!" Jarred turned his anger on our brother. "We all know where he is now, too. He's down at Flagler's, drunker'n a skunk, if ole man Flagler hasn't already thrown him out."

"I know it, Jar."

"The whole town's talkin' 'bout her...everybody knows the truth now." Jarred pointed his bony finger at me. I hung my head again, too guilty to speak. "They're sayin' we all took turns with her, that she let us, that she wanted it."

"Shut up! Shut up, both of you!" Otis screamed, knocking Jarred to the ground. He pinned Jarred's arms down with his legs and sat on his chest, beating his face bloody with his fists. "You dirty bastard! Don't you talk 'bout my sister like that! Don't you ever say it!"

Jarred pushed Otis from atop him. They fell together, like twin timbers, rolling together across the fresh dirt of Ma's grave, mixing blood and earth as they traded blows.

"She killed her, just as if she pulled the trigger herself!" Will cried out. "If she kept her mouth shut, Ma would still be alive!"

"Stop it! Stop it! Stop it!" I screamed in anguish. "I can't stand this any more! I can't stand it!" Pushing past Conrad into the street, I ran through the horrified knot of women, knowing that this time I was running to save my own life.

* * *

"The sedative I gave her should put her to sleep for at least four hours." Somewhere on the fuzzy edge of reality, I heard Ed Nussey speak. I was back in my own bed, in my own nightgown. Someone pulled the eyelet comforter up to my chin.

"There now," a warm voice said. "You just close your eyes. You're back home."

"What do you know about her past?" Ed asked. "From what the deputies at the jail told me, I would suspect that there has been some serious sexual abuse or trauma in her past. Were you aware of anything like that?"

The warm voice slurred unintelligibly, through my drugged mind.

I felt darkness, warmth, and comfort begin to envelope me. I was safe now. I was home. In Jubilant Falls. No one would ever find me here.

* * *

My heart was pounding in my ears, as I threw open the door to the tarpaper shack my brothers and me called home. My folks' bedroom, the only bedroom, was empty. In the big room, nobody sat in the ugly, beat-up couch, or the ragged overstuffed chair with three legs, or at the table where Ma had took her life. Someone had left behind a casserole of chicken and dumplings; someone else had made the attempt to scrub the blood from the wall behind the table, but it had stained a reddish-brown. I knew Conrad would spend Sunday, his only day off from working the mines, painting it. It was just his way.

I shimmied up the ladder, to the attic where my brothers and me slept. When I turned ten, Ma insisted that two old sheets be sewn together to separate the wide attic space.

"A growin' girl needs her privacy after all," she said.

Pa smiled in a way I didn't like. He tried one night to slip his hands down the front of my nightgown, when the boys was out and Ma was working, but Conrad came home early, and Pa had warned me never to speak of it. Still, the curtain went up the next day. It was like a one big permission slip, them two sewn-together bed sheets.

Six years of it, night after awful night; he left me alone only the week before I got my period and nights when Ma was home. Pa come home punch drunk from Flagler's Tavern, climb the ladder, with the boys lying right on the other side of those sheets, and say those awful words that I never forget.

Hold still, honey.

Hold still, and this won't hurt.

Don't scream…someone will hear you. I'll be done, soon.

Don't scream, or I'll hit you again.

Don't scream, damn you…don't scream!

No, I wouldn't scream anymore, because I was getting away. I yanked the sheets from the nails that attached them to the ceiling and, real fast, put all my stuff into it. Another dress, some underwear, the quilt from my bed that Ma had made. I took Conrad's Bowie knife from beneath the mattress that he and Otis shared.

No more whispers. No more secrets. Like Jarred said, everybody knew the truth, now. But everybody was wrong. It wasn't my fault. I had to leave— Pa said if I ever told anybody, he kill me. I told, and now Ma was dead. The whole world knew. I swung my bundle over my shoulder. It wouldn't happen again. Nobody would ever do that to me again.

Downstairs, the screen door rattled on its hinges as Pa staggered in drunk, as usual.

"Marian!" he bellowed. "Marian, you teasing little slut! I know you're in here."

I froze. Below me in the big room, the chicken and dumplings crashed to the floor as Pa fell against the table, bellowing like a bull. "Where are you, you little whore?"

I stepped to the top of the ladder. "Up here, Pa." I slid my belongings from my shoulder and knelt at the edge. Slowly, I pulled out Conrad's knife.

"I told you never to say nothin' to nobody, didn't I?" Pa slurred, as he started up the ladder. "Well, you little slut, you done got me fired. Ain't got a job now to support your ass or them worthless brothers of yern, all because of you 'n' yer big mouth."

"No, Pa. That ain't my fault." The words came out calmly, as I locked both hands around the knife handle and raised it above my head. If I couldn't do it right the first time, he'd kill me, and nobody ever find my body. "You did it all to me and I ain't lettin' you do it anymore."

Pa was laughing, as his head came up through the opening in the attic floor. "And how you gonna stop me, Missy? I can break your neck with one—"

I shoved that knife into his chest, as hard as I could. I felt something hard, then a warm wetness as the blade went in. It slid back out so easily, I thought I missed. Then blood went everywhere – Lord, I never seen so much blood – as Pa fell backwards down the ladder, breaking every rung.

I watched for a minute, while he lay there, trying to get up, trying to stop the blood from coming out that big, old hole, making funny animal sounds and reaching up for me, wanting help. I never seen nobody die before. I felt so apart from it, as I watched, not caring or nothing, like when Conrad gutted that deer he got last winter when Pa wasn't working. After a while, Pa's body went limp in the red pool, his eyes still and shiny like glass.

Even as he lay dying, that twisted old bastard never once said he was sorry, never once begged for my forgiveness. His mouth would move, and there be blood coming out, and his eyes would look all panicky. But I just stared at him. Stared and watched him die.

I used to think about getting back at Pa. I used to think I run away, or I kill him, just like I did now. I used to plan it at night, when he be laying on top of me, rutting like a pig. I had all kinds of different ways to do it; rat poison in the thermos of coffee he took down to the mines was one. I kept a knife under my pillow, 'til he found it.

I thought when I did really kill him, when it really happened, I feel like I won. I thought I be proud of getting him away from me forever. But I wasn't. I was scared, more scared than I ever been in my whole life. I killed both my parents.

I picked up my stuff all rolled up in them sheets, jumped down from the attic, and ran into the woods. Nobody would ever find me, I vowed. Nobody would ever know who the real Marian was.

And, for a long time, nobody did. I put myself through secretarial school at night, while working days in a munitions plant in Charleston during the war. When the war was over, I moved to Ohio, got a job in Plummer County at the hospital as the secretary on one of the wards, then met and married the best looking resident on the floor.

Dr. Montgomery James was not only a doctor, he was a war hero. In France, he earned a Bronze Star and a Purple Heart for going in under German fire to save a fellow soldier who been hit in the chest by shrapnel. Monty took a bullet in the leg for his trouble, but managed to drag the wounded solider to safety.

We were so happy. Montgomery James was tall and handsome, with dark, red hair and a face like Tyrone Power. He knew everything about me, except that I killed Pa, and he loved me anyway.

After a few years, I had more money and prestige than I ever dreamed. For once in my life, people envied me. I couldn't let them down. I couldn't let them see that down underneath all the fancy clothes, the fancy car, and the money, I held a darker secret than anyone could imagine.

But the voices were right. It took nearly fifty years, but they found me. Now everybody knew the truth.

* * *

"Mother, I really think you ought to see a psychiatrist."

"I do not need a psychiatrist!" Shakily, I pulled my handkerchief from the sleeve of my bed jacket and clumsily dabbed at my lipstick. I had not left the sanctuary of my bedroom since my arrest, but remained propped up on my pillows, unable to speak to anyone for two days. The voices kept me there. Beneath my comforter in my own bed, they stayed quiet, particularly when I had company. But when I was alone and out of bed, the voices came: Ma with her hair tied back and in her coffin clothes, walking the floor beside me; Pa in his pool of blood, reaching up for me whenever I tried to step on the floor.

Marian, they said. *We know the truth. We know the truth.*

So I stayed in my bed where I was safe.

Until Kay came to visit me with the children, with all her supposed concern and her silly idealism. I hadn't protected her or her children. By ruining myself, I had ruined her, too.

"I don't need a psychiatrist!" I repeated, handing Andrew and Lillian a box of Godiva chocolates, a gift from Ed and Ellen Nussey.

"Please, don't give the kids so much sugar, Mother. Andrew, leave your sister alone." Kay wrestled the box from the children and put it back in my lap. "Kids, why don't you see if Novella has any goodies for you in the kitchen?" The children clamored noisily from the room, and Kay closed the door behind them. "There is obviously something in your past that caused you to break down at the jail."

"I don't think that's anything you need to concern yourself with," I said, folding my arms.

"Mother, they have medications that can help people with these illnesses. Mental illness is not something to be ashamed of any more!"

"I am not mentally ill!" I yelled, slapping the covers.

"Of course not. Who are these people they said you were asking for at the jail? Your brothers and your parents? What is that all about? "

"They're lying. I have no family—you know that."

"I don't know if what I do know about you is true anymore, Mother. I can't believe you knew what was going on with Aurora Development, or that you had anything to do with the attempt on Jess Hoffman's life. No one could get anywhere close to you to lay a hand on you, Mother. You were curled up in a fetal position and screaming, when the deputies took you to the hospital."

"What does that prove?"

"If you're mentally ill, which, of course, you say you're not, it could prove you weren't responsible for your actions. It could lead to a reduction in charges." Kay arched her eyebrows. "Attempted murder charges, Mother."

"I am aware of what the charges are. Martin Rathke will fix everything...."

"It appears that Martin Rathke has been fixing things for quite a long time now, Mother. I don't think he can get you out of this one."

"But what will everyone at the club think? That I'm completely unbalanced?"

"Then tell me what happened to you at the jail." Kay gave me one of those hard-edged looks that a mother gives to a recalcitrant child.

"Nothing happened at the jail! Why won't anyone believe me?"

"Then why don't you remember?"

"I don't know!" Furious now, I rang the silver bell beside the nightstand. "I think it's time that you and the children leave."

Novella poked her head into the bedroom. "Yes, Mrs. James?"

"Please see Kay and the children to the door."

"Just tell me the truth, Mother. Did you do what Marcus said in that article? Did you hate him so much that you wanted him dead?"

"Novella?"

"Miss Kay, I don't think your mother is up to this just yet. Why don't you and I go downstairs?"

"Out, Novella! I want her out of the house!"

"Yes ma'am." Novella opened the door wider. "Please, Miss Kay."

Kay shrugged. "If that's the way you want it."

Dutifully, she kissed me on the cheek and followed Novella into the hallway. Instantly I was on my feet, my ear against the bedroom door.

"Novella, what in God's name is going on?" I heard Kay whisper.

"Miss Kay, all I know is that she come home with Doc Nussey and Mr. Rathke, weepin' and wailin' like she seen a ghost."

"The arraignment was all over the papers this morning. She didn't see that, did she?"

"No."

For God sake, I didn't need the newspaper. I had clicked on the television news, just in time to see a clip of Martin pushing that TV reporter over. Predatory little snit! Who did she think she was, anyway, asking me those questions? But why don't I remember that? Why don't I even remember going in front of Judge McMullen?

"What about this breakdown? That's what it obviously is, a breakdown," Kay continued. "No one knows about that, do they?"

I didn't hear Novella's answer.

"God, I hope not, for her sake. Well, let me know if anything happens." There was the sound of footsteps and children's voices moving down the hall. I slipped back under the eyelet comforter and, trying to look innocent, ran my silver brush through my hair.

The doorknob turned, and Novella answered once more.

"Did you show them out, Novella?"

"You were listening, weren't you?"

"I beg your pardon?"

"I know you, Mrs. James, probably better than anybody else in this town, and I got a few things I need to get off my chest."

"I did not have a breakdown! Those idiots down at the *Journal-Gazette* have it in for me! My attorney, even my daughter might call this little setback a breakdown, but it's not! Tell me I didn't have a breakdown, Novella, please?" I reached into the nightstand's top drawer and groped for the bottle of gray capsules Ed prescribed for me. It wasn't there. "I really am just a little over-excited, yes, just a little over-excited, what with being arrested and having it all through the papers. My pills, Novella. Where are my pills?"

"You are not hiding behind pill bottles with me no more." Novella folded her arms resolutely and stepped to the foot of my bed. She pulled the pill bottle from her apron pocket and held it tantalizingly in front of me. "You aren't getting these in your mouth, till I'm done with you."

"What?"

"I'm tired of the way you treat Miss Kay. She's standing by you, Mrs, James, and you and I both know you're guilty as sin."

"You can be dismissed, Novella."

"Then do it, but you're going to hear every word I got to say—whether you like it or not." Novella's black eyes flamed. "I knew you when you was just a new bride, Mrs. James, when you didn't know the difference between a fork and a finger bowl. For all your airs and all your stories, I know you didn't come from money. I know you're just trash—I've seen too many white people like you. You made your place in this town on Doc Montgomery's coattails, and you know it. You've never spent your life making sure nobody tarnishes your precious image, even if it means driving the best daughter anybody ever had half out of her mind."

"I am certainly not responsible for—"

"You *hush*! I'm not done with you yet. You set up Mr. Grant to do in Mr. Henning. I know you did. You're a mean old woman, Marian James. You're sick, and you're twisted inside. I've seen too much of the way you operate to not know any different. I don't doubt for a minute that you done set up this whole thing. I don't know nothing about your past, and I don't think I care to. Whatever it was has made you into a monster, and you deserve anything that comes your way."

There it was again, Ma, that awful, screaming noise. Who is it that does that? Why don't she stop? Can't somebody make her stop?

CHAPTER 10

Marcus

Some stories swallow you whole, like Jonah and the whale. Others turn upside down, so that you are Jonah who swallows the whale. When that happens – and it does to every reporter at one time or another – you're so deep inside the details of the story that you can't see the truth. Then you've got to let it go.

And I lost my truth.

Everything I held dear, Kay, my career, and a chance at making something right was dead: and, in the name of ambition and what I called justice, I been the one who killed it.

The first three months after I came home to my parents' house in Chillicothe, Ohio, I spent staring out the window of my childhood bedroom, or staring at their small color television from my perch across the room on the living room couch.

My parents knew very little of what happened. They knew I had a big story by the tail— a story so big it reached back to bite me, and damn near swallowed me whole. They also knew it cost me the woman I loved. I could not tell them more.

I came down for meals, dressed in sweatpants and a torn Packers tee shirt for weeks on end, until my father told me I smelled like old man Dorningham's hog farm, and if I wanted to continue to live under his goddamn roof, I could take a goddamn shower and find myself a goddamn job.

"Yes, sir." I said, staring at my plate of Mom's chicken and noodles.

"Frank," Mom laid a hand on my father's hairy arm. "The boy's had a shock. He just needs a little time and then I'm sure—"

"He's had goddamn three weeks to sit around here and eat my food and watch my television and whine." Dad threw his napkin down on the table. I could still see the blue USMC tattoo through the black hairs on his forearm. "Life's hard. It kicks you in the teeth more than once. There's a helluva lot more people out there who've had to deal with worser things than whatever's eating him. He's got both arms and legs and at least half a brain. There's no goddamn reason why I should be supporting him."

My father was right. I stood in the shower the next morning and felt the water and the soap course over me like a baptism. Once again, I found myself looking for a new beginning. Kay was lost to me forever; I had to accept that.

My sister Calpurnia and her husband lived south of Chillicothe, outside a little town called Antrim. Cal had my mother's love of reading and the tall, angular, good looks of our mother's youth, but she improved on the genetics she inherited. She had her teeth straightened, gotten her hair frosted, and looked like every other soccer mom driving her minivan into the Wal-Mart parking lot. She wore denim jumpers with kittens embroidered on them, white canvas Keds, and cotton anklets to work at her job as a fourth grade teacher in the Antrim Local Schools. Her husband, Dave was one of those affable, bland, blonde guys whose wardrobe mainly consists of golf shirts and khaki pants and who managed to bounce from industrial sales job to sales job without ever affecting the family's standard of living.

That afternoon, she was sitting at the kitchen table drinking coffee with Mom as I came back from the printers with a stack of fresh resumes.

"How's my favorite sister?" I asked, as I kissed her cheek.

"Looks like you're getting yourself back on your feet." Cal smiled, as she eyed me critically. Her southern-Ohio accent seemed to get stronger, the older she got. "That's a good thing."

I loosened my tie and poured myself a cup of coffee. "Yeah. I'm getting there, slowly," I said, dropping into a vinyl-padded kitchen chair between Mom and Cal.

"Calpurnia says Antrim schools are looking for substitute teachers," Mom offered.

I rolled my eyes. "I don't think anybody would want me in a classroom teaching their children."

"You know, the *Antrim Truth* is looking for an editor." Cal fished through the canvas tote at her feet and pulled out a copy of the newspaper. She scanned the page for the ad and when she found it, pushed it across the table to me. "It's not a big paper. It comes out on Thursdays and it's mostly got what the kids at school are doing and what the village council says."

"I don't know." Truth was, I didn't think I wanted to go back to journalism. I didn't have what Jess had, that hard-eyed ability to boil down everything to a six-word headline, to set my feelings aside and make a cold, hard decision on a story, regardless of how it affected someone. But I didn't want to teach and couldn't do anything else, really, when it came down to it.

"Let me think about it."

I patted Calpurnia on the shoulder and, taking the newspaper with me, went back to my room.

I dropped my sport coat across a chair in the corner and, deep in thought, flopped on the twin bed.

Jess. I hadn't thought about him for a while. Just before I left Jubilant Falls, I stood in the doorway of his hospital room, staring at the tubes that seemed to come from every orifice and at the white turban of bandages around his head. His left arm was in traction, held at a right angle above his body, his fingers purple and curled around the plaster-of-paris cast. His neurosurgeon put him into a drug-induced coma, hoping to give his synapses a chance to recover and minimize the damage done by Grant Matthews' Louisville Slugger. There were no guarantees on recovery, Carol told me, and I held her as she cried.

"Would anything ever be the same?" she asked tearfully.

I didn't think so then and, lying on my woven plaid Sears bedspread, didn't think so now.

I heard the kitchen door slam and looked out the window to see Mom, head down and with hands on her hips, stroll slowly down the sidewalk to Cal's minivan. She and my sister were deep in conversation. I slid open the window sash to listen.

"He'll come out of it, Mom. You've just got to give it time," Cal was saying.

"I don't know, honey. Whatever it was, he won't talk about it. Your Daddy was a little hard on him last night at dinner."

"That's Daddy." Cal jingled her keys in her hand and shrugged.

"Maybe this job at your little newspaper will be something he's interested in."

I closed the window and stepped into the hallway where an old push-button phone sat on a small table at the head of the stairs. Automatically, I punched in the number of the *Jubilant Falls Journal-Gazette* newsroom.

"Newsroom. Porter," the cops' reporter intoned briskly.

"Hey, John, it's me. Marcus Henning."

"Marcus! Hey, guy, how's it going? Where are you? We never heard where you ended up and everybody's been asking."

"I'm living at my folks in Chillicothe. No, I'm not working yet, just trying to get my life back together, slowly."

"Don't blame you. That was a nasty time there. Still is kind of, I guess, for some folks."

"Yeah, that's why I called. I wanted to know how Jess was doing."

"He's been moved. He's out of the coma now, and he's at a rehabilitation institute in Cleveland. Carol has taken their daughter and they've moved up there for the short term."

"Who they get to replace Jess?"

Porter made a disgusted sound. "Watt promoted Addison. She's managing editor now."

"You applied and didn't get the job, I take it?"

"Basically. I'm looking around for something else. If I can't move up here, there's no sense in staying, I guess."

"What's Kay James doing?"

"The literacy center director? I don't know. After the trial was over, I never heard anything."

"Did she leave town? Take another job?"

"I dunno."

I listened to him complain for a few more minutes, then hung up. Porter's dreams always exceeded his abilities, and it was no surprise that the publisher, J. Watterson Whitelaw, had promoted Addison. She was good, and she deserved the position.

For a moment, I stared at the phone. I punched in Kay's phone number.

"I'm sorry, the number you have dialed has been disconnected...." A disembodied voice filled my ear. "If you think you have received this message in error, please hang up and try the number again."

So she was gone, too. I gently replaced to phone in its cradle and leaned my head against the wall, my eyes closed.

"Marcus."

I turned to see my mother standing in the stairwell.

"You've got to let her go, son. You've got to let her go."

* * *

"We don't get many with your kind of experience for this kind of a job." Group Publisher Stephen Hamlin looked through his trendy, wire-framed glasses at my résumé. Sitting behind an expensive cherry desk, Hamlin wore an Italian suit, an Ohio State University tie, and reeked of expensive cologne and political correctness.

He poured himself a glass of Perrier and, tipping the bottle my direction, wordlessly offered some to me.

"No thanks. I'm back in the area, and thought I like to try my hand at being an editor," I responded. I rehearsed these answers in the car on the way to Columbus where the regional offices of the Antrim *Truth's* parent company, Choice Publications, were located.

"What brings you to the Chillicothe area?"

I focused on framed picture behind Hamlin's desk of Choice's flagship newspaper, the national daily *America This Morning*, and gave him my canned answer. "It's my home town. My parents live there. I had a relationship go sour and decided to come back."

"Well, divorce happens to the best of us. I think you're very qualified for the job at the *Antrim Truth*, but it's probably a much slower pace than you're used to. However, we're used to our smaller papers being training grounds for some of our larger products, and I think you'll find there's a great deal of opportunity with Choice Publications." Hamlin began to tick off the benefits, but I was only half-listening.

Product? When did a newspaper become a product? Or had I been so spoiled at the family-owned *Journal-Gazette* that I was unaware of the corporate culture that was beginning to overtake the news business? I didn't realize it then, but Hamlin was one of many business types who were invading newspapers across the country. Men and women like Hamlin had never written a word on deadline in their lives, but worked in everything from banking to manufacturing and figured they could apply that knowledge to newspapering. Everything came down to the balance sheet, not the quality of information being provided to the community, not the free expression of opinions, or serving as a record of local government actions.

I wondered how Addison McIntyre was adjusting to her new role and shifted in my seat. Where had Kay gone, I wondered? Why had she left Jubilant Falls? Was the shame of knowing that her mother was behind Aurora Development too much to handle? *Let her go, son. Let her go* – my mother's words echoed in my ears.

"And, if those figures are satisfactory for you, Mr. Henning, I'm prepared to offer you the job as the Antrim editor," Hamlin finished.

"Sure. Sounds great." He probably offered me two dollars a week and all the peanuts I could eat, but I didn't care. It was a job.

And not much of one. The next day, Hamlin and I met with the staff. I had one part-time staff writer, a local woman, Carlene Johnston, who often brought two small children to work with her (at least they were well-behaved enough to sit in the corner of the office and play with a box of Legos), and Doris Overton, my full-time office manager who also handled the circulation and classified advertising. My part-time sports writer, Larry Cochran, worked full time at the local Peterbuilt plant. On my first day, he informed me that, if overtime ever became mandatory on Friday nights, he wouldn't be able to cover football games.

Yes, it certainly was different from the hard-driving newsroom Jess Hoffman ran.

The building was old and decrepit, with the name of the paper painted in an old-style font in a circle on the front plate glass window, and old Linotype machines sat beneath a mantle of dust in the back room. Mice had nested in the nooks and crannies of the old equipment, and the two resident cats, Clark Kent and Lois Lane, were charged with keeping their populations down, although they often found it less stressful to sleep atop the computer monitor on my desk.

The pace was certainly slower. I covered the Antrim village council, the township trustees, and took my own photos, getting them developed at the one-hour photo at the back of the Heidman's grocery store. In my first week, I took a picture of two kids selling lemonade at the edge of town, of a potato from Harvey Schneemeister's backyard garden that he claimed resembled Mickey Mouse, and a grip-and-grin ribbon-cutting photo of the new addition on the Baptist church. Hardly the gritty subjects of a daily newspaper's front page.

The outside world rarely intruded on our front page. Later in the summer, when Saddam Hussein invaded Kuwait, I interviewed

Betty Van Britton whose son was in one of the first Air Force units shipped over to Saudi Arabia. But for the most part, Antrim was its own small, self-contained world.

I put my pages together on my outdated computer each Wednesday night, printing them out and waxing them down on grid sheets to be shipped by truck to the press in Columbus. It was a primitive way to do things, but I figured I was getting back to basics not only personally, but professionally as well.

Nights, I slept on Cal and Dave's couch. It wasn't a bad way to live, and they didn't ask me how long I was staying. By this time it was summer, so Cal was home with the twins, Dodd and Deena, who were just finishing the second grade. We spend Saturday afternoons drinking Kool-Aid in the back yard watching the kids splash around in the blue plastic wading pool, and each Sunday I waved good-bye from the front door as they all bundled into the mini-van to head to the Antrim First Methodist Church.

"Don't know why they call it First Methodist," Dave said, elbowing me one morning and grinning. "Should call it Only Methodist Church."

I think he sort of envied that I stayed at home, pleading heathenism and clicking through the morning news shows in my robe and boxers, while he and Calpurnia greeted visiting worshippers, led Sunday school, and counted the offering after services.

My brother-in-law never seemed to mind that I was there, eating his food, usurping his couch and his privacy. Cal wouldn't allow me to pay rent, or buy groceries, but at least she let me baby-sit the twins and buy pizza on occasion from Mama's Pizzeria as my way to settle the debt.

Before long, however, it was plain to me at least that I needed a place of my own. I broached the subject over a dinner of tuna noodle casserole, after I been at the *Truth* for about a month.

"Oh, let me set you up with Abigail Fairchild," Cal pointed her fork at me. "She's a real estate agent, and she just knows where all the deals are."

"I don't know that I'm ready to buy a house." I had visions of a pushy woman with big black glasses, big hair, and a short skirt chanting "Location, location, location," and cringed. "I'm just looking for an apartment. Maybe I'll go back into Chillicothe to look."

"No!" Dodd and Deena chorused. "Don't leave Uncle Marcus! Stay here! Stay here!"

Cal waved her fork. "Quiet you two. Marcus, you're not going to find many rentals in this place. You might as well buy something and put down some roots."

I gulped and stared at my plate. Buying a house would mean I given up on Kay and, in some ways, a career. I had no intention of spending the rest of my life as the Antrim *Truth's* editor. Even Group Publisher Steve Hamlin had said this little weekly was a training ground, and he expected me to move on at some point.

"I don't think so," I managed to choke out.

There was silence around the table.

"Marcus, it isn't like we don't want you here. You're welcome to stay here for as long as you like to stay," Dave said. "Of course, if I said anything else, Cal would have my butt in a sling."

Calpurnia stood up to take her plate to the sink and playfully smacked Dave across the shoulders as she passed. "He's right—I would! But the kids sure like having you around, and buying a house doesn't mean you're stuck here forever. You buy a house, you find another job down the road, you sell the house. Simple as that."

"I suppose so," I conceded.

"Then it's settled." Calpurnia wiped her hands on a dishtowel and reached for the phone. "I'll call Abigail right now and have her come down Saturday, and we can all pile in the car and go look at houses."

Everyone started talking at once. Dave said something about getting a big kitchen because women liked big kitchens. Calpurnia said no, that wasn't true; it had to be an efficient kitchen, and, in the event I found something I liked, she'd be glad to help me paint. There was a big sale right now on interior latex at the Chillicothe Wal-Mart. Dodd wanted a swimming pool because his best friend Jimmy had a pool with a wooden deck at his house. Deena asked me if I was going to put a swing set in back for when they come to visit.

"Hold on! Hold on!" I cried over the din. "I think this is something I need to do on my own, okay? Just have this Abigail call me at work, and we'll go from there."

That night, after Dave and Calpurnia turned off the news and headed to their bedroom, I pulled the stack of pillows and blankets out from behind the couch and made up my own bed. Lacing my fingers together behind my head, I stared at the ceiling.

This isn't a bad little town, I guess, I thought. It was nice to have family around. There was something so uncomplicated about it that I never had with Kay. My niece and nephew were good kids, not much older than Andrew and unencumbered with his—and his sister's— emotional baggage.

My father and I seemed to have come to a truce, as well. I'd seen him showing off my byline to a customer who'd come into the garage one day. We even sat beside each other on the bleachers, when we go to Dodd's T-ball games.

My job was easy. My life was easy. It had been four months since I left Jubilant Falls. To be truthful, until the house-buying thing came up, Kay hadn't crossed my mind in a couple weeks. Maybe I *was* healing. Maybe I *had* let her go this time.

Then why did I still feel so empty inside?

* * *

"I understand you might be interested in buying a house."

I looked away from my computer screen briefly, to see a lithe, young, blonde woman standing in front of my desk. She certainly didn't look like your average real estate agent. Her hair was cut short just below her ears and two curls swung towards a bright, open smile that seemed to light up her whole face. She wore tailored white cotton pants, a simple, pastel tee shirt with matching leather sandals, and carried a clipboard with a list of available real estate. A small pastel macramé bag hung across her shoulder. She could have been a kindergarten teacher, or somebody's mother, like Calpurnia.

"You must be Abigail Fairchild," I said, standing and leaning over my desk to shake her hand. "Nice to meet you." Her hand was small, soft, and warm; I couldn't resist wrapping both my hands around it.

"Yes." She smiled, and I reluctantly released my grip. "I attend the First United Methodist Church with Calpurnia. We're in United Methodist Women together. She said you might be interested in settling here in Antrim?"

I caught a whiff of perfume, a light, lemony fragrance, clean and refreshing and, I suspected, awfully like her. She hooked a lock of blonde hair around her left ear, and I noticed she didn't wear a wedding ring. "Well, I can't say that in complete honesty—" Something about this Abigail Fairchild demanded honesty. "—but I can say I think I'll be here for a little while. Cal says there's not a whole lot of rental places."

"She's right. There's a few houses right here in Antrim that I can show you right now. Do you have some free time? They're within walking distance."

"Sure." I shuffled some papers around on my desk and grabbed my jacket from the nicked and chipped coat tree in the corner of my office. "Let's go."

Antrim's downtown had a hardware store at the south end of Main Street, followed by Mama's Pizzeria, Linda's Home Cooking Café, the post office, Heidman's Grocery and Video Rental, and several antique and junk stores. The *Truth* and the First National Bank sat at the north end. Abigail pointed south.

"There's a house I think would be just right for you, off Riley Street," she said, checking her clipboard.

Antrim residents numbered about 4,400, most of them living on the few streets that ran like spider's legs from the main drag. Antrim was too small for zoning; many of the houses had been built in accordance with the owner's personal style or ability, during the time when dusty, wagon paths from the outlying township were still the main thoroughfares. There were older, clapboard houses, a few doublewide trailers, a few more shacks, and a couple brick ranches built in the 1950s. At the edge of town, a federally-subsidized apartment complex was located, housing the chronically infirm and unemployable, but it was nothing like the East Side of Jubilant Falls. Amongst a couple blocks of older, well-kept homes sat a new village and township government center of nondescript concrete, home to village and township offices, the sheriff's substation, township fire, and EMS equipment.

When the good times came to Chillicothe, a small coterie of middle class homes began to spring up at the north end of Antrim, within comfortable commuting distance of large employers like the Mead paper plant and Peterbuilt and a short drive from Antrim's downtown. This was Dave and Calpurnia's neighborhood.

"I need to make one thing clear to you, before we get too deep into this."

"Yes?" Her large, doe eyes fixed on mine, and her lips parted slightly to reveal perfect white teeth. An overwhelming urge to kiss her filled my head, a need to see if she tasted as sweet and lemony as she smelled.

I inhaled sharply and shook my head. This was not the reaction I was supposed to have. "Um, I, ah, I'm not planning on staying in Antrim for the rest of my life right now," I managed to stammer.

"Oh, I understand. Calpurnia told me that, when she called me. I've found a couple properties that might interest you. The property owners will rent to you for a year. Then, if you're interested in buying the house, a portion of your rent can go toward the down payment. That way, if you get another job soon—Cal said that you reporters move around a lot—you won't be stuck with a house you have no equity in."

I nodded, relieved. "Why do I think you and my sister have planned my life out for me?"

Abigail blushed. "Let's go look at houses."

We looked at three that afternoon, all, like she said, within a comfortable walking distance of the *Truth*. I don't remember any of them; I just remember by the end of the afternoon, leaning over a kitchen counter, looking into those beautiful, trusting, brown eyes and – as I softly kissed her lips – thinking I could feel again.

* * *

For our first date, Abigail insisted on cooking me dinner at her place. I was a little surprised, knocking on the door of her apartment, the converted second floor of one of Antrim's antique shops.

"You mean to tell me that as a big successful real estate agent you doesn't own some sprawling compound outside of town?" I asked, as she took my coat.

Abigail blushed endearingly and smiled. "I own this building, and the rent from the store downstairs pays my mortgage. That way, I can spend most of my income on what I really love." She led me through the living room and pointed toward a far wall, festooned with blue ribbons and photos, all a variation on the same theme: Abigail in English hunt clothing and holding a blue ribbon, standing beside a huge, muscular horse I assumed was a thoroughbred. Photos of Abigail crouched low over her horse's neck in mid-jump over a hedge, a white fence, or a small ditch. Abigail in a colorful polo uniform riding a smaller horse. Abigail leaning against a stall door and smiling for the camera, as the big brown horse nibbled a carrot from her hand.

"My, you're quite the horsewoman," I said. "I'm assuming that big fella is a thoroughbred?"

She nodded. "That's Mayhem, my stallion – his full name is Fairchild's Midnight Mayhem. The polo pony I don't own any more.

My goal is to own a ranch and raise thoroughbreds. After dinner, we can go out to the farm where he's boarded, if you like."

"I think I like that."

"Well, let's eat then. I hope you like lasagna." She pointed to a small table in the corner of the living room, set with good china, wine glasses, and a single candle in a brass candlestick.

Our conversation was tentative and exploratory as we ate, negotiating that first date minefield. Like me, she been raised in the area and never married, but had come dangerously close. Shortly after graduating from college, she'd been left at the altar by the high school boyfriend everyone assumed she marry. They worked together at a Ross County bank; he been on the fast track to a vice-presidency; she been a loan officer. After the disaster, he transferred to another branch, and Abigail began her real estate career.

"Calpurnia said you had a bad relationship?" she asked.

"Yes. I was involved with a woman who lost her husband in a plane crash. She had two kids and a third she—I mean they—were trying to adopt, when he died." No need to tell Abigail that I been sleeping with Kay long before her husband died or the sordid details of Aurora Development and the major's extra-marital affairs.

"Three kids. That would have been a lot to take on." Her brown eyes shone sympathetically.

"Yeah. There was a lot of baggage there, and it just didn't work out." Amazing how I could gloss over it now, when just a few months ago I felt as though my still-beating heart had been some-one's dinner.

Later that evening, we got into her Ford pickup and drove out into the countryside to the farm where Mayhem was boarded. In the semi-darkness of the barn, I drew her close and kissed her. Feeling her body against mine, her small, soft breasts and taut, muscular legs, I felt consumed with my need for her.

Looking down into her brown eyes, I ran my fingers through her blonde hair. "You're enough to make a man want to start again, Miss Abigail."

And so I did. We spent every waking moment together: lunches at Linda's Café, family dinners with Calpurnia, Dave, and the kids; evenings at Dodd's Little League games, holding hands in the bleachers. We end each evening with a long, languid kiss at the door of her apartment.

"You know, you don't have to go home," Abigail whispered one night as we said our goodbyes. There was something slightly illicit about these goodnight kisses. Even though hers was the only apartment above the antique store and we had no fear of any other tenant walking in on us, our goodnight kisses seemed stolen and deliciously dangerous at her door at the top of the stairs.

Her lips were swollen and her lipstick smeared, as she leaned back into the doorframe. Her breath was sweet, and her blouse, slightly rumpled, showed the edge of a lacy bra.

I traced the lace with my finger and kissed the soft underside of her jaw.

"As much as I want to, I better not," I whispered softly.

"Oh, why?" Abigail grabbed my lapels and didn't let me answer for a moment. Like Sampson, trying to maintain the last of his strength, I planted both hands on either side of the doorframe. I knew if I let my hands slide inside that blouse, I'd be a goner.

Our lips parted again.

"Please, baby, stay," she asked again. Visions of waking up beside her began to dance through my head – a night of delight; her soft skin against mine; falling asleep with her head on my chest, sated from sex; waking early, as the sun came up and leaning over the bed to trace the soft shoulder with kisses until she awaken.

Suddenly, it wasn't a blonde smiling face that turned over to face me in my fantasy. It was Kay's red hair fanned across the pillow and her face, her blue eyes, one framed by that small scar that rolled toward me.

"I can't," I rasped. "Not yet."

Abigail stuck her lip out in a mock pout. "All right, if you say so—this time."

"You realize, when it happens, I'll have to put it in the paper," I managed to joke, adjusting my jacket and stepping back from the doorframe, putting about a foot of sexually charged air between us.

She laughed and slipped her key into the lock. "G'night Marcus." She said.

"Goodnight, Abigail."

The door opened. She kissed me again and was gone. I staggered down the stairs and out to the car.

Calpurnia was sitting at the kitchen table, nursing a cup of hot chocolate and grinning like a Cheshire cat, when I got home.

"Well? How are you and Abigail doing?" she asked, expectantly.

"You planned this, didn't you?" I answered.

She smiled again and sipped from her cup. "I really didn't think about it when you started house-hunting, but after you two had dinner together, I could see you make a cute couple. She's such a sweet girl, isn't she Marcus?"

"That's only half the problem."

Within a week or two, I settled on a small, two-bedroom house that the owner was willing to rent to me for a year before deciding on a final purchase price. It wasn't a bad, little place: two bedrooms, one bathroom, a smallish kitchen and dining room, with no major flaws that Calpurnia and Abigail weren't able to fix within the first weeks with a coat of paint and a few decorative, female frou-frou things. The backyard was fenced and bordered with petunias. I would have to buy my first lawnmower, although Dave said I could borrow his until I found one. To me, the house's major selling point was, of course, location; it was just across the street from the government center, so I was able to pick up the sheriff reports and fire runs on my way into work in the morning.

I had my furniture, which I hadn't seen since leaving Jubilant Falls, delivered. My parents, Cal and Abigail, the twins, and Dave all came over one Saturday to help me unpack and move in, bringing enough food to feed the whole village. By sunset, the place looked as if I lived there for years rather than hours, and I was waving goodbye to my parents, Cal, Dave, and the kids with my arm draped comfortably over Abigail's shoulder.

She pulled me close and looked up at me. "Happy?"

I didn't respond.

Abigail stood on her tiptoes and tried to kiss me, but I turned away. A mantle of permanence was settling around my new front yard, like the evening dew, followed by a vague scent of fear. Or was it just me? I had a house in the same, small town as my sister and her family, a decent job, and this beautiful woman in my arms; what was wrong with me? Why did cold chills run down my spine, and why did I feel that someone was turning the key on the ball and chain around my ankle?

"Hey! I asked you a question!" She rocked back down on her heels, sounding hurt.

"I know. Here's my answer: I think so."

"What's that? You *think* so?" She pulled back and leaned against the porch rail, still smiling, but her eyes were a little hurt.

"This is going to sound all wrong, but this whole thing, this coming back home, taking the editor's job, meeting you and finding this house. It's all been too easy. I'm not used to that."

"What? You want misery?"

"I don't know. With my last job, my last relationship, everything was so hard, so twisted, and such a roller coaster. This all seems so, well, *normal.* "

"What's wrong with normal?"

"Nothing! Normal is great!"

"Then why don't I believe you?" She walked into the living room and scooped up her purse from my battered couch. I followed her inside. "You say you're happy, but when I try to kiss you, you turn away. I do everything but beg you to stay overnight with me, and you say no. What is it? Is it me?"

"Listen Abigail, I don't mean anything by it, I mean, you're a wonderful person, and I love what you've done to the house. "

"But you obviously have trouble with someone who's, as you say it, *normal.*" She hooked her fingers, making parentheses in the air. There was a sarcasm there I hadn't heard before.

"No, it's not that. It's—I'm—"

"I get the idea, Marcus. We've only been seeing each other for about a month now, so I'm not going to push you. But if all I am is a great cook and a good house painter, or if you're just going out with me to please your sister, I'd like to know that up-front, just for my own protection." She slung her pastel purse across her shoulder and headed toward the door.

I gestured hopelessly. "I wasn't sure. I didn't think you—"

"I just wanted to, to," Abigail blushed, but not out of embarrassment. "To take our relationship to the next level, or see if you were interested in that. If you're not, that's okay. "

Oh God, I really blown it now. This wonderful woman wanted to give herself to me, and I was still so terrified of what I experienced with someone else that I couldn't see straight.

"No, it's not that. It's the fact I'm an idiot, the kind of guy who looks gift horses in the mouth and then asks for a veterinarian's evaluation. You just have to accept that in me." I stepped closer and held out my arms. "Please, stay. I want you. I really, *really* do." *When all else fails, beg,* I told myself.

"Marcus, ssshhh." She put her soft hand across my mouth. "You're tired, and I'm tired, and before I say something I regret, I'm going to go out to the farm to muck out Mayhem's stall and feed him, then I'm going home. I'll see you tomorrow, okay?"

I nodded and took her hand from my face, kissing it as I did so.

"Just one more thing, Marcus."

"What?"

"There's very little normal in the world. Open your heart up. Enjoy it." Abigail smiled, a little sadly I thought, and closed the door behind her.

My arms fell limply at my side. God, when would I ever learn? There was something so good, so uncomplicated, and, damn it, so normal about the woman. And she wanted to make love to me! Why couldn't I just accept her sweetness and her simplicity? I certainly didn't have any qualms jumping into the sack and giving it to a married woman. Why did I want to have that same, sordid, obsessive love I had with Kay James?

The engine of Abigail's pick-up truck turned over, and the lights came on. From my front window, I could see the taillights and her personalized license plate that read ABIS TRK, as she pulled away from the sidewalk. I watched until the taillights turned at the corner and disappeared, then I walked back to the kitchen and pulled out a Tupperware serving bowl of Calpurnia's potato salad from my fridge. Grabbing a fork from the drawer, I flopped into a kitchen chair and began to eat directly from the bowl.

So what *do* you want from this relationship? I asked myself. She's beautiful, she is a good cook, and there's just something about that open, trusting face that I found irresistible. Or did I? And why not? Was it fear? If we broke up tomorrow (and could anybody say that we were truly a couple at this point?), would I regret it? I wasn't sure.

Maybe she was right. Maybe I needed to sit down with her and lay everything out, where I stood and where I wanted the relationship to go, just for her own protection. I wasn't ready for any kind of commitment; I saw that now. I had to be honest about that to her. Tomorrow, I promised myself I'd call her and tell her up front what was going on. It was the right thing to do, right after my cold shower.

On the countertop, the police scanner crackled to life. When I first came to Antrim, I convinced Hamlin to buy a police scanner for the office. The previous editor had been content to catch his police news on Tuesday mornings, or on television, but I wanted to give readers a little more timely stories whenever possible. I also bought a hand-held scanner for myself, in case something happened at night. Most of it was the occasional heart attack or fender-bender accident, but sometimes I got lucky. Once, I had been able to compete with the local daily, when three boys from Chillicothe High School stole a car and went joyriding through the countryside, plowing into a tree late one Wednesday night. They came away with their lives, but just barely, and I came away with a lead story for that week's paper that already wasn't a day or so old.

"Four-one-seven, respond to Collins Schoolhouse Road at the railroad crossing. Report of a vehicle struck by a train there," the dispatcher intoned. "Caller is the train engineer. He reports one injury, possibly a fatality. Another vehicle has rolled into the ditch. Unknown injuries there. Fire and EMS please respond."

I tossed the potato salad back into the fridge and listened to the dispatcher repeat the call. While my instincts about women were sadly lacking, I knew when to jump on a story. I found a reporter's notebook in my brief case, grabbed the scanner, and headed for the car.

Across the street at the government center, the fire and EMS vehicles were beginning to come alive. I waited until the last ambulance pulled from the bay and followed it up the street and into the darkened countryside.

* * *

Collins Schoolhouse Road was at the western end of Ross County. Like most country roads, it meandered across fields and small creeks until it climbed a sharp rise, made an abrupt left turn, and descended sharply into the next county. Just before the county line was a railroad crossing, so seldom used that even I had succumbed to the habit of not looking before speeding across.

Quickly, I surveyed the scene. The remains of a Buick lay mangled on the track, illuminated by the train's headlight and the spotlight of a sheriff's cruiser. A white sheet had already been placed over the driver's compartment; the poor SOB who either didn't see the train or tried to beat it would never make that mistake again. An older man, I assumed the train's engineer, stood talking to a deputy. To the right in a ditch, a blue, Ford pickup truck lay on the passenger side. Firefighters circled the vehicle, working to pull the driver out and get the truck back on all four wheels again.

An EMT jumped from the ambulance and ran toward the truck in the ditch. A group of firefighters stood around it, working to get the driver out. I swung my Nikon up to my eye, looking for a money shot. Things would change vastly from the time the *Chillicothe Gazette* would print their first story and the time I could print mine, but a good front-page photo could stand the test of time. As I twisted my telephoto lens, the truck's license plate came into focus: ABIS TRK.

I dropped the camera and ran towards the scene. "Abby!" I screamed. "Abby!"

Firefighters had Abigail fastened to a backboard, as they pulled her from the wreckage.

"Abby, are you all right? Are you all right?" A volunteer firefighter blocked me from coming any closer, as Abby, her face bruised and swollen and holding her left arm close to her chest, was strapped onto a gurney.

"Sir, you're going to have to stay back. Are you a family member?"

"She's my—I—we're —she's a friend of mine," I managed to choke out. I tried to jump around him to get closer to see how she was doing, but the firefighter's big, meaty hands stopped me.

"I'm going to have to ask you to step back, sir," he repeated. "She's received some broken bones and some bruises, so we're going to transport her to the hospital. You can talk to her there."

I nodded dumbly. EMT's wheeled her close to me, to load her onto the ambulance. They stopped briefly beside me.

"Abigail, are you okay? What happened?" I managed to ask, laying a hand on her shoulder.

She smiled weakly. "I'm okay. I think my arm is broken. I went for a drive after we talked, and that car in front of me I guess didn't see the train. I slammed on the brakes, so I wouldn't hit him, and rolled the truck. Is he okay?"

Before I could answer, an EMT spoke up. "Let's worry about getting you to the hospital right now, Miss." Turning to me he said, "You can follow us in your car. We're not going lights and sirens."

I leaned over to kiss her. She was loaded into the back of the ambulance. "See you at the hospital," I said.

Several hours later, Abigail's left wrist was in a cast. Thankfully, it wasn't her arm as she earlier suspected, and her head was fogged with painkillers as I helped her up the stairs to her apartment above the store.

With her good, right hand, she grabbed my shirtfront and pulled me into her living room, her lips locking drunkenly on mine. I stepped back and brushed her tousled hair from her glazed, brown eyes. "Abigail, not tonight. You're hurt. You're wired on Darvocets."

"I've been wounded worse than this, riding dressage with Mayhem," she slurred, throwing her head back and parting her lips seductively. "And, besides, I want you Marcus. I want you now."

"Let me put you to bed, and we can talk about this in the morning."

"Yes, Marcus. Put me to bed." With her one good hand, she deftly undid the buttons on my shirt. Abigail pushed the facings of my shirt aside, and her hands slid greedily, drunkenly, over my chest.

"Abigail, this isn't—I can't—"

She slipped fluidly to her knees. For a moment, I thought she passed out; instinctively, I grabbed her under her armpit, and then gasped, as I felt her teeth bite the flap on my fly. "Oh my God."

The next thing I knew, our clothes left a trail from the living room to her bed. Cupping her breasts in my hands, I traced the bruise on her left cheekbone with my lips, moving to the soft hollow of her collarbone, then her perfect, small breasts.

Softly, seamlessly, she rolled me onto my back and straddled me. I grasped her hips and guided her toward what we both wanted. We came together, in that small dark room, our breathing synchronizing as our movements built toward a crescendo. Guttural moans filled the room, as Abigail's back arched, and we exploded together. She collapsed on top of me, and I wrapped my arms around her.

"Oh, baby, I think I love you," she slurred. In a few moments, the Darvocets completed their task, we slipped apart and Abigail drifted into a deep, drugged sleep.

I lay listening to her regular, deep breathing and knew in that instant that I couldn't stay. I slipped from the bed and gathered my clothes. Fishing through a kitchen drawer, I found a pencil and a notepad. "Abigail, I'm sorry. You deserve better than me," I wrote and scrawled my initials across the page.

I tiptoed down the stairs and slipped into my car parked underneath a streetlight. The realization was as clear as the full moon shining on Antrim's empty Main Street. I could have stayed here. I could have led an easy life with a beautiful, uncomplicated woman. But it wouldn't have been love, not the love I knew would have been possible, the love I had before.

Turning the ignition, I made a U-turn in the middle of the street. I was heading toward the highway and back to Jubilant Falls.

CHAPTER 11

Kay

"This court finds the defendant is incompetent to stand trial at this time. She shall be remanded to the custody of a mental health facility, until such time as she can be declared competent."

With a swing of his gavel, Judge David McMullen – a man who had been a dear friend of my father's and who had, with his wife and daughters, once spent a Christmas holiday in the Virgin Islands with us – brought the first nightmare to an end.

For Mother, then, it was over.

I made sure she had a private room. Even in her insanity, she would want only the best. Even if she recovered, Mother would never be tried for the stabbing death of her father. I made some discreet inquiries and found that Marvin Gillespie's death so many years ago had been ruled accidental.

Conrad Gillespie was the last surviving brother and easier to find than I imagined. Jarred had succumbed to lung cancer in his fifties; a heart attack had claimed Otis a few years later. Conrad had moved just a few miles up the road from the little coal town Mother had grown up in, opened a construction business after the war, and raised a family of six children with his British war bride, Cora.

One Saturday, I left the children with Novella, who agreed to stay on, and met Conrad in the day room at the mental hospital where Mother would spend the remainder of her days.

She was sitting in a wicker chair by the window, staring vacantly out the ivy-bordered windows. Her fingernails, no longer perfectly painted, picked nervously at the hem of her blouse. She still looked well put together; the white blouse was ironed crisply, her hair was combed and styled, and a small gold dove held a pink-flowered silk scarf around her shoulders. The staff saw to it that her appearance would always be impeccable.

"Mother?" I touched her shoulder. The nervous finger picking stopped, and she looked at me. It was a few seconds, before she recognized me.

"Oh, hello, Kay," her words were slow and soft, the results of the antipsychotics she was taking.

"Mother, I have someone here to see you." I turned, and Conrad stepped forward, clutching his Gillespie Construction ball cap in his hand.

"Hello, Marian."

Mother looked back and forth between Conrad, the brother she hadn't seen in fifty years, and me, the daughter who now knew all her closely-held confidences.

"Everybody knows now, don't they?" she whispered, reaching for our hands. "It's not a secret anymore."

Tears brimmed in Conrad's eyes, as he knelt beside her chair. "No, sis. It ain't a secret no more."

"They came for me, Conrad, just like the voices said they would."

Conrad laid his head on her arm, to regain his composure. Tentatively, she touched his thinning, gray hair with a wrinkled hand and looked at me.

"This is my brother, Kay. Have you met Conrad?" she asked, her eyes vacant from medication.

"Yes Mother. I have. I'll let you two visit for a while." I touched her shoulder. "I love you, Mother."

She smiled back at me with vacant eyes, patting my hand.

I left them to catch up on the years and went to the cafeteria for a cup of coffee. After about an hour, Conrad found me.

"She's bad off, ain't she?" he asked, rolling his Styrofoam coffee cup between his large, calloused palms.

I nodded. "She'll never see the outside world again. The scars of the abuse and then the effort to keep her father's death a secret has just festered too long."

"We all knew that she killed him and run off. She had to. She couldn't have stayed there in that house, with Ma dead."

"But what about the police?"

"There was a chicken casserole broken all over the floor, when we came home. We put the pieces of that around Pa's body, before we went for the police. My hunting knife was missing, but it didn't take any rocket scientist to figger out where they'd find it, if anybody *could* find Marian. There weren't no fancy police investigators back then, and I'm sure that they were just as glad as everyone else to see Marvin Gillespie gone."

"That's harsh."

"It was a harsh world we lived in then. The company that owned the mines owned everything back then. They owned the company, owned the shack we lived in, they even ran the school and the store where we bought our food and clothes. They printed money we spent there. The scrip they made, that was our money. It was a hard world, Kay. A hard world. You know what a governor is?"

"If it's anything other than the political one, no."

"A governor is something you put on an engine to keep it from going faster'n it needs to, a control. It reins in the power of an engine, like you rein in a horse."

"Okay."

"Our pa had no governor on his life. He go after the first thing that caught his interest and, like anything that runs wild without some kind of restraint, his interest wasn't very often pure, or very honest. He was like a lot of men back then in the coal camps. He spend his check, what the paymaster didn't dock for the grocery bill at the company store, on hooch at Flagler's Tavern, and when he couldn't spend it on hooch, he go back in the hills and get him some 'shine. And when he be damn near blind drunk like that, he was an animal. He get in fights with anybody who looked at him wrong. He come home, and on nights when Ma was working...." Conrad stopped and hung his head.

I reached across the table and laid my hand on his arm. "You couldn't have stopped it, Conrad."

"Pa only kept his job because Ma would go beg the boss to let him stay. He couldn't work more than two or three days a week, when he was on a bender. Don't think them miners was all like that. They was so beat down...their lives wasn't nothing but working hard for a few pennies. They were all looking to make their lives, everybody's lives in that camp, a little better. When something happened to make that world a little less hard, people looked on it as a blessing."

"But my mother never knew that."

"No, she never did. We tried to find her. I don't know if she changed her name or anything, but we looked for her for almost 10 years before we give up. Maybe if we tried harder, if we looked longer, she wouldn't be here today."

"You don't know that. For the most part, Mother had a good life." I told him about Daddy, the practice, the huge house on the north end of Jubilant Falls, my marriage to Paul, the children – all three of them – and finally, Paul's death.

"You ain't had it easy either, have you?"

I shrugged. "Who among us does?"

"It's the secrets we keep that'll eat us alive. That's the one thing I've learned in this life. Marian had her secrets. Your husband had his secrets, and look where it all ended us up." He gestured at the cafeteria's institutional décor.

"Yeah, Conrad."

"That's Uncle Conrad. to you," he smiled.

I smiled back. "We're sitting here just finding out about family we didn't know we had, and we're taking steps to make sure there are no more secrets."

"That's right. No more secrets."

* * *

Despite the relief of Judge McMullen's order declaring mother unfit for trial, I still had two more ordeals left to endure in the Aurora Development case, as the *Journal-Gazette* was calling it.

One went quickly. Grant Matthews never saw a jury, at least as a defendant. When the felonious assault charges against him were upgraded to attempted murder, the man who scarred my face so many years ago curled up like a whipped dog and took the first deal he was offered: testify against Lovey McNair and we'll give you a mere twenty years, rather than life, behind bars.

That left only one more trial. Lovey McNair faced the worst of the charges: conspiracy to commit murder, solicitation to commit murder, fraud, and a total of twenty-three counts of failure to maintain a habitable abode.

The first witness to testify was Ludean Tate. She stepped into the witness box and clearly, but softly, swore to tell the truth, the whole truth, and nothing but the truth. Lovey stared coldly at Ludean, during her testimony, but Ludean lifted her chin, and she set up the scene of her rat-infested apartment, of her efforts to keep it clean, and of how unresponsive the staff at Aurora Development was to her requests.

The next witness was Grant Matthews. Deputies led him into the courtroom, shackled at the wrists and ankles.

Yeah, you're a big man now, I thought, watching him shuffle across the courtroom as his manacles rattled. Hearing Grant Matthews talk about how Lovey had engineered the attempted hit on Marcus turned me cold.

"He was writing a story that was going to make her company look bad. She didn't want everyone in town to know how badly she let some of the apartments get, how repairs were never made," Grant told the court.

"Did you ever suggest that she repair those apartments?" the prosecutor asked.

"No."

Up on that stand, the man who often left me cowering in a corner or screaming for help those many years ago suddenly didn't look very frightening to me anymore.

"And the story ran the day before. It was already in print," the prosecutor asked. "If you were assigned to stop that story from running, you failed, didn't you?"

Grant shook his head. "Not completely. That was only part of the job. The other part was to get Mr. Henning."

Maybe it was the passage of time, maybe it was my own empowerment, I don't know, but Grant Matthews looked like the slimy worm he truly was. I thought about that brick through my window all those months ago. My fear of that night changed from weakness into rage and from that rage to strength. He didn't scare me any more—he couldn't. From my seat in the spectators' gallery, I glared at him throughout his testimony.

"And didn't the defendant have other reasons for wanting the reporter dead?" the prosecutor asked.

Grant paused. "She told me it was because this reporter was bothering her partner's daughter," he began.

"And is it not true that woman was your ex-wife?" The prosecutor snapped.

"Yes, sir." Grant hung his head. I felt the eyes of the courtroom spectators turn my way. I lowered my own eyes and slipped quietly out of the courtroom.

I locked myself in the last stall in the ladies' bathroom and sobbed.

Everything was gone, everything that mattered; I lost my mother, my husband, and the man I loved, all within a year. It was a burden I didn't think I could carry, but what choice did I have? My cries of anguish bounced off the institutional bathroom tiles, until I didn't think I could cry any more.

It only took the jury forty-five minutes to find Lovey McNair guilty of all charges. At her sentencing, Martin Rathke argued that, at her advanced age and with no prior record, she would not be a threat to the community.

"It seems to me, counsellor, that with this lengthy list of charges she has *been* a threat to the community, to members of staff of our local newspaper, and to the tenants of Aurora Development for some time," Judge McMullen thundered.

In the end, she got ten years.

In one of her husband David NcNair's few acts of spine, he forced his wife to sell all her interest in Marlov Enterprises to me, then closed up the house and moved to Florida. I don't know if he ever visited Lovey in the minimum-security wing of the women's prison in Marysville. I know I never did.

And Marcus? After Mother's arrest, he'd gone back to the newsroom, cleaned out his desk, and disappeared. No one, not even the new editor, a woman named Addison McIntyre, knew where he went.

At least they weren't telling me, if they did.

Jess gradually recovered, although it took him a slow six months at a rehab clinic in Cleveland. His pretty-boy good looks were destroyed in the attack. The left side of his face hangs a little now, and sometimes he drools a bit, but once he gets out of his wheelchair, he claims, he's going back to newspapering.

As guardian of Mother's estate, I made sure that all his bills were paid directly from her funds and established a college fund for his daughter, Rebecca. It went a long way in curing the animosity Jess had always felt about me. At my last visit, I couldn't resist asking if they heard from Marcus.

"What do you hear from Marcus these days?" I stared into my coffee, to avoid the embarrassment of seeing his wife, Carol, wipe the saliva from her husband's chin.

"Not a thing. No one knows where he's gone, or what he's doing." Jess's words were slow and measured, but his intelligence was still intact.

"I tried to call his parents in Chillicothe," said Carol. "But I didn't get anywhere. Either they wouldn't tell me, or they really didn't know."

"Ludean Tate has heard from him a few times by letter," Jess said.

"Was there a return address? Is he okay?" I clutched my coffee cup harder, hoping I didn't sound as desperate as I felt.

Jess shook his head. "She wouldn't say. I think it's best that everybody move on, Kay. He's gone for good."

So, I had lost him completely.

I resigned as director of the literacy center, although the board begged me to stay. In the end, I was made an at-large board member and had a hand in choosing my successor. But there were other, bigger issues to deal with in that run-down neighborhood, too. As the new head of Aurora Development, I made sure that all the rental properties surrounding the center were repaired. Ironically, it took less than the bimonthly bill I now received for Mother's care to repair each house.

If Mother had only been strong enough to stand up to Lovey.

I closed up that ghastly rental house of ours in the historic district and moved into Mother's house in the North End. There were too many memories of both Marcus and Paul, and no matter what I did I could never escape them. It was a strange sadness that I carried with me then, knowing that events beyond my control cost me both of the great loves in my life. I went through the lists of *if onlys* and *I should haves*, almost every day. *I should have married Marcus the first time he asked. What if I forgave Paul?*

It was a strange, lonely Christmas. Paul's absence was made even more conspicuous by the deployment of troops to Saudi Arabia in Operation Desert Shield. We still were in the middle of the trial when the First Tactical Fighter Wing based at Langley had been the first unit to deploy to Saudi Arabia that August. I was too wrapped up in the trial to think much about it. No doubt, I thought at the time, all we needed to do was show some force, and everything would all end peacefully.

An event that would have kept me on the edge of my seat for days passed by like so much background scenery. My life as a military wife seemed so far away now, a part of my life I finished with, like high school or my first marriage. The places I seen – the sands of Florida, the beauty of Virginia's Chesapeake Bay, the mountains of Korea – were part of the past.

Now, as the Christmas tree twinkled in the corner, I couldn't help thinking that, if Paul had lived, he would have given anything to be there in the sands of the Saudi desert.

He would have also given anything to see that PJ was here in Jubilant Falls. I hadn't forgotten about that little boy who was so unaware of all the changes he brought about. As I promised Paul, Conrad, and myself, I would still bring that little boy back to the States and make him a part of this family. It was the one thing left to be settled, one thing that would complete the circle.

A few trans-pacific phone calls to Sister Mary Michael at the orphanage in Songtan City, just outside Osan Air Base, sent me in the right direction. PJ's birth certificate had come through and listed Paul as the father, so he was already a U.S. citizen. There were still endless forms to fill out, phone interviews with Korean and American embassy functionaries, and plans to be made.

Finally, just a few days after New Years, twelve months to the day after the death of Paul Armstrong, I left the children in the care of Novella and got on a plane for Seoul.

* * *

"*Shilla hamnida – Sonkkum kalkkayo*? (Excuse me miss, tell your fortune?)" The wizened, old, Korean woman held out her hand to me, gesturing that she would read my palm. Her bottom teeth were missing, and wrinkles cascaded down her cheeks like so many dry yellow creek beds. But despite the man's winter coat that enveloped her tiny frame, I could see her eyes were friendly.

It was two days later, and I was standing on the streets of Songtan City, just outside the Shinjang Mall. I arrived the day before and, after settling into my tiny room at the New Seoul Hotel, fell asleep and slept the sleep of the dead. The next morning, despite the misery of a Korean winter, I decided to walk through the city, just to see what I remembered. I stood outside the oriental-style gates of Osan Air Base, but decided that I couldn't go see the flight line where Paul had met his death. I could imagine plumes of black smoke rising from the twisted metal of his airplane into the Korean sky, and I shivered.

Turning away, I started walking through Songtan City until I found myself in one of Songtan's shopping areas. Shinjang Mall wasn't a mall like most Americans consider a mall, with its food courts and ample parking. Instead, the mall was a few city blocks closed to traffic and filled to the brim with small shops and street vendors, each hawking their wares to anyone who passed by, particularly American servicemen and their families who bought the cheap imitations of Rolex watches, Nike shoes, and Levi jeans. The goods, which ran the gamut from factory seconds to outright fakes, would only last a few weeks to a couple months, but it was difficult to turn those dubious bargains down.

While shopping was better in Seoul's I'taewon market district, my favorite Songtan shop was Mr. Lee's Leather shop, where you could get eel-skin wallets, custom-made shoes, briefcases, and purses for next to nothing. Tailors also made a killing. During our first tour to Korea, Paul managed to get a suit custom made, including the shirt and tie, for less than a hundred dollars.

The time difference was killing me; it was mid-morning, about 10 a.m., but my body said it was one in the morning back in Jubilant Falls and screamed for sleep. Exhausted, I forced myself to keep walking to acclimate myself, knowing that, if I laid down again, I be spending the next night staring wide-awake at the walls.

Sister Michael Mary offered to meet me at Kimpo Airport, the country's only major airport. Instead, I chose to take a bus from Kimpo into Seoul and from Seoul to Songtan City. As I fished through my purse for my Korean phrasebook, I mused that this old woman might give me a little confidence.

"*Shilla hamnida – Sonkkum kalkkayo*? (Excuse me miss, tell your fortune?)" she repeated. Koreans love to have their fortune told. It's not uncommon to see fortune tellers set up with a small chair and table in many of South Korea's open-air markets. While they mostly plied their trade to young couples in love, telling them that marriage was or was not in their future, this old woman had singled me out this morning when business was slow.

I flipped through the pages of my phrase book; amazing how much Hangul, the native Korean language, I forgotten in the four years since Paul and I had been stationed here. "*Mullonijo!* (Sure!)" I said, sat down at her little table, and wrapped my own winter coat more securely around my legs. I flipped through the phrasebook, again. "*Yong-o haseyo?* (Do you speak English?)"

"Yes. Give hand. You listen." The little old woman nodded and took my hand in hers. Her fingertips were calloused, and there was dirt under her nails as she silently poked and prodded the lines in my palm.

"What do you see?"

She stooped perusing my palm and looked at me. Silently, she held out her hand.

"Oh, I'm sorry. Here." I pulled out a couple *won*, Korean dollars, and placed them across her palm.

"*Kamapsumnida*. (Thank you.) I see much struggle in past. Much hurt, but many blessings."

"We all have that, *ajumoni* (aunt). You could say that about anyone."

"Is true, but you. I see something else." She bowed briefly. "I see *mirae*, rendezvous with the future, a completion of the life circle. You are not here for business, yes?"

"I am here to meet my new son."

The old woman raised her arms in glee. "Old aunt not wrong often! I see in your hand!" She pounded her own palm with her dirty index finger. "You adopt baby boy? Yes?"

"Yes."

"Many sons good. Boy have GI daddy?" The government had long kept a tight lid on foreign adoptions of children who were pure Korean; the concept of a multi-ethnic culture was anathema to most Koreans. A father who would not care for his child was also unheard of. That was why so many women who became pregnant by U.S. servicemen were often considered the lowest of the low; without a father to register a child in the family's genealogical record, that child literally did not exist.

There were a number of Korean adoptions right after the Korean War when times were hard and they couldn't feed their own children. Now that times were getting better, the government was considering phasing out all foreign adoptions in the future; that didn't include the Amer-Asian children like PJ.

I nodded. "My husband. My late husband." I whispered. Wordlessly, I pulled the photo of PJ sitting on the old nun's lap from my purse and pushed it across the small table.

The old woman examined the picture closely, then patted my arm. "You good wife, Palm say much happiness awaits after much sorrow. Remember *mirae*."

I nodded and stood, taking the picture from her wrinkled, yellow hand. Suddenly, the jet lag seemed to disappear, and I felt stronger and more confident from those few words. I was doing the right thing – I was honoring Paul's last wishes. For the first time in more than a year, I felt peace.

Later that afternoon, Sister Michael Mary came padding down the wide hall of the Catholic orphanage with her arms outstretched and her blue eyes twinkling. She was a waistless, postmenopausal woman with a round face and rubber-soled shoes, wearing navy blue polyester pants and jacket along with her black wimple.

The orphanage sat close to the underpass from the unimaginatively named National Road One between the Catholic Church and the police station, just a short cab ride from my hotel. Like most buildings constructed after the war, it was western in style. I clutched my purse and the photo close to me during the cab ride, terrified of what was coming. What if he didn't like me? What if I didn't like *him*? What if I found I couldn't bond with this baby? Would my resentment of all of his father's affairs throughout our marriage poison this meeting, or would I be able to look at PJ as what he really was – the little boy who, because of his mixed heritage, had been abandoned through social convention and whose father had died horribly?

"Mrs. Armstrong! So good to see you!" Her strong arms enveloped me in a bear hug. "How was your flight? Did you get rested? It's so difficult to fly and get acclimated to the time zone changes. Can I get you some coffee? I'm sure you're excited to meet PJ. He's napping right now. We've all been so excited to know that PJ is going home with you that we're all in a bit of a dither."

"I'm a little nervous," I said, smoothing my hair. "Scared to death, actually."

Sister Michael Mary laid a strong arm across my shoulders and steered me down the hallway. "Perfectly understandable! Perfectly understandable! Come—let's go to my office. You can get settled there. We've got a few forms yet to fill out, and then we'll have Sister Agnes bring in PJ."

We stopped in front of a door marked with her nameplate and a gold cross. Inside, the office was sparsely furnished with a desk, a few battered easy chairs, and an end table. At one side of the room was a bookcase filled with theological works.

Sister Michael Mary gestured for me to sit down in one of the easy chairs and slipped behind her desk. "Young Paul is a very lucky baby boy," she said, sorting through the files on her desk. "Ah, here is his file. There are very few people who would make this effort to bring him home."

"It's what Paul would have wanted," I said.

There was a knock on the door, and a young nun poked her head in. "Sister, there is a young woman here to see you."

"Please have her wait in the waiting room, Sister. This is Paul Pak's – I mean Armstrong's – adoptive mother, Kay Armstrong. She's come to take him home today. Tell the young woman gently, but firmly, that I am with a client, and I will be with her as soon as possible."

"She's very insistent on seeing you now, Sister." The young nun sounded flustered. Behind her, a woman's voice pleaded tearfully in Hangul.

Suddenly, a small Korean woman wearing a pink pullover sweater and black pants pushed past the nun and into the office. Her hair was cut short just below her ears, and she wore tiny, gold earrings. Her eyes were red from crying. "I must see woman who being new mother to my baby!" she cried in English, bowing and wiping tears from her eyes.

I knew her instantly.

It was the woman who had slept with my husband, who had carried his child and tried to raise him on her own, and who had sent that handful of money to Paul, hoping against hope that he was going to buy her a house for the three of them to live together in America.

We stared at each other across the room, fascinated at finally seeing each other. She wasn't one of the Osan whores—the juicy girls—who worked the bars preying on lonely servicemen, as I had thought for so many years. She looked intelligent and well dressed.

She looked *nice*.

"Kyung-Wha? What are you doing here?" Sister Michael Mary's tone was suddenly soft and gentle.

The Korean woman bowed again, then pointed at me. "I need to see woman who being new mother to my baby."

"How did you know I was here?" I asked.

"Please forgive. You show fortuneteller in Shinjang Mall my baby's picture. She live in my building. She know my story. She tell me." Kyung-Wha said, simply. "I had to see you."

I stepped forward and took her hands in mine. "I'm glad you did. I have wanted to meet you for several years."

Sister Michael Mary nodded to the young nun who backed out the door, closing it behind her.

"Kyung-Wha, you have given up your rights to this baby," Sister Michael Mary said. "You really shouldn't be here."

"Yes, yes. I know," she replied. "I can no stay away. Please, Miss!" she clasped my hand tighter, her black almond-shaped eyes boring into mine. "Let me tell you why I have baby."

We both sat down in the easy chairs and Sister Michael Mary returned to her desk.

"I want to ask you forgive," Kyung-Wha said. "I want you know my story."

She reached across to my chair and took my hands again. What Kyung-Wha was really reaching across was a divide bigger than an ocean or a continent; she was reaching across two hearts, hers and mine. As I met her gaze, I saw a sadness there that was oddly familiar.

We had both loved the same man, she and I; we had given birth to his children, and we had learned of his seemingly congenital unfaithfulness in deeply painful ways. Then finally, we had both lost him.

"What can I say, as mother full of guilt?" she began. "I am mother, without right to be mother. Sending little Paul away is hard, harder than anything I do, ever. But I know you love him. I know he will have life full of love and care and he accepted. He not get that here, because his green eyes and yellow hair mark him outsider here. You know that."

I nodded, still holding her tiny hands in mine. "How did you meet Paul?" I asked.

Kyung-Wha smiled briefly. "My parents run small souvenir shop in Shinjang Market, and I worked there. Nice souvenirs – celadon pottery, carved mahogany. It almost four years ago."

Mentally, I did the math. We had been stationed here then, when Andrew was just a baby. I had agreed to come to Korea for a two-year tour, thinking that if I go with Paul I could keep an eye on him. Stupid me. There had been another woman who worked in the office, a young lieutenant who was enthralled that a senior pilot would pay attention to her.

"Paul come to shop to buy pottery. I wait on him and think how handsome he is. Tall. Masculine. I very attracted to him and he to me. He asked we meet for coffee later. He never said he had wife and children. For that I am so sorry to you."

"It's okay. You weren't the first."

"We sit in café, drinking coffee and making sweet talk. I fall in love with him, and that wrong. We see each other when we could. I had to help my parents, who were old, infirm, and not like that I see Caucasian. They want me to marry Korean boy they choose for me. He is nice, educated, and could give me good life, but he not Paul. Each time we could, we slip away. I give myself to him willingly, because he promise many things. He promise bring me back to the United States, where we live together and go to university. Like a fool, I believe those promises – it is in my weak nature that I do these things. Soon, though, his tour is over, and he going back to the States. He say, 'I send for you.' He promise."

She stopped and wiped her eyes. "After Paul go, I pregnant. He send me many letters, so I have address and write him about being pregnant. He say he happy I have baby, that he come back and get baby and me and bring us to United States. We get married, he said. I save money, for many months. My parents let me stay with them, even though I pregnant and embarrassment. I stay in the house. I not work in shop anymore, but I save money best way I can. Then, when baby come, I name him Paul. By then, I have much money." She made a fist, to signify how much. "I not hear from Paul for several months, so I send picture of little Paul and all my money to him."

"And *I* got that letter. *I* opened it." I said.

"Yes. Paul write me and tell me he lie to me, that he already have wife and two children. 'But what am I to do?' I write back. I never get answer."

Sister Michael Mary spoke up. "Kyung-Wha was like a number of the young women who come to us. She tried for almost a year to raise the child on her own, believing Major Armstrong would return. But in the end, she found it impossible. So when little Paul was how old, Kyung-Wha, about a year?" Kyung-Wha nodded. "Yes, just over a year old, she came to us and gave us her son. She knew that she could not raise the boy any longer and that a new family could adopt him and give him the love he deserved."

"I give Paul to sisters and I go to Seoul to find job in factory. I work there almost a year. Then, my mother gets sick and dies. My father need help with shop, so I come back. The day before I come back, there horrible plane crash. I learn from newspapers it is Paul." Tears welled up in her eyes. "I know you good woman. Paul say so in last letter, when he say he can no longer keep his promises. He say you good mother to his children and loving wife. I know you be good mother to my baby." She covered her face, and sobs racked her small body. "When you show picture to fortuneteller, she know it like one I have in my apartment. She tell me you here, that you my son's father's wife. I have to see you…to ask you forgive."

"There is no need for forgiveness. You did nothing wrong. You just loved someone, like I did," I whispered, laying a hand on her shoulder. "I promise I will be a good mother to your son, Kyung-Wha. For Paul and for you."

There was a small knock on the door, and the elderly nun I seen in the photo Sister Michael Mary sent me, Sister Agnes, poked her head in. "Sister?" she asked.

Michael Mary gestured that she come in, and Agnes stepped into the office, a small boy in her arms, clinging desperately to the nun's neck.

"Here is your son," Sister Agnes turned, so we could see his face. Kyung-Wha and I gasped, simultaneously. His face was unmistakably Paul's, despite the yellow skin, the blonde-streaked hair, and almost-round eyes. He wore little jeans, with an elastic waistband and a flannel shirt. I couldn't help but remember a similar outfit I dressed Andrew in at that age. PJ been in the orphanage so long he didn't recognize his real mother and was clearly unsure of me.

"You are so beautiful!" I cried. I stood up and reached for him then stopped suddenly. Turning back toward Kyung-Wha, I saw she had buried her face in her hands, trying to master her emotions.

I stepped away from the little boy and touched her shoulder. With tear-stained eyes, she looked up at me. "You first. You gave him to me. You should be able to hold him in your arms first."

Kyung-Wha shook her head. "That right not mine anymore. He your son now." She stood and, with grace and strength, walked up to PJ. She touched him lightly on his back. "I wish for you beautiful life, my son. A beautiful life with love and happiness in America." And suddenly, clasping her hand over her mouth to control her emotions, she was gone.

* * *

It was a long flight back. I held my newest son close on my lap, stroking his soft hair as he slept, fingering the alternate strands of dark brown and blonde that marked him as an outcast in his old home. The circle was now complete. He was such a beautiful child. How could I have ever rejected this little boy? When he was awake, his green eyes were sharp, crackling with the same intensity and intelligence that had drawn me to his father, overlaid with that inscrutable Oriental calm.

Paul really was a hero after all. Saving this little toddler from the streets of Songtan was probably the most honorable thing Paul ever did. This son, too, would be a hero someday, just like Paul.

But what about my hero? What about Marcus?

* * *

"PJ, in just a few minutes, we'll be at your new home!" It was early evening, and I began to gather our belongings together. "You're going to meet your big brother, Andy and your big sister, Lillian. Won't that be exciting?"

Our flight seemed to never end. The legs from Seoul to Los Angeles then Los Angeles to Chicago seemed interminable. Now, on a commuter plane from Chicago to Jubilant Falls, it was ungodly. We were both exhausted, crowded into narrow seats. PJ cried, from the moment the plane took off, and I could not comfort him. He knew very little English. (Sister Michael Mary had taught him a few words like 'Mommy' and 'I love you,' but everything else was still in his native Hangul.) Poor baby, he probably thought he was giving up the safety of the nuns and the orphanage to spend the rest of his life airborne.

"Now, now, now…it's going to be okay. No honey, you can't sit in Mommy's lap right now." *Mommy.* I stopped and smiled. I had made the leap; the bond was real. He was now my son. "We're landing, and you need to sit in your own seat and buckle in."

His green eyes, in stark contrast to his yellow skin, widened.

"We're almost home, honey."

With a thump, the airplane touched down, and within moments we were taxiing to the gate. Right on time. I slung my purse across one shoulder, lifted PJ to the other, and joined the other passengers as they shuffled in lock step into the airport.

As I came down the jet port, I saw Marcus.

His tie was loosened to the middle of his chest, and Andrew and Lillian were clutching his hands excitedly. Squealing in delight, the children broke away from him and ran to me.

"Mom! Mom! Is this PJ? Hi, PJ! Did you know that Marcus is really cool? Novella said he once saved his boss's life, and he's done all sorts of cool things!" Andrew and Lillian's excited sentences ran so together, I couldn't tell them apart.

Marcus watched as I hugged the children in turn and introduced them to their new baby brother. "Hello," he said uncertainly.

I stood, strong as a rock, hiking PJ further up my hip. "Hello."

"I called your mother's house."

"It's my house now, Marcus. Mother is still hospitalized."

"I know. Novella told me everything. I'm sorry."

I shook my head. "It would have come out sooner or later. We just happened to be the ones who got the ball rolling. If anyone is to blame, though, it's Lovey."

Marcus hung his head and nodded, scuffing one shoe against the other. An uncomfortable silence surrounded us, as the other passengers rushed by.

"Marcus, aren't you gonna say hello to PJ?" Andrew asked.

"So this is PJ, eh?" Marcus reached for the toddler, but I pulled back, unsure of his motives. This baby would not be a steppingstone back to me, no matter how badly I wanted Marcus back in my life.

Marcus scuffed his shoes again. "Listen, Kay, these last few months have been very hard on me. I've been holed up at my folk's house, and, hell, I even thought I could fall in love with someone else. There's a very beautiful woman in a small town that hates my guts right about now. But it was all wrong Kay – it was wrong for both of us. I've been trying to make sense of why none of it worked, but the only reason I can come up with for staying away is my own ignorance. I can't live without you. Part of you will always be the major's wife, and I've accepted that now. That's includes PJ here. Please, Kay, can we try again?"

"Yes, Mom! Say yes!" Andrew and Lillian bounced up and down.

Tears began to well in my eyes, and I smiled. He was back. The old fortuneteller was right. The circle was now complete.

Once again, it was *mirae*, a rendezvous with the decades to come. Marcus and these three children were my future. And it was all coming together, here and now.

"Yes, Marcus, yes."

We reached for each other this time, the five of us joining together in a group hug, knowing that we were beginning a new chapter as a new family. And this time, I knew we could make it.

Suddenly, a shout rang out from down the corridor:

"It's started! They're bombing Baghdad!"

Marcus and I stared at each other in disbelief and joined the throng of passengers running toward the television set, mounted high above the airport bar.

I was mesmerized, frozen in my tracks, staring at the televised map of Iraq, as the newscaster's voice described the sights and sounds of the massive bombardment underway.

Someone in the crowd, a young man, filled with all the imperviousness of youth, called out. "All right! Let's kick some Arab ass!"

"I fly a thousand miles to smoke a camel!" another young man's voice answered.

Passengers around him did not laugh.

Fear rose and fell like the tide in the pit of my stomach, as I recalled the thousands of training missions Paul had flown. The UEIs, the ORIs, the dangerous missions, the deadly night flying, the exercises upon exercises – this was why they did it. This was the real thing.

I turned to Marcus, hoping to find the same fear within his eyes.

"Fight's on," I whispered, using some of Paul's old cockpit slang.

"The major would have wanted to be there, no doubt." Marcus draped one arm around PJ and me, the other arm around Andrew and Lillian.

"Yes, he would have."

"Something tells me this was what he lived for, wasn't it?"

"Yes."

"It never leaves you, does it? The military life?"

"No, I guess not."

"Let's build on that then."

CPSIA information can be obtained at www.ICGtesting.com
Printed in the USA
LVOW062323270212

270690LV00001B/16/P

9 781608 446940